BLOOD
and
SUNLIGHT

A Maryland Vampire Story

Melanie would love to believe in fairytales. She'd love, in fact, to believe in anything. The twenty-three-year-old college dropout is stuck — stuck in a dead-end waitress job, stuck in her hometown of Ellicott City, Maryland, and stuck with a boyfriend who likes to play dress-up as a vampire.

Vampires. Her world and her reality are turned upside down when she encounters the real thing. Along the way, she meets Lucas, the would-be vampire slayer, his father the sheriff, and ultimately the vampire himself. Melanie learns that fairytales can come true, and evil isn't always where you expect to find it.

BLOOD and SUNLIGHT
A Maryland Vampire Story
by
Jamie Wasserman

Licensed and Produced through
Penumbra Publishing
www.PenumbraPublishing.com

PRINTED IN USA, EAN-13/ISBN: 978-1935563327

Also available in EBOOK, EAN-13/ISBN: 978-1935563310

~AUTHOR DEDICATION~

For Michelle, Alex, Shana, and Baby Number Three — my happily ever after.

I'd especially like to thank my wife Michelle, who read dozens and dozens of drafts of this book. She should, by all rights, be working as an editor at a large publishing house. I'd also like to thank my parents, Joe and Nadia, who surprised me by not only reading the book but telling me how much they enjoyed it. They're not particularly good liars, but they are great parents. I'd also like to thank Gerri Hernandez, Chris Huza, Ron Raynor, Samantha Anamasi, and Katie Catalano — your encouragement and suggestions made this happen.

BLOOD
and
SUNLIGHT

✚

A Maryland Vampire Story

by

Jamie Wasserman

And Little Red Cap thought, "As long as I live, I will never leave the path and run off into the woods by myself."

—*Little Red Cap, The Brothers Grimm*

PART I

Fall

Prologue

"...and they lived happily ever after." The man closed the book and waited.

"Daddy?"

"Yes, darling," he said, smiling to himself. He was never lucky enough to get away with reading just one story.

"I'm not sleepy."

"You haven't tried. Close your eyes," he recited. This was their nightly ritual.

"It won't help." The little girl frowned, sat up in bed, and crossed her arms.

"Would you like some water?"

"No."

"Another blanket?"

"Daddy..." the little girl whined.

"Another story?" the man asked, sighing.

The little girl nodded happily.

"Okay, okay." The man flipped the big book in his lap open to another page. He had already bookmarked which story he was going to read. "Sleeping Beauty?"

"I don't want a story from *that* book."

"Oh?" the man asked, surprised. This book was her favorite, and he couldn't remember the last time she had asked him to read anything else. "Okay," he said, unsure, and reached towards her small book shelf.

"Uh-uh."

"Uh-uh, what?"

"I want the story you know by heart."

The man leaned forward and smoothed back the girl's hair. "The one I used to tell your brother when he was little?"

"Yes, that one."

"I don't know ... it's been a long time since I've told that one. I may not remember it."

"You remember."

She was right, of course. How could he forget? Things were much better then. "It might be a little scary for you," he said, trying one last time to distract her.

"Please, Daddy!"

The man watched her lips turn down at the corners, and he knew he had already lost. He just couldn't stand to see her cry. He kissed the girl on the forehead and took her hand. "You know he's going to be fine, right? Your brother's pretty tough."

"I know."

The man studied the little girl. Even in the dark, her face looked serene, untroubled.

"Okay," he said. "Move over. Let me sit next to you."

"How come?" she asked, scooting over quickly.

"So *I* don't get scared." He crammed as much of himself as he could onto her small bed. "Let's see..." he said to himself.

"Daddy?"

"Yes, dear."

"Is there a princess?"

"Yes, but she doesn't know she's a princess."

"Just like Cinderella?"

"A lot like Cinderella, yes."

The man waited. His daughter's questions always came in twos.

After a short pause, she added, "And, Daddy?"

"Yes, sweetie?" He folded his hands in his lap.

"Are there monsters?" She pulled the covers up past her mouth.

"Yes." He tugged the blanket away from her face. "All fairytales have monsters. But these are a little different. These monsters look just like you and me."

"Then how do you know they're monsters?"

"You don't. Not always," the man said sadly.

The little girl chewed at the inside of her lip, mulling this over.

He looked at his daughter. She had the same worried expression her mother had. It made the man smile at the memory. "Are you sure you want to hear this?"

The little girl nodded up at her father.

"Okay, I think I remember it now. This story begins like any other fairytale. Do you want to start it for me?"

The little girl closed her eyes and snuggled next to her dad. "Once upon a time..."

Chapter 1

Ellicott City is a former mill town cut into the rocky Maryland hillside. The Patapsco River runs alongside the train tracks at the bottom of Main Street, part of the old B&O railroad connection. Every spring, the river banks flood and pour over the cobbled streets. And every fall, part of the shopping district, once home to migrant rail workers, catches fire and destroys another small piece of the town's history. The steeples from a dozen Victorian churches rise above the trees, their bells the only note heard clearly above the Sunday morning tourist exodus. There is much history here, but for the most part the dead are silent, despite the many signs advertising ghost walks and haunted tour groups.

In June, when the rains finally relent, the air is sticky and thick and gets into everyone's eyes and hair. The stores close early but remain lit, warding off the night like garlic. An old wooden train bridge marks one end of Main Street; a rickety, soot-covered mess that sprawls across the road like a gateway into something terrible. It signals a stopping point for tourists.

Just on the other side of that bridge sits the Old Monk, a brick and mortar restaurant thrown together somewhat haphazardly off the main road.

* * * * *

It was only 8:00 pm. The last of the locals finished their meals as Melanie listened to the soft clinking of glasses and plates, and the dull thrum of conversation drifting from an open window. An empty coffee cup sat untouched on her table. It had been at least an hour since a waiter had bothered to check on her, and that was part of the appeal of this place.

She sat in the courtyard in the back of the restaurant, or rather, what passed for a courtyard — discarded patio furniture and an umbrella or two that had no doubt been washed to the back of the building by the nearby

Patapsco River in the latest storm. She sat in the dark, watching the even darker water crest and bubble, half expecting a body to be suddenly cast from its murky depths. She was in that kind of mood. Expecting the worst, and confident that she wouldn't be disappointed.

Soon they would arrive, in long dark coats and velvety sashes, reeking of Marlboros and skunky beer and opium incense, and maybe that would lighten her thoughts, or at least take her mind off the anniversary of yet another missed year of college, yet another year stuck in this town.

She returned her attention to the black cat that sat cleaning itself on the flat-topped roof. She didn't mind sketching the little fur-balls, but if it got within kicking distance, she couldn't be held responsible for her actions. It wasn't just that she was allergic; there was something in her that seemed to bring out the worst in cats. Like she was wearing mouse-scented perfume.

Melanie tucked a newly dark strand of hair behind heavily pierced ears. She had a heart-shaped face and large, bright eyes that made her seem keenly aware and always interested. Melanie was thin and almost always wore black clothes, which gave her a hungry, desperate look that men seemed to love. She felt old, jaded, and over the hill — she was twenty-three.

Tonight she wore cut-off jeans and a sheer tank top; a hold-over from the sweltering afternoon. Though the night had cooled considerably, her body still felt warm, and she figured she'd most likely be drunk or high soon enough that the evening cold wouldn't matter anyway.

She thumbed through her sketchpad, looking for a clean page. She'd need another one soon. With stark and sharp charcoal lines, she began to sketch the cat, who preened and purred at the attention. Just before she could add the eyes, always her biggest challenge, the world went completely dark.

Two clammy hands held fast over her eyes.

"Guess who?" a voice said. It was high and shaky. The hairs on the back of Melanie's neck stood up. "You smell nice," the speaker said, lingering at her throat and nibbling playfully at her ear.

"Hi Bryan."

"Lucian," he corrected. "I told you to call me Lucian." He slumped in the chair next to Melanie.

Blood and Sunlight   Jamie Wasserman

Bryan was tall and skinny and seemed skinnier still in his long black overcoat at least two sizes too large. He wore a crumpled black top hat that covered stringy black hair dried out from too many dye jobs. He was pale and powdered his skin wherever his Mediterranean coloring threatened to poke through.

"What happened to your teeth?" Melanie asked, hurriedly tucking away her sketchbook in her worn backpack serving as both a purse and art portfolio. She didn't mind sharing her photographs, but her drawings felt more personal. They weren't simply something she saw, but something she felt, and she fully believed in keeping those types of things hidden.

Bryan stuck a long finger in his mouth. "I took them out. They were tearing up my gums. I may get mine sharpened. I haven't decided."

Melanie shook her head. She knew Bryan wouldn't go through with it. He even opted for magnetic earrings instead of full piercings. She herself had five tiny silver studs that ran up and down both ears like Braille, and she had been thinking of adding more.

Whatever the reason, she should be grateful Bryan had ditched his fake teeth. Not only did the plastic vampire teeth he liked to wear make him lisp and drool, but they were the cause of at least two bar fights. It made him look *ridiculouth.*

"Did you bring anything to drink?"

Bryan produced a small bottle from a tattered backpack, "Wine. Blood red." He winked.

Melanie smiled despite herself. Bryan could be corny, but it was hard to deny his enthusiasm.

"I like your hair." He rested a hand on her thigh.

"I figured you would." She leaned in to kiss him. She liked the way he tasted, like smoke and Chardonnay. He was dry but sweet.

They met in a summer art class. Night school, of course, because traipsing about in daylight would ruin his finely cultivated pale complexion. Bryan was deeply appreciative of Melanie's series of photographs of garbage cans. Of everything about Melanie for that matter.

On their first date, he stood nervously at the door and waited for her

6

to invite him in. Later he would ask permission to kiss her. She chose what movies they saw and where they went to dinner. She decided when they were finished making love, even if he hadn't. He made her feel strong, and if that meant pretending tomato juice was blood and swearing off garlic, then so be it. Besides, this strange relationship gave her the days totally free to herself.

While Bryan playfully nipped at her lips like a puppy, she studied the turrets from an old castle-like house or church that rose dizzyingly above the legacy oaks on the hillside. Though the way the building sat precariously on the edge of the cliff sickened her, Melanie felt obsessed with locating the property. She imagined climbing into the house on a rope of spun gold, a wealth of untold treasures awaiting her discovery, but subsequent attempts to find it despite detours deep into the woods had proved fruitless.

Tonight, she noticed smoke pouring from a chimney, the first sign she'd ever seen of anyone living there. She had assumed it was long abandoned.

A not so distant howl interrupted them.

"Listen to them, the children of the night. What music they make," Bryan said, doing his best Bela Lugosi.

Melanie snapped back to attention. "It's just Carl."

"You have no imagination." Bryan slumped in his chair and searched his pockets for a cigarette.

Melanie did not understand why so many of her dates had to include Bryan's minion — or posse, or whatever he was calling him these days.

Suddenly, a large black shape landed on the patio, taking out a rusted metal chair. Melanie's cat, sleeping peacefully now in the shadows, screeched and ran up the nearest drainpipe. Melanie didn't even flinch — God help her, this was becoming an all too familiar routine.

"What's up, suckas?" Carl picked up the broken chair and hurled it as far as he could. It landed on the soft ground by the river's edge. He watched it, disappointed, and brushed rust from his hands.

Tonight he was wearing a frilly white shirt and purple velvet pants. His naturally dark curly hair was bleached nearly white. Yin to Bryan's Yang. Melanie often tried to imagine Carl as he was in the Marines; scrubbed,

7

shaved, and pressed into a uniform. The mental image always went up in a cloud of dust when presented alongside the real thing.

When Melanie met Bryan, he and Carl were already inseparable. Carl waited for Bryan after class, and the three of them would drink coffee at the student union or catch the last showing at the Golding Theater. She began to wonder if she were dating both of them and how sex would work.

Back then, Bryan seemed pretty unremarkable. He and Carl shared an apartment near the community college, volunteered nights at the local homeless shelter, and even wrote an article or two for the local paper. His hair was blonde and close cut, and without the goofy plastic Halloween teeth sticking out of his mouth like ill-fitting braces, he might be considered pretty attractive, or at least normal enough to sit next to on a bus.

Bryan always had a fascination for all things morbid — zombies, ghosts, werewolves, serial killers — but his first love was always vampires. After a recent 'pilgrimage' to New Orleans with Carl, he returned completely caped out, looking like a cross between Inspector Gadget and Count Chocula. Melanie hoped it was just a passing phase and that he would soon find something else ghoulish to obsess about. Maybe even her.

In order to appease him, Melanie began ditching the long, flowing hippy dresses she loved for tighter, darker clothing. She painted her bright turquoise eyes with black liner so they'd look more baleful, and took right away to the endless supply of drugs and liquor that Carl provided. Melanie suspected visits into Bryan's albeit limited fantasy world might be the closest she'd come to an exotic getaway.

"What's the plan?" she asked. Though she already knew the answer, she hoped, just once, Bryan might add a change of venues to his limited repertoire. Maybe they could even leave the city, if only for just an evening.

"Where else?" Bryan grinned. "Anybody got any 'shrooms?" He rummaged through his backpack.

"Better." Carl dropped a small plastic baggy filled with white tablets on the table. *Ecstasy.*

His choice of drugs was getting progressively bolder but he had yet to produce something Melanie refused. She wondered if she had any limits; if there was nothing she wouldn't swallow.

Bryan smiled, and he and Carl let the small pills melt on their tongues, then washed it down with swigs of wine. Melanie secretly dropped hers in the back pocket of her bag — she needed to be clear-headed for the walk to Hell House.

Chapter 2

If the legends were to be believed, Hell House, or rather the ruins of Hell House, were a monument and tomb to a terrible evil. The building began life in the 1800s as a monastery, but an outbreak of typhoid or cholera forced its doors to shut. Some say that the dead were interred within its walls.

Hell House reopened in the 1900s as a convent but quickly burnt to the ground under mysterious circumstances — the nuns burned alive with it. Fifty years later it was rebuilt as a seminary, run by priests rumored to practice satanic rituals. Following the mysterious deaths of several students, the place closed and remained abandoned for decades.

Eventually, a caretaker was appointed to guard the property against the onslaught of teenagers looking for a good scare or a secluded place to screw. He carried with him his own set of urban legends — he was a convict, a squatter, a Satanist come to reclaim the property. It was said he brandished a sawed-off shotgun in one hand and a monstrous pit bull on a chain in the other. Last Halloween, the house burned to the ground a final time, and the caretaker disappeared completely into myth and rumors and the Maryland night.

Melanie did not accept or believe anything she couldn't see or touch. Years of Catholic upbringing had literally beat any faith out of her head. So one Saturday afternoon, while Bryan slept, she spent the better part of an afternoon in the cramped Maryland Historical Society building to learn the real history behind Hell House.

The truth, Melanie noted, was far more mundane than the legend. Its real name was St. Francis Xavier College — and it did once serve as a seminary for the Redemptionists, a group of devout Catholic missionaries. She discovered cracked and yellowed newspapers with photos of a lovely Gazebo that overlooked the river, sprawling well-kept grounds, and even an outdoor pool in the back. The school ran uninterrupted for almost a century.

Yes, fires were part of its past, but that was also true for everything in this ancient, fragile town.

The caretaker was a man named August Grund, a Vietnam vet who drove a beat-up pickup and sometimes had run-ins with the police, but always over late-night intruders. He lived in a small, well-kept trailer at the back of the house.

Melanie took a trip to Hell House one spring afternoon and ran into August. He showed her where wild rose vines climbed the chain link fence that surrounded the property, and where to watch out for poison ivy. His 'hellhound' was a half-blind fourteen-year-old Doberman named Linda who licked Melanie's hand and whimpered at her heels. In a final move which ruined almost all the remaining mystique of the ancient grounds, August asked Melanie back to his trailer for a cappuccino.

None of this Melanie shared with Bryan.

Ever since he had discovered the hidden tunnels, Hell House had become his official hideout and playground. Underneath the rotten pile of ashes and timber that was the actual house, the fire exposed a ruined network of underground tunnels, most likely remnants of the old boiler room and later the laundry and electricity tunnels. But for Bryan, they represented a descent into something far more mystical. The unknown. An underworld of his own making. Although Melanie hated every rat-infested step, she refused to take the romance out of his world, and in fact hoped secretly that some of it might even enter hers.

There were easier ways to get to Hell House. Just past the Old Monk, where Main Street ended and gave way to abandoned buildings, the town's only formal restaurant, and the old Legionnaire's hall, a small side road veered off through the woods, ran over the river and stopped next to the defunct mill. It was narrow enough that only one car could pass at a time, but it didn't matter — no one ever took the road anyway, especially at night when the absence of streetlights and the closeness of the trees made it seem dark as a hollow. From there, it was an easy climb up the sixty-six stone steps that led to the seminary grounds.

Bryan preferred the road even less traveled — a mile-long stretch of railroad line that connected Ellicott City to Catonsville.

Melanie didn't mind the dark woods that leaned as close to the tracks as the occasional train would allow. She didn't mind the tortuous walk over rocky ground that caused her to lose her balance and wrench her ankle, or having to hold her breath as she moved silently past the abandoned switch-house where a turkey buzzard made its nest. She didn't even mind having to step over the occasional pile of white deer bones, bleached whiter still in the moonlight.

The part of the walk that made her sweat and shiver with fear was the train tunnel. Built inexplicably above ground, out of concrete thick as a bunker, the tunnel was the only way to get to the house from this direction.

Dark did not bother her. At home in her apartment, she'd let the sun go almost all the way below the horizon before she'd even think about turning on the lights and, even then, she'd only burn candles. But there was something about the tunnel and the dark contained there that was suffocating. It wasn't simply dark; it held within it the possibility that it would never be light again.

Two steps into the tunnel, and the temperature dropped fifteen degrees. Another few steps, and whatever light that remained from the moon or road suddenly vanished, unable to push its way through. At that point, she lost all perspective. All she could do was trust that she was going the right way and continue.

Whatever meager light produced by a cigarette or a lighter never carried far enough — her feet were left to shuffle along the ground in total blackness, kicking up God knows what. Melanie imagined that this darkness was hundreds of years old, boxed in, growing thick with rage. All sorts of malevolent patterns swirled in front of her, reshaping into terrible and hungry creatures. Her fears, which she kept carefully stowed in the back of her mind, suddenly took shape right before her.

When she finally did spill out the other end of the tunnel, she was left gasping for breath and sweating despite the cold. The dark took something from her every time she passed through it.

Though it was a cool evening and already almost midnight, she felt hot and blinded by the streetlamps burning at the old paper mill. Still, she felt comforted by their presence, and her mood lightened instantly.

She looked back into the mouth of the tunnel. Bryan and Carl stumbled out of the darkness, smiling, relieved.

"Hell, yeah!" Carl shouted and bumped fists with Bryan.

Melanie shook her head in disgust. It seemed like such a hollow victory. To her, the trip was the price of admission to a happy boyfriend. To Bryan, it was a test of self.

Melanie rifled anxiously through her bag and found the Ecstasy tablet Carl had given her and dropped it on her tongue like communion. She knew it wouldn't be long before she felt its first syrupy effects. Her blood was naturally slow and thick. Her doctor told her the name for her condition, which she instantly forgot, along with a list of necessary precautions. Essentially, it meant she'd probably never have kids, and she might die if she ever got on an airplane. Her blood was a clotted pool, and anything she put into it eddied and lapped against her veins but hardly waned. She felt light-headed and cold all the time.

Bryan caught up to Melanie. "How is it you always beat us? We went in first."

"I don't know." She had often wondered that too. This time she had even stopped twice just to catch her breath. The air was as dense and murky as swamp water.

"Did you finish reading Feast of Blood yet?" Bryan put his arm around her.

"No."

"What part are you up to?"

"The middle?"

Behind her, Melanie heard a thud and something skitter along concrete.

"Take that bitches!"

Carl was throwing rocks at the mill's barred windows. Occasionally one would go astray and clatter over the roof, landing with a sploosh into the river on the other side.

Blood and Sunlight

Jamie Wasserman

The factory's location was chosen carefully for its proximity to the quick Patapsco River. At its peak, the waters were nearly clogged with dead tree limbs tossed into the current, headed for use in the saw mills up north. That much Melanie remembered from school. For Carl, it was just something else to throw rocks at.

"You haven't even started it yet, have you?"

Melanie looked back to Bryan. "I will. I've just been busy."

"Add it to the pile."

"I said I'd read it."

"Whatever." He took his arm off her shoulder and quickened his pace.

Lately, Bryan had been feeding Melanie a steady diet of vampire books and movies that he told her she absolutely *must* read or watch. At one point, she had them stacked into an elaborate pyramid in the corner of her bedroom. After a while, she got bored with the exercise and simply shoved them under her bed.

"Whatever yourself. It's all the same old crap anyway."

She held her breath expectantly. The last few weeks, she'd been trying to get Bryan to lose his temper. To show some semblance of passion, of being more than just someone who would follow at her heels. That was nice for a bit, but without a little giveback, she often felt lonely. Like she was stuck in a relationship with herself and found she didn't much like the company.

"Forget it. It's no big deal. It's just a book, right?" Bryan conceded as he stopped and waited for her to catch up. "You should sketch this." He pointed to the broken stone steps sunken with moss and ivy that led up to Hell House.

"Yeah, maybe," Melanie said, disappointed, and kicked at the first step that wobbled loosely like a tooth.

"Hey, man," Bryan shouted back to Carl, "You coming or what?"

Carl was struggling to pick up a rock bigger than his head. "You should feel how smooth this stone is."

"What?"

"I'm serious." He rubbed his cheek against the rock.

Bryan giggled. "He's wasted. You feeling anything yet?"

14

Melanie rubbed her arms. Now that Bryan had mentioned it, she realized her arms had been tingling, but now they felt like a thousand fingertips were gently poking her. She touched her ear, then couldn't stop touching it.

"You okay?" Bryan rubbed her back. He had an unlit cigarette hanging from his lip.

"Yeah. I think it's kicking in." Melanie felt a warm sensation pass from where Bryan touched her — it ran from the base of her neck to the bottom of her spine. Her muscles contracted and then released. She leaned over and kissed him, and the warm sensation returned, shooting straight to her toes. There was nothing better than trying a new drug for the first time, feeling its soft medicinal effects cover your brain like a warm, fuzzy blanket. The ultimate in protection from the outside world.

On top of the sudden peace she felt, there was also a stirring between her legs, a desperation of her body to be connected to someone, anyone else. Bryan would do. She took his hands and held them over her breasts. "We need to find somewhere to go right now."

"Go?" Bryan looked confused.

She pulled him up the stairs.

"Oh ... *go*," he confirmed with a grin.

Melanie strode confidently up the crumbling steps and across the grounds. The house held no fear for her as it seemed to for everyone else in this town. This was not hallowed earth, just another grand gothic building reduced to a pit of rotting timber and corroding ironwork. She was all too familiar with ruin, and old enough not to be afraid of campfire stories. She saw nothing spectral here, even at night when dark shadows crept over the hillside, and tiny, rustling creatures crisscrossed the grounds.

But regardless of what time of day it was, Melanie always felt ill at ease walking by the old statue of the Virgin Mary that sat miraculously unbroken in the center of the clearing. The graffiti that covered it like a multi-colored straitjacket did not bother her. It was the way someone had completely blacked out Mary's eyes, giving her the appearance of a Susan Keane painting — something soulless, with a wide, impassive face. For a girl raised on a strict Catholic upbringing, even a wayward one, the notion of an indifferent holy mother was simply too much to take. While she was tripping on the X, the statue seemed larger in size, the spray-painted graffiti blurred together into something pulsing.

Bryan pulled Melanie away from the statue and headed off towards the edge of the grounds. As he walked, he sang cheerfully, "Who's afraid of the big bad wolf, the big bad wolf, the big bad wolf."

"Please. Stop." Melanie gritted her teeth. Her thoughts felt sluggish, purposeless, drifting like cells in a thick stream of warm blood. The singing was forcing her to focus, the last thing she wanted, and on something unpleasant, at that.

"Wait for meeee!" Carl called as he raced up behind them.

Here the ground opened up, revealing the network of underground tunnels that stretched off into nothingness.

Melanie and Bryan had only been brave enough to explore the first thirty feet or so before, but the X was kicking in, and Melanie experienced a comforting mixture of horniness and invincibility.

"Aww, I know what you guys are going to do."

"Go break something."

"Break this baby," Carl grabbed his crotch.

Bryan smirked at his friend.

Melanie took a tenuous step towards the broken ladder that someone had propped up at the tunnel entrance. It seemed to be missing every other rung.

"F-that." Without thinking, Carl jumped down into the dark and landed with a heavy thud. "Ow."

"You okay?" Bryan looked down.

"Am now. Won't be tomorrow."

Melanie took another step and was on the top rung of the ladder now. If she was any less wasted, she wouldn't be doing this. She'd be thinking about ledges and plummeting and air rushing through her hair and the ground rising like a fist to meet her. She'd probably be getting sick.

"Mel?"

"Yeah?" Maybe she wasn't so okay. She could see the bottom, but it seemed further away than it did before.

"You're looking a little green. Can I help?"

"No," she said sharply.

"Whatever. Do it yourself. You always do." Bryan crossed his arms and waited.

He was only trying to be supportive, and she had hurt his feelings. *Nice one, Mel.* "I'm sorry. Yes, actually, I could use some help."

Bryan nodded and tried to hide his smile. He was needier than a new puppy. "We'll climb down together, okay? Just keep looking up."

He helped Melanie to the first step, then awkwardly climbed behind her so she had no way of looking down where all that ground was. She could hear him panting for breath.

So, he wasn't the woodsman, dragging the big bad wolf by the ears into the forest. He remembered birthdays and her favorite kind of plant, the pale swallow-wort. He was sweet and thoughtful, and that was enough. Though it did sometimes make her feel guilty that she rarely returned the favor. Would it have really killed her to read his damned book?

When they finally reached the bottom, she patted his cheek. "Save your energy, stud."

He smiled back gratefully.

Carl was sitting on the ground with one of his pants legs pulled up past his knee.

"Check it out — blood. Want a taste?" After sticking his finger in the wound, he held it up to Bryan.

"Yuck, just go."

"Suit yourself." Carl flicked the blood off his fingers, onto the ground, and wiped his hands on his pants.

For all his posturing about vampires, Bryan would have made a lousy bloodsucker. He couldn't even sit through ten minutes of the medical channel. But if Carl ever crossed over, you'd probably struggle to tell the difference.

He staggered down the tunnel with Melanie and Bryan in tow. As they walked, Carl kicked aside rotting and burned-out timber, and they pressed

17

further than any of them had ever gone before.

The narrow walkway opened into a larger space. The old boiler room. Mangled power lines occasionally crackled as if electricity still flowed through their veins. A rotting mattress lay in one corner, and broken glass covered the floor. Melanie marveled at the level of effort it must have taken to cram a mattress down here, but never thought about why it was done in the first place. In another corner of the room, a chair was inexplicably bolted into the floor.

Bryan found a sweatshirt in his backpack and spread it across the filthy mattress like a blanket. "*Pour vous*, my darling," he said and swept his hand gallantly low.

Melanie put her hands over her heart. "Thank you, *monsieur*." She had to suppress a giggle at his attempt at chivalry, then frowned — this might be the closest she got to being treated like a princess.

She flopped on the mattress, and Bryan snuggled in clumsily next to her. She could feel the heat from his body, his staggered breath. Too many cigarettes, not enough trips to the gym. In a few years, Bryan would look just like Melanie's mother had — leathery, slug-like skin, and a dull listless mouth. She reminded herself to stay in the here and now.

Melanie's legs tingled, and her hands trembled. She ran her hands along the mattress, then Bryan's legs. Her clothes felt too constricting and suddenly heavy. She pulled and tugged at her collar. Her belly clenched, but she wasn't hungry, at least not for food. She immediately tore at Bryan's shirt. She wanted to feel his skin against her, to taste him and be dominated. But even on the X, Bryan was patient and gentle in their lovemaking. When Melanie moaned too loudly, he would ask if she was okay.

She pulled him on top of her, and he fumbled, unused to being the one in control. Across the room, sitting in the ancient chair, Carl groaned softly, watching them. Melanie could see the glint of his eyes, his ring-covered fingers sliding down his jeans...

It wasn't the first time Carl had watched them make love. Melanie wondered if Bryan knew, but he never mentioned it. He definitely seemed oblivious to the constant stream of lewd comments Carl made to both of them. Nobody took Carl seriously. That's probably how he got away with as much as he did.

Regardless, for Melanie it was exciting. She chickened out last semester, after volunteering to be a nude model for a sculpting class, but in Bryan's arms she felt less inhibited and enjoyed the attention. Secretly, she wondered if Carl would ever be brave enough to join in.

Carl moaned slightly and lowered his head. He never lasted long, but the X made him come even quicker. He adjusted himself and staggered back down the tunnel the way they had come in.

Bryan, on the other hand, could go all night. The Seroquel he took for anxiety had robbed him of orgasms but allowed him to keep it up for hours. Much better than the Zoloft he used to be on — he would go months without touching her and, on the few occasions when he did rise to the occasion, would run to the shower immediately afterwards.

Bryan finally fell into a nice rhythm, and Melanie locked her legs around him, pulling him deeper as her muscles tensed. She tilted her head back, and her body shook. Bryan tried to pull away, but she held him closer, rocking her hips against him until they were making love again.

Bryan got bolder — he nipped at her throat like he had always joked about doing. Melanie winced but willed him on. He bit harder and sucked at her neck and then her nipples as she moaned and shuddered.

They continued to make love until their thighs and back ached, until the X finally sweated its way out of their system. Then they fell back on the worn mattress, Melanie's ear against Bryan's chest, the sound of his heartbeat amplified, pounding away, tapping out a long-forgotten message.

Melanie heard glass breaking down the hall — Carl had probably found something new to smash. That was the last sound Melanie remembered before she fell into a deep sleep.

Chapter 3

"Mel! Mel!"

Bryan must have been calling Melanie's name for some time, for though it came in whispers, his voice was urgent and ragged. She looked up and saw him hurriedly pulling on his pants.

"I heard a scream," he said. "Get dressed! Get dressed!"

Melanie listened for a moment, but heard nothing. "Are you sure?"

They both listened intently. All Melanie could hear was the sound of blood rushing in her ears.

"It's just the X. Go back to sleep." Melanie rolled over. She did not like being woken up. Ever.

"I know what I heard." Bryan continued getting dressed, but more slowly and with less confidence.

"Do you have any water?" Melanie smacked her lips together. Her tongue felt like cotton.

Just then, she heard a distinct snapping sound and something that sounded like a rock clattering across a concrete floor. She sat up and met Bryan's eyes.

"Probably just Carl."

They listened together again, but no sound followed. Regardless, Bryan looked spooked. "I heard screaming earlier."

Melanie was sure it was nothing, just a drug-induced nightmare, like the time Bryan woke up screeching about owls after doing mescaline with a Mexican hitchhiker they picked up.

"Let's go. I'll check it out with you." If she had been at all concerned, she never would have volunteered. She would never be the person who ran back into the house to save the family dog from the fire. That was why she didn't keep pets around — nothing should be dependent on her for protection or survival.

She slipped on her denim shorts and sandals and threw on her shirt. There was some light streaming through the tunnel. Melanie realized it must be close to dawn. Her chest felt dry and sticky, and she had a sharp pain in her neck. Bryan had opened a welt. It felt like a really nasty hickey.

"I'm sorry about that," Bryan whispered. "Does it hurt?"

She shook her head. "Dracula."

Now dressed, Melanie took Bryan's hand, and they walked back along the corridor until they got to the mouth of the tunnel.

Melanie was still smirking at her own joke when they came upon Carl sprawled on the ground, his neck twisted at an absurd angle. A small shadowy object sat on top of his bloodied chest. Melanie thought it might have been a cat at first, but as they got closer, the creature looked up. It was a girl who looked about Melanie's age. Her face was dirty and marred with heavy black streaks. Her hair was matted and tangled. Her face was drawn, and her stomach heaved as she took in air. She looked starved. Blood dripped from her lips and down her chin. Carl's blood. "What the hell?"

When the girl saw Bryan and Melanie, she hissed and positioned her hands protectively on Carl's body.

Bryan pushed Melanie behind him and whispered to her, "My backpack. I left it in the other room." He nodded towards the tunnel, "There's a knife in there."

This was news to her. She wanted to ask why, but the girl began to growl, softly at first, from somewhere in the back of her throat, and it was getting louder. She wondered how something so frail looking, so clearly damaged, could have hurt anyone, let alone Carl, a sociopath with military training.

"Carl? You okay buddy?" Bryan took a step to the right, drawing the girl's attention to him.

For a second, Melanie saw Bryan as the shattered knight pushing back the dragon into his lair, if only to spare a few precious seconds so the damsel could escape. Had she been completely wrong about him?

"Go!" he whispered to Melanie.

She backed down the hall, slowly at first, never taking her eyes off the

21

girl. When she was out of sight, she hauled ass back to the room where Bryan left his backpack. She tried to tell herself Carl had just passed out or banged his head, that the girl was probably high on some whacked-out weed. Yes, that would make sense, but her heart still felt like it was trying to pound its way out of her chest. On the way, Melanie scratched her cheek on a sharp metal rod jutting out of the wall, but continued as quickly as she could. The growling was getting louder.

She found the backpack lying at the foot of the mattress along with her bra and Bryan's boxers. She grabbed the bag and ran back, something warm dripping from her face. Melanie thought she might be crying until she rubbed her cheek and saw her hand smeared with red. She felt like there was a hollow space in her throat, that she might be sick — the blood an all too real reminder that she was human, vulnerable, and deliberately heading into danger.

Down the hall, the growling erupted into a series of sharp, precise snarls, and Bryan let out a scream.

Melanie's stomach lurched, and she ran faster, dragging the heavy backpack behind her. When she returned, the girl had Bryan pinned on his back and was slashing at his face with long and broken fingernails. What Melanie initially thought was dirt on the girl's face, turned out to be scars and burns, like she had survived a fire. She remembered the rumor about the nuns who were supposed to have been burned alive here, but this was no ghost.

"Get the knife. The knife!" Bryan yelled, holding up his arms to protect his eyes.

Melanie feverishly dug through the backpack. Retrieving it was one thing, but her hands were shaking so bad, she was as much a danger to Bryan as she was the girl.

She found the knife and kicked it across the floor, then edged away. It landed about a foot away from his grasp. *Add it to the list*, she thought. *One more thing Bryan had asked of you, and you had disappointed him again.*

The girl sunk her teeth into Bryan's arm, and he screamed again, trying to shake her loose. He flailed desperately for the knife, but it sat uselessly out of reach.

"Oh God, Mel, help me!"

Panicked, Melanie backed into a corner. She felt herself peeing and sobbed. She wanted to run but her legs felt cramped and heavy. Instead, she slumped to the ground and covered her eyes like a child.

The girl let go of Bryan's arm and lunged at his throat. With her ear only inches from his mouth he leaned forward and clamped down as hard as he could.

The girl screamed and tried to pull away, but Bryan would not release his hold. She tugged like a mouse caught in a trap until she finally pulled free, bits of her ear still in his mouth. The girl whimpered and bounded out of the tunnel in a single inhuman leap into the night, clutching her wounded head.

"Mel," Bryan whispered, his voice hoarse. He spit and wiped his face on his sleeve, trying to clear his mouth of the girl's flesh.

Melanie rocked back and forth in the corner. The girl was nowhere in sight, and blood poured out of Bryan's neck. His shirt was soaked in gore.

"Mel," Bryan called out again, obviously struggling to speak . He tried to pull himself up, but coughed and choked and gasped for air. "It won't stop bleeding."

But Melanie did not hear a thing. Her body was soaked with sweat and her ears filled with the sound of rushing air. The room grew dark, darker, and then her body shut down, tight as a glass coffin.

* * * * *

It may have been a few minutes or a few hours when Melanie's vision cleared, and the dark room quieted and reformed around her. She touched her legs, face, and chest. Though wet and achy, she was whole. And then she saw Bryan. He lay motionless, his body curled into a question mark.

His cuts were smaller than she would have thought. Tiny half-moon indents on his arms and neck. A dark ring of blood pooled underneath him — far too much to have been created by such simple wounds.

She crawled over to him, "Oh God, Bryan. Lucian. Are you okay?"

He still felt warm, but his face was drawn and pale.

23

Blood and Sunlight   Jamie Wasserman

Across the room, Melanie saw the prone body of Carl. His eyes were rolled back in his head, his neck twisted inhumanly and exposed right down to the bone.

Melanie gasped, though it wasn't the first time she had seen a dead body. After coming home from a night of partying, she'd discovered her mother slumped over. It was a familiar pose for her mom, who usually drank herself to sleep, so Melanie left her there without even a blanket to keep her warm. It wasn't until the next morning when her mom's lips had turned blue that Melanie realized something was wrong. But that was a very different situation — Carl's throat was opened, his head clung to his body by the thinnest of muscle. There was no point in even checking for a pulse.

"C'mon, Mel, get it together," she whispered to herself and bit her lip hard.

There was no way Melanie could carry Bryan out — the floor was covered in broken concrete and shattered glass — let alone get him up the ladder by herself. She ran over to his backpack and rifled through it, looking for his phone. Nothing. She checked his pockets carefully, afraid that the slightest of movements might open his wounds again. Nothing again.

"You brought a knife but left your cell phone at home? Jesus Christ." Melanie paced back and forth, her thoughts a jumbled mess. She wished she had paid her phone bill. She wished she had the money to pay her phone bill. She wished she could bring herself to search Carl's blood-soaked pockets, but she couldn't. She wanted a cigarette and sleep and to be anywhere but right here.

"I need to get help." She touched Bryan lightly on the arm. "I'll be right back, okay?" she said, trying to reassure herself as she climbed into the night.

* * * * *

Melanie carefully sidestepped down the stone steps that led to the road. She was all too aware of what she must look like — bloodied, sweating, and wet. She wondered who would stop for her. There wasn't

24

exactly a large amount of neighbors nearby. Desolate woods, one-lane roads, and rivers and cemeteries were her only options for at least a few miles, and by then it might be too late. Melanie shivered at the cold and at the thought of being left alone.

Though the caretaker had left soon after the last fire, Melanie wondered if someone else might still occupy the small trailer. She ran up the small path that circled the grounds and breathed a sigh of relief when she saw the old trailer still parked at an awkward angle pressed tight against the woods. Though it was dark with the windows boarded over, it looked untouched by the previous fire and still habitable.

She banged on the door with the palm of her hands and shouted out between deep sobs that made her cough and choke, "Please, I need some help!" She collapsed on the ground and cried some more.

"You shouldn't be here," a voice said; it was rich and tinged like cinnamon.

Melanie jumped to her feet and looked around, but didn't see anyone. "Who said that?"

"You *can't* be here." This time the voice was more forceful.

A man stepped forward out of the dark and, for a moment, Melanie thought it might be Bryan, that this was all some kind of sick joke. He wore a faded pair of jeans, a clunky set of combat boots, and a black t-shirt that settled over his shoulders like a second skin. His hair too was black, long, and wavy on top, but shaved closely on the sides. As he got closer, Melanie could see his hair was naturally dark as coal, not like Bryan's, which had a tinge of blue. His skin was so pale, he almost seemed to glow. No amount of powder could give anyone an aura like that. Most striking, though, were his eyes — almond-shaped and so green they seemed to draw in all available light. He would have been at home on a Greek coin, or propped up on a stone column at the Louvre. A simple silver chain disappeared into his shirt.

"I need help," Melanie pleaded again.

"You're bleeding," the man said. He looked to be in his mid-twenties but carried himself so steadily, so confidently, he might have been much older.

No shit. Melanie covered her neck self-consciously.

"No, here." The man brushed her cheek. Melanie shivered at his touch. Though he seemed delicate, his hand was strong and cool and smelled faintly of cedar.

Remembering herself, Melanie said, "My friends are hurt. We need a ride to the hospital."

The man didn't move.

"Please, they're back there in the tunnel. They need help."

"What happened?" The man looked around absently at the empty road, the trees, and finally at the shrinking moon.

"We were attacked."

"By what?"

"A girl, I think." Melanie frowned. Nothing of this night seemed to fit. Maybe it was the X. Maybe Carl was fine, and Bryan was simply waiting for her to return, but her wet jeans and scratched face reminded her otherwise.

"Are you hurt?"

Melanie took a silent inventory of her damages and shook her head.

"You're shivering," the man said.

"Do you have a phone or a car?" she asked.

"No," he said, without further explanation. "Don't worry about your friends. I'll see to them. Are you sure you're alright?"

"I'm fine. Will you help me?"

"You don't look fine. In fact, you look like you might pass out any moment."

"I said I feel—"

His eyes flashed with a liquid quality.

Melanie felt thirsty and light-headed; her legs felt suddenly weak. Before she could finish her thought, her whole body went limp, and the world went dark.

Chapter 4

When she came to, Melanie was lying on a pile of old blankets in a small, dark room. She looked around. Though the windows were covered over in black paint, enough daylight poured through the half-open door that Melanie could see everything clearly. There was a small kitchen, a torn-up couch, and a round table. There wasn't space for much else. In the back, a heavy red curtain separated what must have been the bedroom, maybe a small bathroom.

She knew immediately that this was a trailer. She grew up in a trailer, and the smallness of it, the shabbiness, the low ceilings and flat, unremarkable walls were unmistakable. It was like a renovated mausoleum.

Her whole body was drenched in sweat — the air here was sharp and ghastly hot.

She wondered where Bryan was, where she was for that matter, and what she had been doing. The events of the previous night had just begun to re-enter her consciousness — she saw herself feeling her way through a terrible dark, dropping X, making love with Bryan — but before she could form a full picture, thick, black smoke poured through the open door.

Melanie coughed and hacked and looked around for another exit — there wasn't any. Flames shot through the windows and poured up the sides of the trailer. The metal buckled and hummed with the heat. She realized she didn't have long before the room would fold up like a soda can.

She grabbed the heavy curtain that separated the back half of the trailer and wrapped it around her like a shroud. Her clothes clung tightly to her body, and her legs were sore and tight, making any sort of movement difficult. Without a second thought, she flung herself in the direction of the half-open door. On the way, she banged her hip into the doorknob, then rolled hard to the ground like a giant, smoldering burrito.

The sun hurt her eyes. Even here, in this thickly wooded area, the light came through harsh and white. Before she could get up, a man stepped into view, his face obscured by the bright sun burning behind him. The one thing Melanie could clearly see (and feel) was the long hunting knife the man held at her throat. It had serrated edges, the kind used to ensure that if the intended prey didn't die, it would at least suffer.

"Who are you?"

Melanie swallowed, but even the slightest movement dug the sharp edge of the blade further into her throat.

The man pulled the knife away, then ripped the curtain off Melanie. She rolled into the dirt and then scrambled to her feet. She had to squint under the further glare of the sun.

"You're alive," he said, with more than a little surprise in his voice. A metal gas can sat a few feet behind him. Melanie narrowed her eyes.

Flames shot around both sides of the trailer, grazing the lowest branches of the ancient oaks that surrounded it.

"No thanks to you." She picked up a rock and weakly threw it at him. "Asshole!"

The man calmly slipped the knife into a side pocket on his pants — army camouflage, Melanie noted, to go with his plain army green tee shirt and combat boots. His blonde hair was cropped short like he had just gotten out of basic training, but the nose and eyebrow piercing made Melanie think otherwise. *Skinhead probably, or a wannabe punk.* He had a sharp nose, but his face looked soft, boyish. He wasn't much taller than she was.

"You weren't supposed to be here," the man said, unapologetic.

The entire events of the previous night came rushing back to Melanie. "Bryan," she exclaimed to herself, and ran across the grounds back to the tunnel.

"Hey!" the man shouted and ran after her. "We need to get outta here before the fire department and cops show up."

Melanie looked into the tunnel where she had left Bryan, fearing the worst. Though the ground was blood-stained, the room was conspicuously absent two bodies. She remembered going for help, the trailer, and the strange man, but was shot back to the here and now by the pyromaniac pulling at her collar.

"Get the hell off me!" She slapped at his hand.

"Were you bitten?"

"What?" Melanie pulled back her hand as the man tried to grab it. "No. Get away from me." Melanie remembered Bryan nipping at her throat. How did this guy know?

A faint siren could be heard over the sound of crackling flames and the breeze whipping discontentedly around the trees.

"Is that blood down there?"

Melanie nodded, staring into the empty room. *Maybe Bryan had made it out safely. Maybe Carl wasn't really hurt.*

"Come on." The man grabbed her wrist.

"I'm not going anywhere with you. Get off me!" Melanie pulled away, but the man only tightened his grip. "You're hurting me."

The man released her, and his voice softened, "Any second, this place is going to be crawling with cops. I'll bet you've got a great story to tell them."

Melanie didn't reply. She wasn't even quite sure herself about what had happened.

"Do you have a car here?" he asked.

Melanie shook her head.

"My name is Lucas." He managed a weak smile. "I promise I won't bite. Can I please take you home?" he asked and held his empty hands out to show he was harmless.

The sirens drew closer.

Shit. She'd fail any drug test the cops would make her take right now, and she wouldn't do anyone a bit of good in jail for arson. She could go home, call Bryan ... he was probably sleeping off the X in his apartment, she reassured herself.

Melanie managed a half nod and whispered, "Okay."

"This way," Lucas said, indicating with a jerk of his head for her to follow. He walked quickly to the broken driveway that wrapped around the front of Hell House.

Melanie reluctantly followed Lucas, all the while looking around for any sign of Bryan or Carl, or the man who helped her last night.

* * * * *

Lucas drove an old jeep with a broken T-top stuffed haphazardly in the tiny backseat. The front end was nearly caved in, like he had driven straight into a tree. Though Melanie could have done without the wind constantly tangling her hair, she enjoyed the noisy rush of air to combat what otherwise would have been a silent drive.

Mentally she went through the previous night's events, but found it always ended the same — in a shroud of mystery and smoke and more questions.

Melanie gave Lucas directions to an apartment complex near hers, but far enough away that she still felt safe. She wouldn't mind the walk and needed some time to clear her head.

They drove through the woods, back into Ellicott City, and up past the courthouse where the road widened and gave way to ranch homes and the elementary school. But instead of turning where Melanie indicated, Lucas continued driving straight.

"That was it," Melanie said watching the sign for her street grow smaller.

Lucas kept both hands on the wheel, his eyes steadfastly on the road.

"You missed my turn."

"I need to show you something," Lucas muttered so low under his breath, Melanie could barely hear him.

"What are you doing?"

"I want to show you something." He turned to look at her and smiled. As he did, his whole face seemed to darken.

"Yeah, right." Melanie fumbled with the door. Jumping out wasn't really an option, but maybe opening the door would get him to stop the car.

"Wait!" Lucas pulled the car suddenly over to the side of the road. "Please."

Melanie had the door open, one foot on the road, "Make it quick."

"I really need you to see this."

"What?" Melanie was getting impatient. She might've been scared, but the events of last night left her feeling numb and bold.

"First, what happened to you last night?"

"I don't know." And as far as Melanie was willing to think about it, that was the truth.

"Who's Bryan?"

"My boyfriend." Melanie saw someone peering out the window of the nearest house. This made her feel a little safer.

"He was hurt. Maybe bitten?" Lucas sounded almost hopeful and closed his eyes.

"Yes. Him and another friend."

"A man attacked them, right?"

"No."

Lucas opened his eyes. "What?" He studied Melanie confused.

"A girl." Melanie frowned, it sounded almost ridiculous out loud. To think that anything besides maybe a bear or a mountain lion could have mauled Carl like that would have been unthinkable twenty-four hours ago.

"Did she have blonde hair?" Lucas bit his lip. "How did she look?"

"I don't know. It was dark, and she was pretty dirty." Melanie paused, remembering. "Her face was burned."

"Hmm," Lucas grunted. This clearly wasn't the answer he was hoping for. He grabbed a duffel bag in his backseat and rifled through it. "So, you didn't see anyone else last night?"

Before Melanie could reply, Lucas pulled out a gun from deep in the bag.

Melanie looked back to the house for help, but the curtains were closed, and all the lights were now out. *Great.*

"I need you to come home with me," Lucas said, very matter-of-factly.

She had seen too many Lifetime movies start like this to let him take her anywhere. "Okay. Sure," she said evasively as she mentally planned an escape route. That's when Lucas shoved the gun in her hands. She gasped. He might as well have dropped a live spider in her lap.

"You keep this. I'm not going to hurt you, but we need to talk. Okay?"

Melanie stared at him. He was trying to make her feel safer by giving her some control. It had the opposite effect. Her driving companion had gone from slightly off-balance to downright paranoid and dangerous. She had to think of a way to escape, and fast.

"Do you know how to shoot one of those?"

Melanie shook her head.

"Okay." Lucas took the gun back and threw it in the bag, then dug through its contents again. "Here," he said, throwing something else in her lap. "Mace. That's police grade. Sprays just like a perfume bottle. Just remember to take off the safety before you use it."

Melanie took the mace, twisted the safety cap off, and rested her hand lightly on the button.

"Good. This is going to sound crazy, but I think I know what happened to your friends. Just give me a chance to—" But before he could finish his sentence, Melanie sprayed him in the face and jumped out of the car.

Lucas howled and grabbed at his tee shirt, trying to wipe his eyes. Unfortunately, some of the mace sprayed back into Melanie's face, and she barely made it two feet before she fell to the ground in pain, blinded.

Melanie had only a vague sense of where the jeep and road were. She didn't want to run off and risk getting hit by a car, but she knew she only had a limited time to get away. She felt along the street, hoping to find grass from a lawn, to feel her way towards a house and safety.

Someone grabbed the back of her neck and pulled her to her feet.

"Why'd you do that?" It was Lucas. He sounded more surprised than angry. "Stop moving, damn it!"

He sprayed something wet in her eyes. "It's saline. It'll stop the burning."

To Melanie's surprise it did. She could open her eyes some. Lucas's face was beet red; his own eyes were swollen. They both breathed heavily.

Before either one could say anything else, a police car pulled up behind Lucas's car, lights flashing. The cop let his siren sound once just to let them know he was there. Melanie figured the owner of the house must have called, and she managed a small smile.

"Fuck," Lucas whispered. He still had his hand on Melanie's neck. "Listen," he said, "Keep your mouth shut, or I'll tell them you helped me start that fire back there. And it isn't going to be long before somebody discovers a pool of blood back in the tunnel."

"I didn't do anything wrong."

"That's good. Keep saying that. Cops are known for their understanding and gullibility."

Melanie's smile disappeared quickly. She should have just waited back at Hell House for the police to arrive — there would have been questions, sure, but now she was fleeing the scene of a crime.

"Let me do the talking?" Lucas was more gentle this time. "I won't hurt you."

Melanie bit her lip. She was using every last bit of strength not to claw his eyes out.

The police officer got out of the car and walked over to Melanie and Lucas. He was young, looked more like a military recruit than a cop, and walked with his hands resting stiffly on his belt. "There a problem here?" The officer stopped and regarded Melanie and Lucas. She imagined they must have looked like they had just survived a bombing.

"Shit."

Lucas was all manners now. "Officer Johns."

"Luke? God, cheese and crackers, what happened to you?"

"Funny story—"

"Who is this?" He jabbed a thumb disdainfully at Melanie.

"Ah—" Lucas stammered. He hadn't bothered to ask her name.

Melanie let him sweat for a few seconds and was about to answer when the officer interrupted, "You and Leah quits already?"

"Something like that." Lucas managed a swollen-eyed wink.

Officer Johns smiled big at Melanie, like he knew everything about her all at once. "Gotcha, tomcat. What the hell you guys been doing?"

"Field party last night." Lucas brushed some dirt off his sleeves.

"And your face?"

"She thought my mace was breath spray."

The officer took another look at the two of them and burst out laughing.

"My *name* is Melanie."

Officer Johns took off his sunglasses and wiped his eyes without even a second glance at her. She felt her cheeks flush and put her hands on her hips, demanding to be acknowledged.

"Sorry about all this," Lucas said.

"Get outta here. I won't tell your daddy about this."

"Thanks, sir."

The officer paused before getting back in his car and said, "Hey."

Lucas stiffened.

"Call me next time you party, huh?"

Lucas gave him a big thumbs-up.

The police car pulled away with one last turn of the siren.

When he was gone from sight, Melanie kicked Lucas as hard as she could right between the legs. He dropped straight to his knees, and she grabbed his duffel bag from the backseat. She knew Lucas was crazy, but she wanted to know exactly what kind of crazy.

"More mace," she said, emptying the bag's contents onto the street. "Railroad spikes, the gun. What's this?" She held up a metal rod.

Lucas looked up, both hands holding his injured groin. "Tazer," he groaned.

Melanie dug further. "Garlic bulbs? Wood crosses, more saline..."

"Water." Lucas sucked in air.

"Why water?"

"Holy water."

"Of course. You hunting vampires?" Melanie said sarcastically as she picked up another can of mace and threw back the safety.

"That's what I've been trying to tell you."

Chapter 5

"Who are you?" Melanie asked. Her feet suddenly felt very unsteady.

"I told you — Lucas." He stood up, still sucking in air.

"How did that cop know your name?"

Lucas kneaded his fists into his temple, seemingly engaged in some heated inner-debate over whether or not to tell Melanie. Finally, he blurted, "My dad's the sheriff." He got to his feet on wobbly legs.

"Oh," Melanie said and wished she had a big comfy chair to fall into. "Sorry for kicking you." She wasn't sure what the penalty was for kicking the son of a police officer in the balls, but it couldn't be good.

"And macing me?" Lucas seemed to be enjoying the sudden advantage he had over Melanie.

"No," she said firmly. "You deserved that. Where's Bryan? And Carl?"

"Who?"

"My boyfriend and his friend," she said slowly.

"I don't know." Lucas hung his head a little and ran his fingers over his short blonde hair.

She wanted to kick him again. "You said you knew what happened to—"

"No." He looked directly at Melanie. His eyes were the deepest blue she had ever seen. "I said I think I know what happened to them. I don't know where they are."

"Please," Melanie said, "just tell me." She wanted all of her unanswered questions given to her in a nice little package with a silver bow, to make her unspoken fears just disappear. She looked hopefully at Lucas.

"They were attacked—"

"I know that."

"—by a vampire."

Blood and Sunlight   Jamie Wasserman

If this were a horror movie, a blast of thunder would have exploded around them, but it was a warm, summer day. The sun shone bright and strong, and a light breeze blew through the trees, disrupting a nearby wind chime.

Super. I've gone from dating Dracula to being kidnapped by Dr. Van Helsing. This wasn't getting her anywhere. She began walking away, back towards her apartment. Maybe Bryan was waiting for her there. Maybe this whole thing was just an elaborate joke to get her more involved in his fantasy life. She needed to shower and change clothes and sleep.

"Where are you going?" Lucas called out.

Melanie stopped and looked at him. He seemed small, like a little boy. Some strange part of her wanted to hug him.

"Thank you very much for the ride and nearly kidnapping me, but I can walk home from here."

"Wait." Lucas caught up with her. "The girl who attacked your friends last night, I think that was my girlfriend."

"Get help, creep."

Lucas pulled out his wallet from one of his many pockets. It was hooked to a long chain that disappeared somewhere in his pants. "Here," he said, handing Melanie a picture of a thin girl with wispy, strawberry blonde hair. Her lips were pursed tight, and her eyes were a dull blue, almost gray.

Melanie was glad she hadn't eaten anything in the last 24 hours. Her stomach churned and tightened. She held the picture away from her body like the mere image could somehow harm her.

"Well?" Lucas asked impatiently.

Melanie nodded and said softly, "That was her." The picture was undeniable proof that last night had really happened. She felt unsteady, dizzy. That meant that Carl was dead and Bryan ... *no.*

There was no victory in Lucas's smile. "Do you believe me now?"

About vampires, no — but Lucas did know something. "I don't know." And then something terrible occurred to her. "Oh my God, the burns on her face. Did you do that to her?"

"No," Lucas said sadly. "Sunlight."

"Of course." The street was once again deserted. "Because she's a vampire."

"Look, the police won't do anything until your boyfriend—"

"Bryan," Melanie interrupted. "His name is Bryan." She was surprised at how annoyed she was at Lucas calling Bryan 'your boyfriend.' Maybe because it made him seem less real, closer to being gone. Or maybe ... Melanie refused to follow that line of thinking.

"—until *Bryan* has been missing for twenty-four hours."

"What makes you think he's missing?" Melanie's eyes widened. She was barely ready to accept him being hurt.

Lucas paused and seemed to contemplate a new approach. "Hey, maybe he's home already, waiting for you."

"Yeah," Melanie said, unconvinced.

"He's probably at least already left a message for you. You guys will laugh about this."

Melanie managed a fake laugh.

Lucas's face got serious. "But if he's not at home, could you give me a day? Just one day. That's all I need. There's some crazy shit going on in this town, and I think I can stop it with your help. If you're still not convinced, I'll drive you to the police station myself and have my dad fill out a missing person's report. He's a good cop." He said this last part begrudgingly. "It probably won't even be necessary."

It occurred to Melanie that Lucas might be directly involved in all of this. It was his girlfriend who attacked them, after all. Some sort of sick Bonnie and Clyde thing. Maybe he had Bryan chained up in his basement. Best to get rid of him as quickly and gently as possible.

"Okay."

"Yes!" Lucas pumped his fist.

"Give me your number," Melanie said.

"Why?" Lucas asked, confused.

"I need to go home and get cleaned up. I need to eat and sleep. When I'm ready, I'll call you." She smiled as sweetly as she could.

"No." Lucas shook his head and frowned, almost sadly.

"What do you mean, *no?*" She reached inside her pocket. She had stolen one of Lucas' cans of mace. The safety was off, and she felt secure knowing she could reach it quickly.

"You can't go back to your place. It's not safe."

"And why is that?" Melanie palmed the mace and held it at her side.

"They always go back to their home."

"They?"

"Vampires." Lucas was talking to her as if she were a slow child.

She didn't like being talked down to, especially by a borderline nut job. "So you think Bryan is a—" Melanie's cheeks flushed.

"Yes. If he was attacked, he's one of them now. And your boyfriend ... Bryan," he corrected himself, "is under the vampire's control now."

Brainwashed vampire zombies. Great. She had enough problems to contend with at the moment. She didn't need Lucas dumping his bag of supernatural garbage on her lawn.

"But we didn't live together." *Stop arguing with him, damnit!*

"It doesn't matter. Rest assured, he will come after you eventually."

She crossed her arms and shook her head. *Just tell him what he wants to hear. Think. What did you learn about vampires from Bryan?* "It's daylight and I won't invite anyone in. I'll call you before dark."

Lucas nodded like he was seriously mulling this over. "Okay," he finally said. "I'll drive you back."

"No!" Melanie said a little too emphatically. She continued in a softer tone, "I mean I live just down the street."

"Right." He glared darkly down the street. "I guess that'd be okay. Wait right here." He ran back to his jeep and scrambled through the dashboard, returning at last with a piece of paper with his phone number written on it. "Before dark," he said and held the piece of paper just out of reach.

"Yes, yes." Melanie reached out and snatched it out of his hand, slipping it inside her pocket along with the mace.

"Okay." Lucas backed away a few steps and waved his hand in a small goodbye.

Melanie watched him as he walked back slowly to his car and fiddled with the radio. She caught his eyes studying her in the rear view mirror. When he realized she wasn't going anywhere until he left, he finally pulled off down the road.

As soon as he was completely gone from sight, she ran home in the opposite direction as quickly as she could.

* * * * *

Melanie climbed up the metal stairs to her apartment at the top floor of a non-descript brick building that overlooked thick and aged woods — white oak, pine, and spruce. Melanie had learned the names of all the trees to help make them more familiar and the woods a less strange and dark place.

Her backpack was lost in all the confusion of the night before. Besides her keys, Melanie made a mental note of the things she'd have to replace — her favorite lipstick, a sketchpad (thank God she didn't sign her work), charcoal pencils, her license, and — *shit* — the lighter her ex brought back from Paris. She was glad she had the sense to hide an extra key in the flowerpot next to her door. Nothing ever bloomed; the pot was nothing more than a wet and muddy pool that stained the floor, the victim of countless over-waterings. Melanie liked to think of it as suffering from too much love.

The apartment was big with high ceilings and came pre-furnished with sturdy wood furniture, the kind used in college dorms. The real sell to her, though, was the loft — she threw a mattress up there, right against the painted railing. Her regular bed went unused most nights, as Melanie preferred to sleep in the loft, where the air was warm and remained sweet with vanilla incense despite the fact she hadn't burned any for months. When it rained, the drops plinked against the skylight and reminded her of the first trailer she lived in after her dad died and before her mom started drinking.

She opened the apartment's metal door; it felt heavier than she remembered, and she had to use her shoulder to un-stick it from the frame. The air was stale and dull, and she reminded herself she had only been away for a day, not a month. The door shut on its own with a resounding thud and, though it locked automatically, she drew the chain for the first time since she'd lived there.

Immediately she ran to the answering machine, but it displayed a solid red light — no messages. She called Bryan's apartment and got a busy signal. Excitedly, she dialed again, but the phone just rang and rang. She tried to think of someone else she could call, but came up empty. Only now did she realize how small her circle of friends was, how much she depended on Bryan to fill the gaps in her life.

She needed sleep to be clear-headed, but opted instead for a scalding hot shower. She tossed her clothes right into the trash. She wasn't so rich that she could afford to simply throw out clothes, nor did she own an extensive wardrobe that could be easily replaced, but she wanted nothing to do with them. They had what Bryan would have called 'bad juju,' and she knew she wouldn't be able to wear them again without thinking about what had happened. Later, she promised herself, she would wait at Bryan's apartment until he came home.

The shower felt great. Her skin turned red, and the bathroom began to fill with steam. But as it did, she remembered the smoke pouring through the trailer and then Bryan missing from the tunnel. She turned the water to cold and rinsed off as quickly as possible. Afterwards, she retreated to the loft where she knew it would be warmed from the early afternoon sun pouring through the skylight.

Still wrapped in her bath towel, she collapsed on the mattress, feeling achy, exhausted, and a little out of breath. A white cordless phone lay next to the mattress. She picked it up and held it to her chest, curling in a ball like a cat.

"Vampires," she said to herself, and actually managed a little laugh. This whole fucking town has gone crazy. She cursed herself for not calling the police immediately — she wasn't guilty of anything, she had nothing to hide.

Sighing, she summoned up her courage and pressed '9-1-1'. There was a psycho on the loose. Even if Bryan wasn't missing, she had been attacked, and Carl was dead. She'd have to leave out the bit about being high on X when it happened and come up with an explanation as to why she waited so long to call, but this was the most logical thing to do.

The police had never been Melanie's friend — or Bryan's for that matter — and she wasn't sure how he'd feel about her calling them. They had been pulled over more times than she could count, chased out of cemeteries, and fined once for tossing cigarette butts on the ground. One cop had grazed her breasts during what she thought was an unnecessary pat-down. But this was different — this wasn't something she could handle on her own, and part of her still believed that the police were there to help.

"911, what is your emergency?" The voice was patient and steady. It might have belonged to a man or a woman.

"Um," Melanie mumbled, struggling to figure out how to begin. She shuddered with a sudden chill and pulled her towel closer to her. "I want to report a missing person." She couldn't understand why she was only giving part of the story, like something was steering her away from telling the truth.

"How long has the person been missing?" The voice remained flat and collected.

"Since last night." Melanie on the other hand felt anxious, and a thin layer of sweat collected at the back of her neck.

"Ma'am?" The operator asked, and Melanie realized she must not have been paying attention.

"I'm sorry," Melanie said and felt close to tears.

"What's your address, hon?" There was sympathy in the voice now.

"Don't you have to wait twenty-four hours?"

"Not to take a statement."

Melanie took a deep breath and gave the address. She had done the right thing.

"I'm going to send an officer over right away." The operator paused, then asked, "Are you okay?"

"Yes," Melanie said with a sniff. "Thank you."

She hung up the phone and, instead of getting dressed, pulled the heavy comforter over her despite the heat. She'd have at least twenty minutes before the police arrived. Maybe more. She'd just close her eyes for a moment.

Bryan was okay. This will all get worked out. Maybe I can even convince him to go apple picking, or for a run along the river. Maybe this terrible experience will put an end to his vampirish hang-up.

Maybe they could even become a normal couple. She saw herself and Bryan backpacking in Paris, drinking wine at an outdoor cafe along the Champs-Élysées. His hair was long and auburn, the black dye all washed out now. She wore a flowing white dress that billowed around her. She closed her eyes and fell asleep before she could make it to the Eiffel Tower.

Chapter 6

When Melanie woke, the sun had long since set, and someone was pounding on the door. Whoever was knocking had apparently been doing it for quite a while and was clearly unhappy about that fact. *The police!* Melanie remembered, jumping to her feet. She still had on her towel.

"Coming!" she shouted as she raced down the spiral staircase from the loft to her bedroom. She paused at her closet, wondering what would be appropriate dress for filing a police report. Something solemn, perhaps. Darker colors would not be a problem. Maybe she should wear white to convey a sense of innocence.

The knocking became louder and more frantic.

"Just a minute!" Now it was Melanie's turn to be annoyed. She opted for a gray sweatshirt she bought her freshman year in college at the bookstore and a pair of blue sweat pants. She looked frumpy and what she felt was appropriately disheveled.

The knocking was replaced with what sounded like a series of sharp kicks. Plaster actually flew off the hinges.

"Jesus Christ, I said I'm coming!" Melanie shouted as she opened the door. Before she could say another word, a man rushed through the door in a darkened blur and knocked her to the ground.

He immediately grabbed her by the throat. Melanie couldn't breathe or shout. Her eyes teared up and her vision blurred. She grabbed at her attacker's face and dug her nails into his cheek.

The man howled and relaxed his hold, allowing Melanie to back-peddle and retreat behind the couch.

He got to his feet and snarled. It was a snarl that had no business coming from a human mouth. Melanie wiped her eyes so she could see him more clearly. It was Bryan!

"Bryan?" she croaked and clutched at her neck.

His clothes were covered head to toe in mud. His eyes were black and red — no whites, no milky gray. He rubbed his bleeding cheek, then licked his hand, his tongue carefully taking every drop.

"What's wrong with you?"

Bryan shook his head side to side like a bull, dark blood dripping from his nose, then paced back and forth.

"I went to look for help, but you were gone. I called the police," she warned. "They should be here any minute."

Bryan growled, a menacing gurgle that emanated from the back of his throat. *Just like the girl from the night before.* His pacing grew more frantic, though his eyes never left her.

She took another few steps back. She remembered the mace in her pants, now lying in the bathroom trash, along with her stained clothes. The phone was upstairs, and she had a baseball bat under her bed, left behind from her last boyfriend — none of which were any help right now.

She eyed the front door. If she could slip by Bryan, she could get help. Everything would be all right if only...

At that moment, Bryan let out a terrible shriek, then threw the couch aside like it was made of straw. He held out his hands with deliberate purpose — he meant to kill her. Melanie tried to move, but her feet felt cemented to the floor. She put up her arms in a useless attempt at protection.

Bryan was across the room before Melanie even had a chance to scream. Seconds before he could wrap his hands around her throat again, his skull exploded in a fine mist of red and chunks of brain and bone.

Melanie didn't move a muscle. Bryan collapsed in a heap at her feet. She slowly looked up — a dark figure stood in the doorway, a silver gun in his hands.

Without thinking, Melanie turned and ran for the bathroom.

"Melanie!" a man's voice called from somewhere in the living room.

Melanie turned the lock and dug through her pants for the mace. She backed away from the door and fell backwards into the bath. "Leave me alone!" she screamed.

The man knocked on the door with the palm of his hand. "Melanie,

44

it's me. Let me in!"

"Go away!" She gathered her knees to her chest.

The knocking stopped. The voice got softer, "It's Lucas. I'm sorry. I only took my eyes off your door for a second. I got here as quick as I could."

She looked up. "You followed me?"

"I had to. You were in danger."

Melanie rocked a bit on her heels, then wrapped her arms even tighter around her chest. She felt light-headed. There was simply too much to process. She closed her eyes and mentally spelled the first word she could think of, a trick Bryan's shrink had given him for handling anxiety.

D-E-S-S-E-R-T. No, Melanie corrected herself, *arid, desolate, not an after-dinner treat. Only one 'S'. D-E-S-E-R-T.*

"You got a cigarette?" Lucas asked.

Melanie took a deep breath. "Is Bryan okay?" She used the shower curtain to pull herself to her feet.

Lucas was quiet.

"Is he—" She couldn't say the word out loud.

"Never mind, I found a pack. Do you want one?" He slid a cigarette under the door.

"Tell me if Bryan is okay!" Melanie felt like screaming. She caught a glimpse of herself in the mirror. Her face was covered in blood. Bryan's blood.

"Um, no." Lucas paused. Melanie could hear him taking a few steps away from the door. "He's dead. I killed him. But I had to. He would've killed you. You know that, right?"

D-E-A-D. The word didn't seem real when she spelled it out, just an odd assembly of vowels and consonants. It demystified the word, reduced it to its simplest components, and took away its power to hurt. Melanie crawled over to the cigarette and picked it up. "I need a light."

Lucas slid a pack of matches under the door. "Can you open the door now?"

Melanie lit her cigarette and inhaled deeply. Her throat felt sore and raw, and she coughed and choked when the warm smoke hit her lungs.

"Melanie? Are you okay?"

O-K-A-Y. Or was it Just O-K? Reluctantly, she threw the cigarette in the toilet and got to her feet. She paused at the door, her hands touching the wood as if it might burst into flames at any moment. She pressed her head against the cool frame and grabbed the door-handle, but stopped at opening it. "Call the police," she whispered.

"What? Open the door I can't hear you."

"Call the police!" she shouted, far louder than she intended, and she winced at the pain it caused. She had phoned the cops before Bryan was dead. *D-E-A-D.* Now it was too late. She felt like she owed it to him to see it through, to come clean on everything that had happened.

"We can't do that. They'll ask a lot of questions. Listen, I can take care of this—"

"Call the goddamn police or I'll tell them you attacked us, that Bryan was only protecting me." Lucas seemed determined to make her an accessory — first arson and now murder.

Lucas was quiet. Melanie heard him pacing back and forth.

"What will you tell them if I call?"

Melanie slumped on the floor and wiped her face with her sweatshirt. She hated that thing anyway. "The truth." She was being deliberately obtuse and didn't care.

She touched her neck; it was tender and sore. Black marks were already forming. Bryan would never have hurt her. *What happened to him?*

Melanie heard more pacing and then something heavy sagged against the outside of the door. Lucas sighed, "I stole the gun from my dad. He's gonna kill me."

Melanie was irate. She wanted Bryan to be whole again, she wanted this to be all over. She didn't want to hear about Lucas's petty crap. "That's your problem."

Another sigh, then the floorboards creaked, and Melanie heard more pacing. She wondered why the neighbors hadn't called the police. Gunshots weren't exactly a common phenomenon here.

A few moments later, she heard Lucas talking to someone but too soft for her to hear. After a minute or so of straining, Lucas yelled, "I called my dad." It startled the hell out of her. "He'll be here in a few minutes." Lucas stomped noisily off before she could say anything.

She decided she needed to clean herself up, and then wondered if this would be interfering with a crime scene. She caught herself nervously humming 'I'm gonna wash that man right out of my hair,' before the morbidity of what she was doing sunk in. *M-O-R-B-I-D-I-T-Y.*

She took off her sweat shirt and added it to the pile of bloody clothing in the trash. After slapping water over her face and hair, she threw on a white tank top she had left hanging on the shower rack. Her nipples showed through the shirt, but she was beyond caring. She was close to shaving her head when Lucas knocked on the door again.

"I did what you wanted. Now will you please open the door?"

"Go away." Melanie finally had a level footing. She had successfully pushed aside whatever a normal person would be feeling now — grief, anger, shock. *G-U-I-L-T.*

"Damn it!" Lucas shouted and kicked the door hard.

"Leave me alone!" Melanie shrieked and found herself unraveling again.

"I saved your life!" Lucas kicked the door again, and it buckled off the frame. "Now open the door, you ungrateful bitch!" He added another kick for emphasis.

Melanie was scared and tired and, to her surprise, a little ashamed. Lucas had saved her life, but he had also killed her boyfriend. He brought her home, but only after he almost burned her to death. He seemed to mean well, and Melanie remembered her mom's favorite expression, 'The road to hell is paved with good intentions.'

Lucas softened his voice. "I'm sorry. I'm just freaking out a little. Please," he said. "Please come out and sit with me."

Melanie weakened. If he wanted to hurt her, he could have done it by now, three times over. *Give the guy a break,* she thought. *He just murdered someone in order to save you. That's a heavy load to carry. You'd be freaking out too.*

Blood and Sunlight   Jamie Wasserman

She slowly unlocked and opened the door, and was surprised to see Lucas was crying.

He rushed to her and rested his head against her chest. His hair was soft, not prickly like she imagined it would be. He wrapped his arms around her, pulling her uncomfortably close, his hands resting where her bra strap would be. For one terrible moment, she suspected he was faking it.

"I'm sorry, I'm sorry, I'm sorry," he sobbed.

Melanie stroked his head and gently led him over to her bedroom, away from the body of her boyfriend. They sat on the bed, and Lucas laid his head in her lap. She rubbed his neck until he stopped sobbing. Melanie wanted to cry and scream and shake her fist in rage at the sky, but it somehow felt selfish. Lucas needed her. She screwed up her courage and pushed aside her own feelings until she could be alone, until she could piece together what had happened into something that made sense. She found, to her surprise, she wasn't entirely ungrateful for Lucas — it saved her the trouble of ripping her hair out in bunches, tearing her clothes in grief.

They sat like that in silence until someone else knocked on the front door. Melanie jumped at the sound, but Lucas was the picture of calm. He sat bolt upright and smoothed out his shirt. Melanie wondered how he could switch gears so quickly, then got her answer.

"My dad," he said and walked quickly to the door. He took a deep breath, ran his fingers pointlessly through his cropped hair, and opened the door. Melanie lingered outside her bedroom, not ready to see Bryan's body again.

* * * * *

Melanie understood immediately why Lucas seemed scared of his dad. He was in uniform, but it wasn't like any police uniform she had ever seen. It was all black with high boots that rose almost to his knees. He didn't wear a badge or nametag or anything else that would put anyone at ease. His hair was colored like pepper and hung in long strands across his forehead, which he constantly pushed out of his eyes. He was smiling, but Melanie could only think of the wolf in Little Red Riding Hood. *My what big teeth you have.* His eyes were constantly moving, and too dark to make out any color. He looked like a sadistic boy scout or a demonic priest. Melanie thought about locking herself in the bathroom again.

"Whatcha done now, son?"

Lucas stared at the floor and fidgeted, his hands buried deep in his pocket.

He stuck a finger under Lucas's chin and forced his head up. "Answer me. Now."

Melanie noticed his middle finger was cut off at the knuckle. It made him seem more human, flawed. Vulnerable.

"He saved my life, that's what he did." Melanie felt like she had to stick up for Lucas, but wasn't sure why.

Lucas's dad looked her up and down, more slowly and thoroughly than courtesy would dictate. Melanie felt suddenly all too aware she wasn't wearing a bra.

"Who's that?"

Lucas whispered, "Melanie."

"Speak up, boy!"

"My name is Melanie." She balled her hands into fists.

The officer dropped his hand from Lucas's chin and grinned stupidly at Melanie. "One pair between you." He caught sight of Bryan's bloodied body and wiped his mouth. "This is no good."

He stroked his chin, sizing up the situation and walked over to Bryan and nudged him with his boot, "Damn it."

Melanie winced and tried looking away. A dark circle of red had spread around Bryan's head like a halo, and the image was burned on her retina. She saw it repeated countless times on the white plaster of the ceiling ... *C-E-I-L-I-N-G. 'I' before 'E' except after 'C'.*

"Is there an ambulance coming?" Melanie wrung her hands.

Officer Tyler's eyes narrowed. "For what? He's dead. You shoot him, or did my dumbass son pull the trigger?"

Melanie's eyes sank to the floor. *D-E-A-D. Dead, dead, dead.*

Lucas took a deep breath and exhaled slowly. "I did," he muttered.

"Of course you did." He turned and slapped Lucas hard, knocking him to the ground. His hair was wild and his cheeks flushed.

Melanie took a step forward, but Officer Tyler's sharp look was enough to stop her in her tracks.

"My gun," he said holding out his hand.

Lucas reached behind him and pulled out the silver-handled weapon. He handed it to his father, then promptly buried his face in his arms.

Lucas's dad leaned next to Lucas and said more gently than Melanie would have thought he was capable, "I can't keep doing this." He righted Melanie's table and blood-stained couch, then plopped himself on the edge.

Melanie tried staring out the window. Drops of blood stood out against the white blinds and the surrounding wall. There was nowhere safe to look anymore.

"Get me the phone," Officer Tyler said to no one in particular. When Lucas didn't make a move, Melanie scrambled for one. Anything that might bring other people to the apartment.

As he dialed, his angry gaze never left Lucas, who cowered on the floor.

"Hey Tina!" Officer Tyler said, getting up from the couch. "How's that momma of yours?"

Melanie heard some chatter on the other end, then Officer Tyler said, "You tell her to hang in there." He pushed past Melanie into her bedroom and shut the door. "Prick," she muttered, and then realized she was stuck out here with Bryan's *B-O-D-Y.* Panic was beginning to creep in again.

She looked at Lucas still shaking on the floor. She wanted to hold his hand, to share and lessen the wave of anxiety coming over her, but knew that would only wound his pride even further. She slumped against the wall, close to the door, hoping maybe she could hear what was being said, but Officer Tyler's voice was low and smooth, like silk, like a dirge. Melanie shuddered and made a mental list of what she'd pack if she were leaving for France in the morning. *Passport, camera, francs. Where would I get French money here? What was the exchange rate?*

That line of thinking kept her relatively calm until Officer Tyler finally emerged from the bedroom and looked down at Melanie.

"You sleeping with my son?"

"Excuse me?" she snipped and started to rise to her feet, but Officer Tyler pushed her back down. He knelt in front of her, inches from her face, "Are you sleeping with my son?" He spread the words out slowly.

"No." Melanie folded her arms; it was her only option for defiance.

"Where's Leah?"

She shrugged. "I don't know."

"You kill her, too?" Officer Tyler shouted to Lucas.

Lucas sniffled and managed to say, "No."

"Who's the corpse?"

Melanie's face blanched. She thought she might get sick despite her empty stomach. *C-O-R-P-S-E.* Through gritted teeth she said, "My boyfriend. Bryan."

"Uh huh. You sure Lucas ain't dipping his wick in your ink?"

She shook her head.

"Family?"

Melanie looked up confused. "What?"

Officer Tyler sighed and spoke even slower, "Does Bryan, your boyfriend, have any family?"

She honestly didn't know. She knew his dad was dead and his mom was a drunk just like hers had been. But judging by the hours Bryan kept, and the lifestyle he led, he didn't seem suited for quality time. She had never met any of his family. "No one who cares. Just me," she said finally. *A-L-O-N-E.*

"Is there anything else you want to tell me?"

Melanie felt like she was back in Catholic School. *No monsignor.* Then she remembered Carl's neck, hanging by the thinnest of threads. It was too late for honesty though. "No," she blurted out and immediately sensed Officer Tyler knew she was lying.

"You sure?"

Melanie nodded her head.

"Nothing that's going to come up later?"

"I said no!" she snapped.

"Good." He got up and paced the room. "You wanted to see other people, and Bryan was angry. Bonehead over there showed up to take you out and brought me along. He was just all excited for me to meet this new girl of his. Bryan arrived, flipped out and tried to strangle you." He looked back at Melanie, "That is how you got those marks on your neck, right?"

"Yes." Melanie bit her bottom lip. He was good.

"I tried to pull him away but he was crazed. I drew my gun and warned him to desist. When he wouldn't listen, I shot him dead."

Lucas looked up suddenly. "Dad, no."

"Shut up. You didn't leave me much choice, didya? Next time you wanna kill someone, use your own goddamn gun," Officer Tyler fumed. "Got it?"

Next time?

"There'll be a few questions, but I'll take care of most of it." Officer Tyler headed to the door and then bent down next to Lucas, stroking his head. "I know you had a good reason. We still got some talking to do." He got up and opened the door and said with his back to the room, "I'm going outside to wait for the van. And one more thing," he yelled from the door. "Come up with a reason why the goddamn body in the living room is covered in mud like it just crawled outta its own grave. I'm not that creative."

Melanie rocked back and forth on her heels. *A-L-O-N-E. Alone, alone, alone.*

Chapter 7

There were questions. Lots of them. But anytime the investigating policemen got too in-depth or too close to the truth, Officer Tyler interjected with a question of his own, which derailed all trains of thought. He didn't let the other police separate Melanie and Lucas, so their story never wavered. *A good cop, indeed.* Melanie wondered how many other crimes he had covered up for his son.

When it came time to take Bryan's body away, Officer Tyler ordered Melanie and Lucas upstairs. "Y'all don't need to see this," he said waving away the other officers' protests.

The front door opened and shut several times. The shadows in the room darkened to oblivion. Melanie and Lucas sat on the floor next to each other, but not touching, trying hard to block out the noises downstairs. At some point, Melanie fell asleep. Her dreams were vacant, colorless and lonely. When she did snap herself awake, her neck ached, and she found herself even more exhausted than before. Lucas remained in the same position, teeth clenched, hands clutching at the floor as if he were sitting in the first car of a roller coaster teetering on the edge of a dark precipice.

It was almost midnight when Officer Tyler trudged up the stairs. He was out of breath and disheveled. The day had taken something from him. "I had them clean up a bit downstairs," he announced, sounding almost apologetic. He looked at Lucas. "My shift ends at one this morning. I want you over at the house afterwards. Got it?" He headed back down the stairs.

Lucas nodded, and then found some courage. "Dad!"

Officer Tyler paused with his back to them.

"Thanks." Lucas tugged at his ear.

Officer Tyler ignored him. "Your sister's been asking about you. Wouldn't kill you to stop by the house more often, neither." He trudged heavily down the stairs and out the front door.

Lucas looked at his watch. "11:50," he muttered to himself.

Melanie realized she had gone the whole day without eating again. "Do you want some coffee or something to eat?" She didn't want to be alone.

"I should go." Lucas stood up and wobbled on his feet a little.

"You've got some time. You have to be hungry. Please."

Lucas met her eyes for the first time since he shot Bryan. "Uh, yeah," he said, nodding with understanding.

They walked in silence to the kitchen, almost tip-toeing. Melanie snuck a glance around the apartment. The furniture had been moved and put back slightly askew — it gave the room an unfamiliar, unnerving feel. The living room had been scrubbed hospital-clean, but dark spatters and stains still covered the carpet and couch. It looked like an old map, the kind with vague and watery shapes for continents and a legend declaring, "Here there be dragons," over the unchartered portion of the world.

* * * * *

The kitchen was merely a thin sliver cut out of the living room and separated by a high wall that doubled as a table. Melanie found the room unbearably white and spent as little time there as possible. But now she welcomed the distraction as she clattered and knocked around pans and dug deep into cupboards that hadn't been touched for months. Lucas sat at the bar, staring off into space.

Melanie decided on scrambled eggs, the one meal she could make well, unless she counted mac n' cheese from the box. She haphazardly broke eggs and whipped them into a froth, enjoying the sizzle of butter as it melted on the pan. She threw four pieces of bread into a toaster she couldn't remember buying, and sent the egg batter rushing over the pan. Smoke rose instantly, and she stepped closer to the stove, enjoying the warmth. She was a constant blur of movement and noise.

Moments later, she set two plates down on the table and settled onto one of the high and wobbly barstools Bryan had salvaged from an old restaurant that burned down. The room fell back into an uncomfortable silence with Lucas pushing his food around on his plate and Melanie contemplating the same question over and over ... *What now?*

She glanced over at Lucas. He looked back at her for a long awkward moment. "I'm sorry for the knife thing."

Melanie wanted to laugh. That paled in comparison to the events that followed.

"And for..." He looked backed down at the table. "Well, I'm sorry."

Melanie nodded solemnly. "Thanks for saving me."

Lucas set his silverware down across his plate, forming a makeshift cross. She wondered if it was intentional. She needed conversation. Fast. "The fire," she blurted out.

Lucas looked up, a little ashamed. "Forgot about that. Sorry about that, too."

"What were you doing?"

Lucas perked up, apparently just as grateful as Melanie for a change in topics. "Vampires need to sleep just like us. They need somewhere to go during the day to protect themselves from the sun. I was just eliminating some possible resting places."

Vampires were a familiar topic. Bryan could talk for hours about vampire myths and sightings.

"So how long have you been chasing vampires?" It sounded almost like a pick-up line, but Melanie wanted to escape her own reality for a bit. It was one of the things that had made Bryan so appealing to her.

Lucas looked up and half-smiled. "Four months."

Melanie nodded. What she really wanted to ask was, "Kill anyone else?" and the image of Bryan's blood-rimmed eyes popped in her head.

Lucas poked his food a few more times and set his fork down. He took a deep breath and looked up at Melanie. "My girlfriend..." he finally began.

"Leah," Melanie jumped in, eager to shake the images from her head and wanting to prove to Lucas she had been listening.

"Leah." Lucas's face brightened. "We hung out at Red's a lot. She liked to do karaoke. Plus we got free drinks. The bartender had a thing for her."

Blood and Sunlight

Jamie Wasserman

Red's Tavern was a rundown bar that sat on the opposite edge of the city limits as the Old Monk. It was as far away from Main Street as you could get without actually leaving town. It was a spot for locals — a ramshackle, claustrophobic dive with dark wood furniture and a small stage where loud bands sometimes performed. Melanie didn't think Lucas's piercings would have gone over well in there.

"She could really sing. That night she did 'Shadows of the Night,' the Helen Schneider version, which is a whole lot tougher. You'd never think a voice like hers could come outta someone that small." Lucas looked down, pushed away a thought, and continued. "The whole night I felt like somebody was watching me. Know what I mean?"

Melanie shivered a little. She imagined Bryan at the window, pressing a bloodied face against the glass. She nodded, urging Lucas to continue.

"We sat and talked for a while, then headed out to my car. She said I was too drunk to drive and wanted the keys. It's stupid, I know. I shoulda just given them to her. We got into a huge fight over it. She ran off down the street, and I chased after her. All I wanted to do was talk. Get back home. I reached out and grabbed her arm."

The shattered front door groaned on one good hinge, which made Melanie jump.

"We argued for a bit. I said some things I probably shouldn't have. She slapped me. Her ring scratched my cheek and drew blood. I grabbed her by the shoulders. I just wanted to get her to calm down, to hold her. To tell her I was sorry." Lucas drew a deep breath. Melanie watched his shoulders rise and sag heavily.

"He came out of nowhere. He wasn't much bigger than me, but he was strong. It was the blood, I think. The blood had summoned him like some kind of incantation. He..." Lucas swallowed. "He beat me pretty bad. I remember Leah screaming. All I wanted to do was get to her, to protect her, but he didn't stop. He broke two ribs, bruised me up pretty badly." He touched his side, testing for a lingering pain.

He rubbed his hands together, warming them against an imaginary chill. "That wasn't the worst part. I watched them leave together. Leah was holding his hand. Her face was totally calm. I didn't know it then, but I think he had her under some kind of spell. They say the eyes..."

Lucas turned his own sad blue eyes directly at Melanie. She looked away at the chipped counter.

"The power is in a vampire's eyes. That's how they control you. They walked off together into the woods. I called her the next day, but she didn't answer. I wanted to apologize, to make sure she was okay. I stopped by her place. It didn't look like she ever came home."

"You drove the next day with broken ribs?" Melanie found herself getting caught up in the story.

Lucas's face went slack. "I didn't want things to end that way. She belongs with me." Lucas gnashed his teeth. "We belong together..." His voice trailed off. He folded his hands in his lap and continued. "I hung out at the same bars we used to go, even drove out to her sister's place in Mt. Airy. Nothing. It was like she just disappeared."

Melanie walked over to the door and elbowed it shut. In her mind, Bryan's mangled body drifted away from the window and down the stairs.

"I finally caught a break while I was doing some midnight fishing in Oella."

Oella was even smaller than Ellicott City, and situated just up-river. Like Ellicott City, it was built around a mill. The town was all but deserted now, with a thousand trees to every person. Most folks didn't even consider it a separate entity.

"What were you doing fishing in the middle of the night?"

"Best time to catch trout. They feed at night to avoid all the damn lines. Unfortunately, all I'd pulled were gizzard shads and those damn eels. Ever since they opened up the river, the water's been lousy with them."

"Lucas." Melanie needed to be distracted, and Lucas's fishing lecture was driving her straight back into the arms of the former corpse in the room.

"Sorry. I was out there an hour, maybe two, when I realized just how quiet it was."

"It *was* the middle of the night."

"The woods don't shut down. Crickets, coons, the deer. Hell, it's all you can do to hear yourself think. All the animals love it then. They've had to adapt. Too many people during the day, hunting and tearing up the countryside. We could learn something..."

Lucas tapped a finger on the table with a faraway look in his eye. After a beat, he shook his head and continued, "All that silence, once it registered, really spooked me. I packed up my stuff to leave, when I heard it."

Melanie shivered. A leftover chill from the open door, she told herself.

"It was just a twig snapping, but it might as well have been played on a surround-sound — that's how quiet the night had become. And then I saw them. They were just a blur, hauling ass through the woods. It actually took my brain a few seconds to process what I'd seen. But I'd know that strawberry blonde hair anywhere. And she was with him."

"Him?"

"The vampire."

Of course, he was running alongside the mummy and a werewolf drinking Pina Coladas.

As if reading her mind, Lucas said, "I know it sounds crazy. I didn't believe any of this before I saw it myself."

Melanie blushed and looked down. She wasn't used to being so easily read.

"I trailed them to the burnt-out girls' school."

Melanie and Bryan used to smoke weed there and take pictures of the ruins before it was converted to a park. They even had sex in the old cast iron tub that used to sit improbably in the middle of the grounds. *Bryan*, she said to herself. She closed her eyes and tried to focus on Lucas's story.

"They were gone by the time I got there. It was like the forest just swallowed them up." Lucas stopped abruptly. "Let me finish, Melanie."

She looked up with a guilty expression on her face. "I didn't say anything."

"It's not hard to tell what you're thinking. Your forehead gets all crinkly. And you bite your cheek when you're trying to stop yourself from talking."

"Great." Melanie frowned.

"No, it's cute." Lucas grinned.

Melanie blushed. *Okay, maybe being easily read isn't so terrible.* "So what happened?" she blurted, thinking flirting with someone so soon after the body of your ex was removed from your apartment was in bad taste. *Martha Stuart should do a special on it.* Melanie realized she was on the verge of giddiness — all that stress needed an outlet. She wondered if Lucas's chest was smooth.

"I checked out those woods for hours. Didn't find a thing. I know how to track. My dad used to take me hunting. Well, before I accidentally shot his finger off."

Aha.

"I went back every night for a month. A week ago, I found them again. About a mile east, near Hell House."

Well at least that explains why he was trying to torch the place. Melanie scrunched up her nose.

"No doubt this time. She had the same crazy look as Bryan..." Lucas clenched his fists.

Melanie set her fork down. *Stop saying his name, damn it!*

"She was alone and moving through the woods so slow, you could barely tell she was moving at all. About thirty feet away was a large deer. Six or eight points at least."

Melanie didn't know what that meant, but nodded anyway.

"I watched Leah get closer and closer, but the deer didn't even look up once. You ever try sneaking up on a deer?"

Melanie suppressed a giggle. No, but she did go cow tipping once with her ... ex. She decided that was a safe word. There was a host of terms to choose from, none of which would immediately call to mind her most recent, the one she had dated longer than any of the others, the only one she would have even vaguely considered marrying, maybe, someday in the very distant future, if nothing better came along.

"When she was about twenty feet away, she leaped forward and grabbed the deer by the neck. People can't do that. They can't." Lucas shook his head. "After, she wrestled the damn thing to the ground, then ripped out its neck with her teeth."

Melanie swallowed and touched her own swollen neck.

"She lapped up the blood that poured outta that deer like it was a saucer of milk. I stepped forward to get a better look. I guess part of me couldn't believe what I was seeing. Anyway, I must've startled her. She looked up, shrieked, and took off."

"Did you follow her?"

"She'd just tackled and killed a deer with her teeth. Hell, no, I didn't follow her." Lucas leaned back in his chair and folded his arms. He looked pleased with himself.

"So based on that, you think there's a vampire out there?

Lucas frowned. "There's more. I've been reading up. Everything fits."

"Br — my ex wasn't a vampire. He didn't have sharp teeth. He didn't turn to dust when you..." Her voice trailed off when she saw Lucas's wounded look. "Maybe it's like rabies."

"Rabies don't make people eat live animals."

"I said *like* rabies. It could be something else."

"What?"

"I don't know. I'm not a doctor." Melanie hated herself for arguing. Lucas may have been well-meaning, but he was crazy, and this wasn't a discussion she could win.

"When you have eliminated the impossible, whatever remains, however improbable, must be the truth. Sherlock Holmes said that. And he's one of the best detectives out there."

"Sherlock Holmes is a fictional character, and so are vampires." Melanie felt hungry again. "And I read that book, too. I know who said it." She hadn't actually read the book, but she had seen one of the movies. It was in black and white, and she fell asleep before Holmes announced who the killer was.

"Something bit Bryan and made him act crazy. That same thing bit Leah, and they all acted the same way. Crazed. Bloodthirsty."

Melanie gnawed at her cheek, then stopped when she saw Lucas studying her. "If this guy you're talking about was a vampire, why didn't he bite you? Why didn't he bite me?"

Lucas looked up. "Wait, you saw him?"

Melanie cursed herself for mentioning the man who had saved her. She was only fueling Lucas's imagination. "I saw *someone* last night."

Lucas jumped to his feet, excited. "What did he look like?"

"I don't remember," Melanie lied. She could still smell cedar.

"Curly black hair? Sharp nose?"

It was more wavy then curly, Melanie thought. *And it was a Greek nose.* "I'm sorry."

Lucas frowned. "Would you recognize him if you saw his picture?"

"You got his picture?" she asked concerned. Vampires didn't have a reflection, and they didn't photograph; she knew that from every movie she had ever seen on the subject. *I guess digital doesn't apply.* Why was she even trying to protect this man, she wondered.

Lucas looked at his watch, "Shit. I have to go."

"Why?" She felt a surge of panic.

"My dad," Lucas said softly and closed his eyes. "I'll come back, okay? If I can." He said the last part ominously.

"No!" Melanie imagined Bryan back outside her apartment, pounding a filthy fist against the door, wanting in.

"Melanie..." Lucas started.

"Can I stay with you?" Melanie's eyes teared up. The question surprised her. All she knew was that she couldn't stay here.

"Are you sure?" Lucas did his best to hide a smile.

"I'll sleep on your couch. On the floor. Please."

Lucas looked disappointed, but said quietly, "Yeah, of course." Then he paused. "Melanie, you ever been hunting?"

Chapter 8

Melanie stuffed a week's worth of clothes into an old army duffle bag she got from a thrift store. She hadn't realized just how much of her clothes were black. The word *funerary* came to mind. Then she added a toothbrush, deodorant, and a hairbrush, but gave up on make-up — Lucas had seen her covered in skull fragments; missing a few days of eyeliner wouldn't be a big deal. She decided she would stay as long as Lucas would have her. The thought of having to walk by a blood-stained carpet every day that reminded her of her boyfriend was just too much to take.

As an after-thought, she also grabbed her work uniform and a purse she hadn't used since high school. The weekend was almost over. Tomorrow at this time, she'd be back at The Hidden Fox, serving lattes to ungrateful old ladies or unpacking new books in the storeroom. She almost looked forward to the tediousness.

"Hurry up!" Lucas shouted near the door. He was growing increasingly impatient. A moment later, he appeared in the doorway. "Can I help you with that?" he asked, nodding to the bag.

Melanie knew he wasn't being chivalrous; he was just scared of being late to see his father, but she handed him the bag anyway. He smelled strongly of thick sweat and fear. It wasn't entirely unpleasant.

With the green army bag slung over his shoulder and his camouflaged pants and buzz-cut, Lucas looked as if he were heading off to war. And maybe he was.

Melanie looked around her apartment and at the broken door; she could probably kiss her security deposit goodbye. It was a selfish thought, she decided, and made a mental note to call the super tomorrow to get it fixed.

On her way out, she saw the blinking red light of her answering machine. She punched the button, and a disinterested male voice said, "This is Officer Rolley. I stopped by earlier to take your statement. Please contact me as soon as possible."

Great. Why couldn't I have seen that earlier?

* * * * *

Lucas's apartment complex was right off the interstate, sandwiched between a tiny strip mall and an adult bookstore. When the bookstore had first opened, there were protesters from a local church group, and Bryan and Carl showed up just so they could cross the picket line. They bought a dozen dirty magazines and walked out slowly, daring one of the people to make eye contact or say something. Melanie sat in the car, bored. The church group didn't deviate from their slow circle in the parking lot, and eventually Bryan got fed up and tossed the magazines at them. Carl broke a bottle against an expensive Hummer, and they peeled out. Pretending to be a vampire, Melanie supposed, was easier — you created your own fun. You didn't have to rely on anyone else for excitement.

Melanie let go of the memory reluctantly as Lucas swung the car in front of a set of flat, two-floored apartment buildings done up in that sturdy but forgettable post-war brick that made up most of Route 40. He cut the engine and wiggled a key off his ring, handing it to her. "I'm on the top floor, 2-B on the left."

"Aren't you coming in?"

"Can't." Lucas pointed to his watch, then stuck the key back in the car and started the engine. *Get out,* was the hint.

Where was the chivalry now? Melanie wondered, as she wrestled with her bag wedged in the already crowded backseat. As soon as she slammed the car door shut, Lucas raced away without so much as a second glance.

"No, don't worry about me. I've got it," she muttered to herself and began dragging the bag across the oil-stained parking lot.

A moment later, Lucas screeched back into the parking lot and jumped out. "Bolt the front door and take care," he said taking Melanie's bag and the key as he rushed up the stairs. "Don't let no one in when I'm not with you."

She had to run to keep up, and was winded by the time they reached his apartment. He opened and held the door, setting her bag down. She had to press closely by him to get inside. "Good luck!" She held up her hand, waving like an idiot. He nodded glumly.

She leaned in and gave him a kiss on the cheek. "Thank you."

He blushed and lightly touched his face.

That should buy me at least a few more nights at his place, she hoped.

Anyone watching them might think this was the end of a first date, but inside Melanie was a wreck. She would be whatever Lucas wanted as long as it afforded her the luxury of not having to stay inside her own head.

Lucas touched her arm and promised to be back soon.

Melanie drew a deep breath, summoned up her courage, and felt along the wall for the light-switch. After accidentally turning on an overhead fan and then the porch and kitchen lights, she was rewarded as the living room finally brightened up from yellow fluorescent track-lighting that seemed to occupy every classroom she had ever entered.

The apartment was a near copy of her own, with a living room adjacent to a tiny kitchen, a small bathroom at the end of a hallway, and a single bedroom next door. Melanie frowned at this. Lucas had a good-sized porch, but the view was of the rear entrance of a Dunkin' Donuts, so she drew the blinds and padded her way around the rest of the apartment. There was no loft and no bar, but Lucas had somehow managed to find a table small enough to fit in the kitchen. Most of the rest of the furniture was built out of unfinished wood and cinderblocks.

The other main difference between Lucas's apartment and hers was that almost every available space was crammed with books. She threw her bag into the kitchen, which somehow remained miraculously clear of clutter, and side-stepped her way to the couch.

There were no posters or artwork on the wall, no TV staring dumbly in the corner. The place almost looked like a cell. All that was missing were bars on the window. Melanie picked up an open book from the large plywood shipping crate that served as a coffee table, anxious for a distraction.

"The Vampire's Kith and Kin," she read. It was a library book, wrapped in a plastic cover like an uneaten sandwich. They were all library books, it seemed. This one was heavily marked and highlighted.

Melanie opened the book to a random page and read the boldest and most heavily marked entry. *Although, as we have seen, there are many methods and many variants, it is certain that an effectual remedy against the vampire is to transfix his heart with a stake driven through with one single blow, to strike off his head with a sexton's spade, and perhaps best of all to burn him to ashes and purge the earth of his pollutions by the incineration of fire.*

"Aha," she said throwing the book back on the crate and stretching out on the couch. She wondered if Bryan's book was in there, the one he had been nagging her to read. But she realized she could no longer remember the title. *I was a lousy girlfriend,* she thought.

Part of her wanted to explore the bedroom, maybe even shower and change, though she couldn't bring herself to be naked in Lucas's apartment. Maybe later, she thought, when she wasn't so damn tired. But she was, and the adrenalin that worked its way through her system soured and made her muscles ache. She curled into a ball, pulled a couch cushion protectively to her chest, and fell asleep.

* * * * *

Melanie woke to the sound of the door slamming. To her surprise, she had been dreaming about a castle high atop a craggy cliff, with the ocean crashing below. It would have been quite beautiful, but her dream was in black and white, and it made the castle look ominous and haunted. She was glad for the disruption of Lucas's return.

She glanced at the clock on the wall — it was 2:00 am. Lucas hadn't been gone very long. He went straight to the kitchen and set about preparing himself an ice pack. Melanie expected at least a black eye, but he looked just as smooth and unblemished as when he left. She had to admit that she was a little disappointed, but didn't know why.

"Everything okay?" Melanie asked sleepily when it was obvious Lucas wasn't going to say anything. She sat up on the couch and rubbed her throbbing temples. "What's the ice pack for?"

Lucas sat on the far edge, grimacing as he rested his back against the cushions.

"What happened?"

Lucas sat forward and winced as he lifted the back of his shirt. Melanie could just make out a heavy red line running down his back. Pushing his shirt further up, she found more and more welts, some of which were spotted with blood.

The cuts were concentrated around his shoulders and upper back and reminded her of those Medieval woodcut drawings from Sunday school of monks whipping themselves over the shoulder with Birchwood branches.

She didn't say a word; she simply took off his shirt and gently dabbed the ice pack to the heavier marked areas. He flinched but didn't push her away. To Melanie's surprise, the wounds excited her. Maybe it was because Lucas was cut but still whole, because he survived. Because he returned.

Without thinking, she leaned in and gently kissed one of the lighter marks. And then, when he didn't stop her despite the pain he must have felt, she kissed another. His skin tasted different than Bryan's; saltier, like metal and rust. She was so absorbed in his body that she had almost completely forgotten he was there. It had just been Melanie and a broad expanse of skin and heat.

That is until Lucas turned around and pulled Melanie to him, kissing her roughly. He tasted sour, like Southern Comfort and aspirin. This was too intimate, too soon. She felt guilty as if Bryan might walk in the room any moment; then angry — Lucas had rubbed away any traces of Bryan's last kiss in one fell swoop. She tried to push him away but he grabbed her wrists and pinned her to the couch.

She bit at his shoulder until she drew blood. He yelped and released his hold and Melanie rolled on top of him and scratched his face and pounded at his chest. She let Lucas have everything she had held back — her grief and anger — and he allowed her. She slapped his face and ripped his shirt. She swore like she was possessed, speaking in tongues, speaking in the strange but all too familiar language of sorrow. And then, just as quickly, she stopped and her shoulders sagged and she cried.

Lucas sat up and wrapped his arms around her then laid her gently back on the couch. As she continued to sob, he slid his hand into her pants. She grabbed his arm to push him away but was surprised at how quickly her body responded.

She grabbed the back of his head and pulled him to her chest, willing him on. Lucas rubbed against her, kissing her neck. With his other hand, he continued to stroke her until she finally came, loud enough to wake the dead.

When he was done, Lucas kissed her forehead. "Sorry," he mumbled and walked down the hall to the bedroom. The door didn't shut — it was an invitation.

Melanie sat up on her elbows, a mixture of pleasure and shame and anger buzzing through her veins, making her feel light-headed and tired all over again. She loved sex, loved the way it focused all of her attention on one thing and one thing only — pleasure. With the proper administrations, she was no longer a college drop-out or a waitress at a shitty bookstore. She wasn't struggling to pay rent on an apartment in the town she grew up in and had never left. Her boyfriend wasn't dead. Even Lucas was gone. There was no past, no future, only present and it was limitless and electric. Every one of her senses buzzed and stretched with pleasure. But when it was over, she always found herself exhausted, soaked with sweat, inexplicably disappointed, and all too alone. It didn't matter who was next to her, because she could never find the right words to convey that sadness.

She lay there for a bit feeling antsy and sick, debating on what to do next. If she hung around for a while, she wouldn't feel as guilty about what had happened. She could think of this as a relationship that went south and not just another bed she tried to hide in.

She looked to Lucas's open bedroom door for a long time. Home was not an option and, she realized, she really had nowhere else to go. Finally, Melanie got up and headed towards the bedroom, tiptoeing just in case she decided to change her mind at the last minute.

Lucas was already in bed, his back to the door. Melanie slipped in next to him, enjoying the scent of sweat and cologne that came off the sheets and vanilla perfume. She wondered when Leah last slept here.

"Good night, Melanie," he said without moving.

"Night." She pulled the sheet tightly around her and inched back so she was nearly touching Lucas. Everything, she decided, would make more sense in the morning.

* * * * *

Sun poured uninterrupted through the open window in Lucas's bedroom. He was already up, lying on his side, lightly stroking Melanie's neck. The digital clock on Lucas's floor read 10:15 a.m. She had to be at work in less than an hour.

"Hi." She looked at him, forcing a smile, the sour taste on her lips an unpleasant reminder of last night. She rolled over with her back to him, guilt overcoming her. She couldn't look Lucas in the eyes.

"You did get bitten. Doesn't look too bad though. How'd you get it?"

Melanie sat up and covered her neck. "Bryan. During ... you know. Before he was attacked. Just got a little carried away." Her stomach grumbled. Her body at least was back on a normal schedule.

Last night was a one-time thing, Melanie told herself. *A release to the worst day of my life. Besides, it wasn't like we actually did it.* She swung her feet to the floor and started to head out of the room.

Lucas caught her arm. "I think I can find him."

"Find who?"

"The vampire."

"Lucas, I have to pee."

He let go of her arm. "Oh, sorry."

Melanie took her time. She didn't want to hear about vampires anymore. That was something best locked away with Bryan, six feet underground in the soft brown earth. She peed, brushed her teeth, used all the hot water in her shower, and changed into her work clothes. The bruises from where Bryan grabbed her neck looked yellow and anemic, but no longer felt tender. She was healing despite herself.

Let Lucas wait. She'd get a ride from him to the bookstore and bring her stuff. At work, she'd call maintenance and have her door fixed. She had a distant cousin in Reno. Maybe she could crash with her for a while. Maybe she'd go back to art school, call her grandma, finally visit her mom's grave.

The smell of pancakes and bacon wafted under the door, and Melanie's stomach rumbled anew. She followed the scent to the kitchen where Lucas was busy setting his tiny table and cooking breakfast. He looked up and grinned when he saw her. "Hungry?"

Melanie nodded and noticed that the books had been neatly stacked in front of his already full cinderblock bookshelf. He had made room for her. Melanie suppressed a smile and sat down.

"Do you eat deer?"

Melanie scrunched up her nose. *Even if I did before, I sure as hell won't anymore.* "No." She shook her head at a greasy plate of meat.

"I've also got bacon and sausage."

She took a big sip of orange juice, nodded and wiped her mouth. "Bacon. Please."

"The Hidden Fox," Lucas read, setting two plates on the table.

"Hmm?" Melanie mumbled, mesmerized by the food. God she was hungry. She tore a huge piece of pancake off and shoved it in her mouth.

"Is that where you work?" Lucas pointed to Melanie's shirt, which was now covered in crumbs.

"Um, yeah." Melanie gulped down the rest of her juice.

"Do you need a ride?"

"Actually, that'd be great." Melanie was glad she didn't have to ask.

As if reading her mind, he added, "I can pick you up, too if you want, and take you back to your apartment. Or you're welcome to stay here as long as you want. Wherever you'd feel safer."

"Thanks." A few more days wouldn't hurt. She did hate to be alone.

"And then we can talk about my plan to catch the vampire."

Lucas may as well have shattered a mirror across the table. Melanie was having enough problems just dealing with reality — she didn't need make-believe monsters thrown into the mix. "Jesus Christ, Lucas. No. There is no vampire. There is no bogeyman in the closet. And there is nothing, I repeat nothing, living under your bed."

"I know that." Lucas frowned. "The bogeyman's a cautionary tale. Don't eat your vegetables or the bogeyman'll get ya. But the vampire—" Lucas looked up excitedly. "Wait. The pictures. I never showed you the pictures!" Lucas ran into the living room and slid out a box full of papers from underneath the sofa. "Here!" he said, shoving a handful of black and white eight-by-tens at Melanie.

"They're blurry," she said, thumbing through a series of shots of a man walking through the woods. The pictures reminded her of those shaky photos of Bigfoot. "And I thought vampires didn't photograph."

Lucas frowned. This clearly puzzled him as well. "Not all the books are right. They photograph, and you can see their reflection, I think."

"What about silver?"

"That's werewolves."

Melanie didn't want to ask if Lucas believed in werewolves, too. "So how do you kill them?" God help her, she was feeding his dementia.

Lucas pulled a wood case from under his couch. "With these," he said, opening the box. It was velvet lined and filled with sharpened stakes, a gleaming axe, small vials of water, several crucifixes, garlic, and a spade.

"What if you're wrong about these, too?"

"Then I'll die trying," he said, very matter of fact. In Lucas's vision, there were no other options. She almost admired his conviction.

The last photograph Melanie viewed was slightly clearer than the others. The man was facing the camera and almost seemed to be smiling directly at her. He had wavy hair and wore a tight black tee shirt. In the photo, his shirt looked dirty and worn, not sleek like she remembered.

"That's the best one. You can almost see his fangs."

Melanie quickly slid aside the photographs. This didn't prove anything. A coincidence at best.

"Melanie." Lucas folded his arms and paused for dramatic effect.

"What?" She was annoyed. This was beginning to feel like a visit to the principal's office.

"Last night you said you had another friend with you. Carl, right?"

Melanie flushed. Her stomach knotted.

"But you didn't tell my dad about that."

She froze and wondered if he was looking to blackmail her. *Good luck, creep, I've got nothing.*

Lucas paused, giving Melanie the opportunity to reply but, getting none, plowed forward. "What happened to him?"

She remembered Carl's limp body, his head dangling from his neck like a broken Ken doll.

"He was killed that night," she said softly. And by *your* girlfriend.

"Are you sure?"

"Yes, I'm sure. You think I'm making this up?"

"Of course not. But the body was gone by the time we got there the next morning."

"So?" She swallowed some orange juice, guilt sticking in her throat, making it difficult to swallow.

"So who carried him out?" Lucas leaned back in his chair, smiling, smug.

Melanie wondered that too. It couldn't have been Bryan. He was too weak to even stand. Though he was strong enough to squeeze the very breath out of her later. And he passed out just watching Melanie get a tattoo — a small musical note on her ankle. It was hard to imagine him lugging a dead body through the woods.

"I don't know." Truthfully, Melanie realized, she was grateful. *Out of sight, out of mind.* Whoever had removed the body had done her a favor, no matter how gruesome it seemed. *Hell, who's to say it wasn't Lucas who did it?*

"But you said you saw somebody else last night."

The image in her head of the man who helped her was growing more distant, blurrier, like the photographs in front of her.

"Is this him?" Lucas fanned the photographs in front of Melanie.

"I don't know. Maybe."

Lucas frowned. "Could you draw him?"

71

She tensed. Had he found her sketch book?

"Forget all the vampire stuff. You have to admit, this guy, whoever he is, is at the center of all of this."

Melanie nodded, as if agreeing, but secretly wondered how much it would hurt if she jumped off the deck.

"Melanie?"

"What?" she snapped hoping Lucas might get the hint and drop this whole line of questioning. In her mind, she was running down the road with her arms thrown in the air like the little gingerbread man.

"Will you help me?"

"No. I'm sorry. I think I need to leave here. Maybe move out to the desert." *Flat earth and a vast expanse of blue sky. Nothing could sneak up on you in the desert.*

"The desert?"

"I've been thinking about it for a while now," she lied.

"Really?"

"Yeah."

"That's too bad." Lucas looked downcast.

Melanie heard herself start to say 'It's not you, it's me,' but then thought, *I shouldn't have to apologize. I'm the victim.* "I just think this is something the police should be handling."

"Yeah right." Lucas snorted then clasped his hands together and stared out the window.

"I am sorry," Melanie said.

"Whatever. It's fine." Lucas pushed away from the table.

"I should get my things for work." She stood up and bit the inside of her lip. She was expecting more of a fight. Lucas didn't seem to be one to let something go so easily. She was actually a little disappointed. "It's just, enough people have gotten hurt already."

"I said it's fine," Lucas snapped.

Melanie wrung her hands together. "Don't get me wrong. It's not that I don't want to find out what happened. It's just—"

"Melanie, what do you want from me?" he interrupted.

Honestly, she didn't know. Begging would be nice. Even anger. Something to show he needed her. That anyone needed her. "Can I still stay here?"

"Yeah," Lucas sighed. "As long as you need."

Well, that was something, at least.

Lucas opened the front door for her.

"I'm not saying no."

"Okay."

They walked in silence to Lucas's jeep. He got in, fiddled with the radio, couldn't find anything he liked, and shut it off.

Melanie shifted nervously in her seat. She didn't want to go back to her apartment; not just because of the horrors that awaited her, but because she'd really be alone. Sure, she'd been on her own for over five years now, but there was always a boyfriend a call away, a hook-up passed out on the couch. She had carefully orchestrated a steady succession of men with no breaks in between. She had been chain-smoking her way through relationships. At the moment, Lucas was all she had.

She played with the lock on the door, adjusted the strap on her seatbelt, and then fiddled through her purse for a non-existent cigarette. When she looked up at Lucas, he smiled weakly at her and backed out of the parking lot.

"What would I have to do?" she finally asked.

Chapter 9

Lucas dropped her off five minutes early for work. He had errands to do — the hardware store, a hairdresser, and a locksmith. Melanie didn't even want to think about what was on his shopping list.

Lucas apparently didn't work. His dad paid his rent and bills, and gave him a small allowance. This didn't gel at all with what Melanie had seen of the man. Lucas hinted that the money may have come from his mom, but she seemed absent in the picture, possibly dead. Melanie did not want to learn any more about Lucas's personal history than she had to. If he wanted to discuss the best way to sharpen a stake or how to string a necklace of garlic bulbs, fine; she just didn't want to compare scars.

The Hidden Fox, where Melanie worked, was a small bookstore with an even smaller café. The owners were well-meaning hippies who didn't have an ounce of business sense. They over-ordered books, held expensively catered signings for author friends who rarely sold a single copy, and drank too much of their liquor stock to make any kind of profit. The busboys sold weed out of the kitchen — and on occasion some of it made it into the customers' food. The dishwasher was on work-release from prison.

There was one other waitress who Melanie shared shifts with — Sasha, though Melanie suspected that wasn't her real name. She had big boobs and tied up her work shirt to make them seem even bigger. She leaned over customers' tables so they'd get an eyeful, wore too much perfume, played with her hair while talking, and chomped on gum while she waited for orders in the kitchen. Melanie hated her.

Sasha got all the male customers — the business guys in suits on their lunch hour, the early morning pervs who wanted to grab the new copy of Hustler and didn't have the guts to go to the adult bookstore, and the stay-at-home dads who treated the place as a kid-friendly Hooters. Meanwhile, Melanie was left with the uptight old ladies who dropped crumbs all over the tables and floor, the flustered housewives, and the lonely fat girls who read romance novels in the corner. It suited her fine — they were cheap tippers, but not once had any of them pinched her ass.

When Melanie arrived, Sasha was sitting on the counter in a short skirt, showing off her panties to any customer in the store. In this case, there was only one person there, a hunched figure sitting in Melanie's section.

Sasha smacked on her gum and cracked a bubble. "He asked specifically for you. Refused to order. Said he wanted to wait. He was completely rude. Good luck." She smirked.

Melanie tied on her apron and walked over to the table. The man's hair was graying, and Melanie could see two large hands clasped in front of him. It was Officer Tyler. He had dark circles under his eyes, and his hair stuck out at the sides. He looked like he hadn't been to sleep at all last night. *Just great.*

Melanie decided to treat him like any other asshole customer — with practiced indifference. "Can I get you anything?"

He leaned back in his chair, and Melanie heard the wood groan. He was a big man — not fat, there just seemed to be a lot of him. He was in plain clothes; a pair of work pants and heavy boots, and a shirt with a cartoon of a deer wearing a hunter's hat.

"What's good?"

"Depends on who's cooking."

One of the busboys popped his head into the circular kitchen window. It was Antoine, the rat-faced kid who had dropped out of high school. He was staring at Officer Tyler.

"What do you like?"

Melanie shrugged. "The corn muffins are nice." They were one of the few things the hippies got right. They were thick and moist and drizzled with butter. They were cooked fresh before every shift, and supposedly came out of a Civil-War-era recipe book.

"Alright then."

She nodded and headed off to the kitchen.

"Melanie," Officer Tyler called out. "Have a seat when you're done."

He kicked out a chair from the table, motioning for her to sit.

Melanie's eyes flashed. "How did you know I worked here?"

"Cop, remember."

"Yeah well, you can call me at home if you want to talk. I'm busy." It was wishful thinking to assume Bryan's death would just go away.

Officer Tyler made a deliberate show of looking around the empty café and the even emptier bookstore. "I'll try not to keep you."

"Fine." Melanie bit her lip and walked on stiff legs back through the kitchen door. She was worried that Tyler had found Carl's body. How would that look? She tried to remember her rights. *Bear arms, be silent, happy. Crap.* She didn't remember a damn thing from civics class. She felt like one of those ducks at the carnival that bobbed stupidly up and down in a tank of water, waiting for a snot-nosed kid to snatch her up.

"Hey," Antoine called, half-hidden in the shadows by the freezer. "What's that cop want?"

"How do you know he's a cop?"

"He busted me before. What's he doing here?"

"Eating."

"Did he ask about me?"

"Why would he ask about you?"

Antoine mimed holding a joint.

Melanie shook her head.

"What about Marty?" Marty was the other busboy; he was soft spoken and kind of simple. He smoked way too much of his own stuff.

"No. He's here for me."

"Why?"

Melanie paused. This was the longest conversation she'd ever had with anyone who worked there. "My boyfriend was killed this weekend."

Antoine nodded. "Okay, cool." He whistled his way back over to a stack of clean dishes waiting to be put away.

And that's why I never share anything. She grabbed the nearest muffin and threw it unceremoniously on a plate. Undoing her apron, she walked back over to Officer Tyler's table.

"Sit," he said. "Please."

From the corner of her eye, she caught a glimpse of Sasha swinging her legs on the counter. Her underwear was red. *Slut.* Melanie glowered at her.

"You seem like a straight shooter, so I'm not gonna bullshit you. I love my son..."

Yeah, I've seen the way you love him.

"But he ain't right. He gets into a lot of trouble, and there's gonna come a time when I can't clean up after him. His last girl, Leah, had a calming influence on him. I haven't seen her around in a while." He smoothed back his hair. "Maybe you heard or seen something?" he asked hopefully.

"No," Melanie said sadly. The truth was too ridiculous. *Yes sir, she's roaming the woods at night looking for unsuspecting people to kill and drink their blood. Oh, and she murdered my friend.*

"Seems like she just up and disappeared. She's a good kid. Lucas ever talk about her with you?"

Melanie looked down. "Not a lot, no."

Officer Tyler stared at Sasha still swinging her legs on the counter and then turned his attention back to Melanie. "I worry. When you have kids, you'll know. You'll spend your whole life trying to protect them from the world, and come to find it should have been the other way around."

What the hell did that mean?

Officer Tyler cut his cornbread in two and pushed half of it towards Melanie. He took a bite, closed his eyes and nodded. "You were right. This is good."

She picked a small piece off and popped it in her mouth.

"We tracked down Bryan's mom. Didn't seem too upset though. She kept asking about insurance money. Didn't seem to understand I was a police officer."

Melanie had only vague impressions about what Bryan's mom was like. He didn't talk about her very often, but this seemed to agree perfectly with what she had imagined.

"He ever get physical with you before?"

"No." Melanie shook her head. Maybe she should have lied.

Officer Tyler looked puzzled. This wasn't the answer he expected. "What really happened?"

She bit her lip. The lines of reality had blurred of late. It was hard to tell what was real and what was part of this other world people had created for her. "He got hurt last night. I went to look for help, but when I finally found someone — Lucas — Bryan was gone. He showed up at my apartment last night and just came at me. That's the truth." And it was, at least as far as she understood it. That was the part that made sense.

"Where'd he get hurt?"

Melanie debated on whether to mention Hell House, then thought better of it. She'd also have to explain the fire, and she didn't want to get Lucas in even more trouble. "We were hiking the tracks. He wrenched his leg."

"Just the two of you then?" Officer Tyler raised his eyebrows.

"Yes," Melanie said, staring at the table and then popping another bite of corn muffin into her mouth.

He drummed his fingers on the table, watching Melanie. After a long awkward moment he finally said, "You ever feel like you got up to take a squirt in the beginning of a movie and when you get back to your seat, it's already over?"

"All the time." She laughed nervously.

He finished off the cornbread with a large bite and wiped his hands on his shirt, then pulled a card from his pocket. "You think of anything else, you hear from Leah, or you just want to talk, let me know."

Melanie picked up the card. It had a small shield in the corner and neat silver print. She turned it over. In careful handwriting, he had added his home phone number. Melanie committed it to memory. It wouldn't be the worst thing to have a cop in your corner. "Thanks Officer Tyler."

"Trevor." He tapped his fingers on the table one last time and then stood up, seemed about to say something else, then nodded a goodbye.

This was not the conversation Melanie envisioned having. He dropped a fifty-dollar bill on the table, more in tips than Melanie earned on her best day.

As he left, Officer Tyler stopped by Sasha, who was still popping gum and kicking her legs on the counter, and whispered something in her ear. Her whole face flushed red, and she jumped down.

When he was gone, she wandered over to Melanie, clutching the bottom of her t-shirt. "Who was that prick?"

"Cop." Melanie wiped the table and watched Sasha out of the corner of her eye. She pulled out the knot that tied up her shirt.

"What'd he say to you?" Melanie asked, keeping her voice flat and disinterested.

"He told me to close my legs, I look like a whore."

Melanie snorted, and Sasha stomped off to the kitchen, probably to get high.

* * * * *

The rest of the day was wonderfully ordinary. Melanie waited tables, helped out customers who had placed special book orders, and cheerfully mopped up the floor. At the end of her shift, she found time to listen to the guest poet that Magdelina, one of the hippie owners, had invited to read in the afternoon.

He was a thin guy with a patchy goatee and dark circles under his eyes. His hair was slicked back in a vicious widow's peak. All that was missing was a beret and a striped turtleneck to look like the perfect stereotypical poet. His poems were all about a lost love.

She normally didn't go for that kind of sappy drivel, but she actually found herself close to tears. She wondered if she would ever inspire that kind of devotion in anyone else. Hell, she'd settle for a haiku.

Lucas took that moment to enter the bookstore. Seeing her close to tears now, he rushed over and grabbed her arm as if she were in danger of fainting. "Are you okay?" He brushed the hair from her eyes. "What happened?"

Melanie rested her head on his chest and closed her eyes. Maybe this could fit, maybe this is where she belonged. "I'm fine."

Lucas took her hand. "You ready?"

She nodded and left as the skinny poet warbled on. She guessed the poem didn't end happily, otherwise he'd be at home with the girl, not moaning on and on at a shitty coffee shop. It was always better to leave during the intermission.

Melanie decided she wouldn't mention Officer Tyler's visit to Lucas. He was probably just being an overprotective father and, if he was right, well then Melanie just didn't want to know.

As she and Lucas walked hand in hand to his car, the sun was setting and the clouds were thick and grey as soot. Wherever sky managed to break through the gloom, it lit up orange and red like a house on fire.

Chapter 10

"That is the stupidest idea I've ever heard," Melanie said, and smoothed out her hair. Though Lucas was thoughtful enough to bring her a hat to wear on the windy drive back to his apartment, her hair still floated away from her head.

Lucas had spread a map of Maryland over his tiny kitchen table. Ellicott City was too small, too insignificant for its own map. Melanie longingly followed Route 95 with its bright blue lines drawn out like a vein towards Florida.

"Melanie?"

"Hmm?" She looked up startled. "What?" She was on an empty stretch of white beach. The water crested at her feet, exposing sand crabs and small clams. As the water receded, she watched them burrow feverishly back into the sand.

"Do you see the pattern?"

She looked back at the map. Small red Xs formed a neat circle lashed around the heart of Main Street like barbed wire. Each X marked a supposed sighting, an attack, a death. She touched a finger to the red X where Carl was killed, where Bryan was attacked. It seemed too neat, too orderly a way to account for the loss, the horror she remembered. "It's still a miserable idea."

"You'll be perfectly safe. I'll be there the whole time."

Melanie was hurt and didn't bother to hide it. "It sorta feels like you're putting me on display."

"All I'm asking is for you to just sit and have a drink. Nothing else. I'll be right there. We let him come to us. Just like a deer blind."

More hunting references. Great, I guess that makes me the bait.

Lucas wanted Melanie to hang out at one of the bars on Main Street and wait for the vampire to approach her. She'd indulge him in small talk, stroke her neck every once in a while, or do whatever the hell it took to get a vampire turned on. Once he was properly riled up, she'd invite herself back to his coffin, but at the last minute make an excuse as to why she couldn't be eaten that night — she was on a low protein diet and so wouldn't be nutritious, she had garlic for lunch, et cetera. Lucas would track them the whole way and return during the day to dispatch the vampire while he slept, when it was safer.

Of course, this wasn't exactly how Lucas had explained his plan to her, but she already felt sour about the whole escapade. This was far from the adventure Melanie had pictured. In her mind, when Lucas first proposed hunting vampires, she imagined the two of them walking through the dark woods at night, a flashlight cutting through the gloom. They would explore the entrances of caves, rummage through the ruins of the original mill; check for tracks and telltale droplets of blood, or a billowing white scarf caught in a tree branch. Of course there'd be no victory, no vampire caught in the proverbial net, but she had hoped for romance. Holding hands to stave off fear, working together with someone towards a common goal. All of that sounded just lovely.

Lucas stroked her cheek. "You're his type. Thin, fair-skinned. Alone. He'll find you, I just know it."

Great, why don't I just tattoo 'victim' across my forehead?

"And then?" Melanie asked, suspecting that turning him over to the police wasn't even in the top-ten list of things Lucas had planned.

"We stake him, cut off his head, stuff it full of garlic bulbs, then burn the body."

"Uh huh." Melanie remembered shopping with Bryan for fake plastic teeth and foundation that would make his skin look paler. She never imagined she'd look back on those days wistfully. "But Bryan was killed by a bullet."

Lucas nodded and winced at the memory. "Yeah, I thought of that. The people he bites, they don't come over the same. They're like wounded animals. They can't control themselves. They're weaker. But this one, I think he's more..."

"Traditional?" Melanie added.

"Exactly. Like Typhoid Mary."

She shrugged and shook her head. She'd given up pretending to understand Lucas.

"He carries the disease, but he's not affected by it. Maybe he was born with it. Or maybe his system has found a way to adapt to the illness, to achieve some sort of balance." He walked over to his pile of books and dug out a ragged spiral notebook. "Look here." He opened the book to the first page. The sheet was covered with cramped and detailed handwriting, lines crossed out, rewritten, circled, starred and, oddly enough, cartoonish pictures of animals. It looked like something a chemistry professor might do if he was whacked out on acid.

Melanie leaned over and read what she could. "Known: Fangs, hemato ... hemato-fo..."

"Hematophogus."

"Hema-to-phogus."

"It means he drinks blood."

So why didn't you just say, 'drinks blood,' jerk? "Cold-blooded? How do you know he's cold-blooded?"

"When he touched me, his hands were cold."

"Of course."

"That's important. See, what if the folklore got it wrong? What if he isn't dead? People just thought he was because, you know, the blood drinking, and running around at night, and icy hands? What if there's a more natural explanation?"

Melanie stared blankly, so Lucas continued. "Take lizards. Lizards are cold-blooded. If they want to get warm, they have to rely on the sun. See? And their heartbeats are slower. Much slower. Some can even regulate them. They could make their heart beat so slow, you might even think they were dead. That got me thinking—"

"You have cold-blooded down twice." Melanie took up the notebook from Lucas and read with more interest.

"Well yeah, I meant like mean, cruel. A killer."

"Uh huh." She looked back at the notebook. "Strong, fast... What is this a picture of?" She pointed to what looked like a cross between a Danish muffin and an angry pig.

"Razorback gorilla."

"Uh huh. And this?"

"A rattlesnake's rattle."

It looked more like a spotted Octopus. "Why?"

"It has the fastest muscle movement of any creature. And it uses almost no energy. The secret is that the muscles it uses don't require a lot of oxygen. See, it's the breathing that slows us down. Even the muscles have to breathe. So maybe if the vampire can regulate his heartbeat, he can also regulate his breathing. Or maybe he just needs less." He said the last bit almost hopefully and with a tiny bit of admiration.

She continued reading, "Not ... dead?"

"That's what I was saying earlier. Once I started thinking of him as more of an animal or a genetic freak, I realized he must have to follow the same rules as you or me. He walks, talks, eats, sleeps. So he must have a brain. And brains don't deal well with dying. They turn to soup. Just a gray mass of pulpy—"

"I got it. Nocturnal?"

"The only times I've seen him were late at night. Just like the vampire bat—"

"You're not nocturnal. You were out at the same time."

"Okay, not in the strictest sense, but you saw the burns on Leah's face. I did some research. There's a skin disorder called Porphyria. It's triggered by exposure to the sun. They probably won't go up in a cloud of dust during the day, but they'll burn and blister, they'll weaken. They might even get stomach cramps or diarrhea."

Ew. Lucas was beginning to kill some of the romance for her. Sure, she wasn't as fanatical as Bryan was about vampires, but still there was something to be said about a green-eyed demon sweeping you away into the mists of the unknown. Even if he only wanted you for a snack.

"See, if you discount the more outlandish myths about a vampire — turning into mist or a bat, summoning the dead, you've got a creature whose abilities can all be equated with something in the animal kingdom. He's just an incredible collection of them in one package."

"So, he's not immortal?"

"I don't know." Lucas frowned. "It wouldn't be unheard of. There's a kind of sponge that can live thousands of years. And there was this oyster—"

"Unknown: Stakes, holy water, garlic, crosses," Melanie interrupted, not enjoying the seafood comparisons one bit. 'Gun' had been added in a different color pen underneath, probably recently. Melanie didn't comment.

"Yeah, well, I'm kinda going with Western European folklore here. If he lives, then he can also be killed. Maybe some Seventeenth Century peasant got it right."

So every way to stop him is an unknown? And that doesn't seem like a problem to you? "What if he's Jewish?"

"What?"

"Why would a cross or holy water bother a Jew? Or what if he's a non-practicing Catholic? Or Muslim? Ooh, what if he's—"

Lucas snatched the notebook away from Melanie, "You're not taking this seriously."

She thought those were perfectly legitimate questions. "Sorry. Please?" she asked reaching for the book.

He reluctantly handed it back to her. "You can't completely discount mysticism. Just because you haven't seen it, doesn't mean it doesn't exist."

Melanie was okay with that line of thinking.

In the middle of the paper, written in red and traced over in heavy black lines, Lucas had written 'Destroy the earth!' Melanie wondered if that was his ultimate goal. First vampires, then the world! "What's this mean Luke?"

He blushed. "I didn't mean it like that."

"Okay." Melanie crossed her arms and waited for an explanation. She wondered if she should call Homeland Security.

"Vampires don't tend to move around a lot. They pick an area and stay there. When they do move, they have to take soil from their home with them."

"Why?" *And how would that work? Did Dracula stuff his trousers with dirt before he went out to ravage the local virgins?*

"I ... don't ... know," Lucas admitted, spacing the words out. "But it's one of the core legends."

She knew she was going to regret asking this, but did so anyway. "Core legends?"

Lucas smiled and thumbed through the notebook until he found a map of the world. Each continent was covered in Xs and dates. "Every culture, every society, has some kind of bloodsucker in it. From the Adze in Ghana to the Zmeu in Moldavia. And these different folklores all have their own set of rules, some of which occur over and over again. Those are the core legends. We're talking countries separated by too much ocean and too many centuries for the stories to be based on anything else but simple fact."

"That vampires are real?"

"Yes," Lucas slammed the book closed.

"So ... dirt?"

"Dirt."

"What do you intend to do with the dirt?"

"Well, not just the dirt. Their homes. They need a base, somewhere safe. Somewhere they have ties to."

"So you burning down half the town..."

"Precisely."

"And the rest of the core stuff?"

"Blood, Fire, and Earth," he said, counting each word on his fingers.

"Sounds like a rock band."

"I suppose," Lucas conceded. "And possibly water."

"Right. Holy water for our Jewish vampire."

Lucas scowled at her.

"Well, you've certainly thought this out." She glimpsed back through the rest of the page. There were plenty of words she didn't understand — 'thermoreceptors', 'draculin' which sounded vaguely mysterious and literary, and 'reproduction'? *Now we're talking.*

At the bottom, Lucas had drawn what appeared to be a dragon with a forked tongue twice the length of its body. *Now that could come in handy!*

So Lucas wasn't completely deranged. His demons were built differently from Bryan's — they were made of flesh and bone. There were no extraordinary ingredients in their construction, but the end effect was the same — evil, masked in skin, stalking the night. It was oddly comforting to her to be on such familiar ground.

"Fine, I'll help," Melanie finally agreed, but only because she thought the chances of finding that man were slim to none, and maybe because, secretly, she did want to see him again. It also seemed to excite Lucas. He rubbed her neck and then stroked her cheek.

Lucas leaned in close to her and whispered, "Really?"

She nodded again and closed her eyes, expecting a kiss.

It beat sitting around in a graveyard all night waiting for Bryan to 'rise,' fending off the chill night air and mosquitoes. She could just sit in a warm bar and get drunk.

"Awesome! We'll start tonight!" He pecked her forehead and ran off to the bedroom. "I've got to get ready," he said excitedly.

"Fun," Melanie said to herself. She mentally went through her wardrobe. *What do you wear to catch a vampire?*

"Lucas?" she called out.

"Yeah?" he shouted.

"Where did you even get holy water?"

"eBay."

"Of course you did," she muttered to herself.

* * * * *

Lucas chose the Orange Brewery, a trendy restaurant adorned with bright wood flooring, a high ceiling with exposed metal piping, and a large copper tank that gurgled happily as tourists filed into the upstairs bar. The restaurant sat smack dab in the middle of Main Street, surrounded by an upscale baby clothing company and a pricey jewelry store. The exterior was well-lit by flood-lighting while large bay windows poured even more light onto the sidewalk. It made the heavy stone front of the building look inviting and warm.

The basement bar was a different story. Accessible only by a long, rickety wooden staircase in a small alcove just past the kitchen, most tourists didn't even know it existed. Once it was probably a storage room for wheat and flour from the original mill. Or maybe it served as a jail before there was a jail. With so many nationalities pouring in to the city in those first days, there must have been confusion, resentment, fights.

Sometimes, on her darker nights, Melanie liked to think that this room served as a place to store the bodies of the immigrants who dropped dead right on the factory line, or a secret chamber to torture those who would not work. Certainly, with its thick, impenetrable stone walls that occasionally dripped water, low claustrophobic ceilings, and dismal yellow lighting, the room could pass for a dungeon in any Vincent Price movie. Melanie loved it instantly.

The downstairs bar was tiny, especially considering the size of the restaurant above. The bar itself ran the length of the room; a dark slab of mahogany knotted improbably right into the ancient stone. There was only room for six tables, each one more worn and battered than the last. There were a few lanterns hanging loosely in the corners of the room, their wiring exposed. The room reminded Melanie of Luray Caverns, a cave she visited on an elementary school fieldtrip, in what now felt like a lifetime ago.

She found a long, flowing white dress at a thrift store, thinking it made her look virginal. That would appeal to any man, vampire or not. It was open-necked of course with puffy sleeves that hid her hands. She would have been at home on the English moors, chasing Heathcliff through the heather. Unfortunately, Lucas was not a brooding, dark-eyed rogue — he was moody with barely one foot in reality, but she'd settled for even less before.

Earlier, she had rummaged under Lucas's bed, looking for cash and cigarettes or something she could pawn, and found bright red lipstick that must have belonged to Leah. Lucas did a double-take when he saw her wearing it, but if it bothered him, he didn't say a word.

He set up camp upstairs at a table nearest the stairs. This way he could watch everyone who went down to the bar. If someone looked suspicious, he'd follow them and signal Melanie. He was decked out in camouflage again, which made her wonder if he owned anything else.

In the basement, Melanie chose a seat next to the far wall, with her back to the bar. This sealed off two means of attack. God help her, she was starting to think like Lucas.

The first two hours were quiet. The only people who came in were tourists who made a wrong turn looking for the bathroom. Even the bartender spent most of his time in the back, occasionally dragging heavy-looking boxes back and forth.

Melanie sipped red wine because it made her cheeks look flush and her lips fuller. She smoked her remaining pack of cigarettes, lighting one off the other until nothing was left but clumpy ash and stubbed-out butts. When the cigarettes were gone, she dipped a finger in the ash tray and drew stick figures in obscene positions on the table.

The bartender raised an appreciative eye at her artwork, and she continued, getting more and more elaborate and lewd until even the ash was gone. She wanted another drink, but Lucas had carefully instructed her to keep a level head — and took away her wallet to make sure she'd stay that way.

An overweight man huffed down the stairs and asked the bartender for change for a five, and then huffed back up. A couple argued for a bit at the end of a bar over how many seashells were appropriate to display in their house. And around midnight, the bartender fell asleep while leaning against the wall, and knocked over a stack of glasses when he jarred himself awake.

It was after one in the morning. *Last call.* Melanie gathered her things and realized, with more than a little of the old Catholic guilt returning, that she hadn't thought about Bryan all night. In fact, she had spent the evening hunting vampires, which seemed like a betrayal unto itself. She was tired, bored, and lonely. If she was going to spend her nights sitting alone in a bar, she sure as hell didn't need to keep Lucas around. She stomped up the stairs to find him.

She had to clear her throat just to get his attention.

"Is it time already?" He looked up from his journal, in which he was furiously scribbling notes.

"Mm-hmm." *Some guard,* Melanie thought.

"Let me just finish this."

Melanie sighed audibly and crossed her arms while Lucas continued to scribble away. "They're closing."

"Just a sec," he said without looking up.

"I want to go home." The strain in her voice was showing.

Lucas looked up and put down his pen. "What's wrong?"

"I'm tired. Can we please leave?"

"Yeah, sure."

He got up and draped an arm around her. "So, any possible suspects? Get any good leads?"

"Did you see anyone go downstairs?"

"Uh, yeah. There were a few."

Melanie broke away from Lucas. "No you didn't. You were busy writing in your little diary."

"It's not a diary. This is my casebook. All the great detectives have them. *Everything* is in here."

"Casebook, huh?" She rolled her eyes. "No, Lucas. I didn't see any possible suspects. Nobody turned into a bat the entire night. I did see someone order a Bloody Mary. Should I have slept with them?"

Lucas frowned, "You're mocking me."

"Well, duh." Her voice was getting progressively louder. More than a few people in the bar turned to look at them.

"You don't have to do this, you know. I can get some other girl."

"Yeah, right." She rolled her eyes.

"What's that supposed to mean? You don't think I could get someone else?"

She smirked and let out a snide "Ha."

"Well, screw you then!"

He pushed past her and stalked off towards his jeep. Melanie now had the undivided attention of everyone in the bar. She glared back at them and then chased after Lucas. He was her ride home.

"Lucas!" she called out. She had to run to catch up with him. She wasn't used to men being so overly-sensitive. Hell, Bryan might have been a doormat, but he knew how to dish it out.

"What the hell's your problem?" she asked when she finally caught him.

Lucas was already in the jeep with the engine idling. He didn't look at her as she climbed in. He peeled out before her butt even touched the seat. Melanie struggled to get her seatbelt on as Lucas gunned the engine and raced up the curvy road that led out of Main Street.

"So what, now you're not speaking to me?"

He reached over and turned on the radio at full volume. Bob Seger blasted from the tinny jeep speakers: *'Caught like a wildfire out of control ... till there was nothing left to burn and nothing left to prove...'*

To hell with you then. Tomorrow she'd start apartment hunting.

Lucas gripped the wheel so tight, his knuckles turned white, and he drove like a madman, weaving in and out of traffic. With the low doors and an apparently broken seatbelt, Melanie found herself clutching wildly at the dashboard, trying to hold on. She didn't give him the satisfaction of yelling at him to stop, even though her stomach heaved every time he took a hard turn.

At last, Lucas came to a screeching halt in front of his apartment. If he had asked, Melanie would have told him to drive her home, but he didn't, and she'd be damned if she was going to open her mouth first.

He stomped up the metal stairs and let the door go in her face. Red-faced and pissed, Melanie was ready for a good screaming match. She caught the door and shoved it open so hard it left a mark on the wall. She shouted, "What the hell, Lucas?"

Lucas had his back to her as he played with his answering machine.

She balled her hands into fists and waited.

After hitting a few buttons, he said calmly, "I'm going to bed. There's some blankets and a pillow in the closet. You can sleep on the couch."

Melanie's mouth dropped. "What is your problem?"

He shook his head and walked off to his bedroom. "Night."

"Jeez, Lucas. I was just kidding, okay?"

Blood and Sunlight   Jamie Wasserman

He slammed the door behind him, leaving Melanie alone in the apartment.

All this because I made fun of him not being able to get a girl? Or maybe I wasn't being enthusiastic enough about his vampire hunting? Christ, everyone needs a reality check every now and then. When Bryan and Carl thought about robbing the local blood bank, she was the one who threatened to go to the police if they did. They may not have been happy about it at the time, but after they sobered up, even they realized it was a stupid idea. Lucas needed to get over himself.

What was most frustrating was that Melanie knew Lucas had a temper. She had seen flashes of that back in her apartment. She didn't mind a good screaming match. That usually made for great make-up sex. But Lucas's silence really set her teeth on the edge.

On the rare occasions when she and Bryan fought, he would at least have let her yell until she was spent. He would even bring her flowers the next day, never mind that they were probably borrowed off a fresh grave; it was the thought that counted.

She was left to go to sleep alone, tense, keyed up, and a little horny. Tonight, she reasoned, she had nowhere else to go and, even if she could bring herself to go back to her own place, she had no way to get there. This was all pretty typical. She didn't just hit rock bottom, she brought a pick-axe with her.

She gingerly sat on the couch, still stunned. Tomorrow she'd get the hell out of there and try to figure out what to do next. Maybe she needed to be on her own for a while. No more men. At least no more crazy men. This couldn't continue. She would be seventy and chasing after ogres under bridges. It was too painful to think about.

Melanie wished desperately that Lucas had a TV set. She needed a mindless distraction. Instead she grabbed the nearest book she could find — a thick medical-looking textbook called *Wintrobe's Clinical Hematology, Volume 2*. It was nothing but pages and pages of information about blood disorders. She made it up to the part on Thrombocytopenia before sleep finally overtook her.

Chapter 11

Lucas was gone when Melanie woke up. Her back ached from sleeping in a tight ball on the sofa, and she was more anxious than ever for a good fight. And then some making up. But the apartment was quiet and gray with morning — and no Lucas. *Out burning down the city,* Melanie thought, and then remembered she was out of cigarettes.

She made a cursory search of the apartment. No TV, no radio, no computer. *God, how does anyone live without email?* She finally found a portable CD player and a small case of discs. *Finally, something to interrupt the silence that still lingered from the night before.*

She thumbed through the CD's — Allman Brothers, Jimmy Buffett, Thin Lizzy, Lynyrd Skynyrd. Lucas was a redneck. The hunting and camo-wear should've been a clue, but Melanie had hoped he was just troubled. Troubled was sexy, redneck was not. She tried to shove that thought to the back of her head. She settled on Pink Floyd's *Dark Side of the Moon* and went to get dressed and figure out how she would make it in to work that day.

In the bathroom, Melanie rummaged under the sink, hoping Leah had left behind a box of tampons. Her stomach was cramping, a good sign the hag would soon be here. She found a pink toothbrush, a sample-sized bottle of Narcisse perfume and, *thank God,* a barely opened box of tampons. Underneath was a small red purse with thin spaghetti straps. Inside she found some lotion, a nail file, a cell phone whose battery had long since died, a set of keys attached to a frightened looking troll doll, and Leah's wallet.

She opened the wallet — there were credit cards, an un-cashed paycheck from a temp agency, a driver's license, and a picture of Leah next to a younger looking version of herself standing in front of a waterfall. Tucked on top of the picture was a dried out four-leaf clover. *Fat lot of good it did her.*

Melanie could not imagine leaving the house without half of these things. Wouldn't Leah be back for them? This thought made her shiver.

She pulled the license out and read the address — Leah lived only a few minutes away from her. She slipped the license and keys into her pocket and tucked the rest of the things carefully back under the sink. She had no idea why she took them, except that maybe she felt like she should be doing something more for Bryan — investigating, interviewing, avenging her dead lover. Lucas didn't seem up to the task, and no one else seemed to care.

After a shower and a breakfast of stale bread, Melanie made a cursory search of Lucas's bedroom for cigarettes and some more pocket money. The boy didn't even have posters on the wall. His clothes were neatly hung in his closet, what little there was of them. More camouflage gear. He must have cleaned out the local army surplus store. She dug through his drawers. *Christ, even his underwear was camouflage.* Exactly how that would come in handy, she couldn't imagine. She did find a twenty-dollar bill in his nightstand drawer and a pack of Camels. She pocketed both, called a cab, and went outside to wait and smoke and sulk.

* * * * *

At work, Melanie kept looking up at the door, expecting Lucas to walk in, maybe even with flowers or chocolate. She didn't care how girly that sounded. She knew she wasn't the heroine. She wasn't even the best friend. She was the quirky acquaintance who gets dumped or killed. A short morality lesson before the movie continued. But just once, she thought, she deserved a little more pampering, a little more screen time.

But Lucas did not show up and, aside from the sight of Sasha arriving for her shift in a floor-length skirt and a shirt buttoned to the neck, nothing eventful happened.

Melanie knocked off work at six that evening, made a dinner of customers' leftovers in the kitchen, and debated whether to show up at the bar to help Lucas and apologize — for what, she still didn't know — or to spite him and call it quits and go home.

Ultimately, curiosity won out, and she decided to go anyway. *Let him see what he's missing.* Maybe she'd even meet a man who owned suntan lotion and liked to jet-ski, who didn't sleep under floorboards or sharpen stakes for a good time. Besides, she wanted to blow the last of Lucas's money.

She called a cab to take her to the Orange Brewery. She liked being driven around, even if it was only five minutes away. She plastered Leah's make-up on, slipped on a flimsy tank top that showed off her small breasts, and slipped into a tight-fitting skirt that would have made Sasha blush. She vaguely wondered what possessed her in the middle of her grief to pack something so slutty, but soul searching wasn't her thing. Chasing down thoughts usually lead to dark, ugly places, and tonight would be about fun.

The cab driver whistled when she got in.

"You're dressed to kill," he said.

Melanie smirked and lit one of Lucas's cigarettes despite the no-smoking sign on the window. The cab driver didn't offer any complaints.

* * * * *

To her surprise and mild disappointment, Lucas was not already there in the bar. He had abandoned her altogether. She frowned. *No big loss,* she convinced herself. She had enough of Lucas's money left for one drink, maybe something fruity and served with an umbrella, so she decided to stay, grabbing the same table she had the night before. Only an older couple sat in the bar, drinking coffee and chatting in low whispers.

The bartender raised an appreciative eye when he saw Melanie, and didn't charge her for the drink. When he brought it round to her table, he sat down with her, knocking back a shot of Jack Daniels.

He wasn't the type of guy Melanie normally went for — he was darkly tanned and well-built and supremely confident. *Healthy* was the word that came to mind. She generally liked boys who were skinny, pale, and drawn, and who wore more make-up than she did. The bartender was a good head taller than she was, with dark blonde hair that looked messy but probably took hours to get just right.

95

"You've got beautiful legs," he said.

She smiled and looked at her drink. It was said in an appreciative manner, not smarmy, so she crossed her legs, revealing a little more thigh.

"Tony," he said, offering his hand.

"Hi, Tony." She lit a cigarette and exhaled a puff of smoke. "Yvette," she lied. She used the alter-ego Yvette whenever she wanted to appear mysterious and sophisticated. When she wanted the boy to really work for it.

"You waiting on somebody, Yvette?"

"Sure," she said. "A vampire." She laughed at her own joke.

Tony leaned back on his chair, his shirt riding just a bit above his belt revealing a toned, flat stomach. "Look no further," he said and grinned so wide, Melanie could count every one of his teeth.

Melanie's face went slack. "Wait. What?" Suddenly she didn't feel so sure of herself.

Tony leaned forward and took the little plastic sword from her drink, eating the pineapple and cherry pieces whole. Some of the juice ran down the corners of his mouth, and he licked it slowly.

Melanie felt a cold bead of sweat drip down her back. The bar, she realized, was now empty. If she screamed, she wondered, would anyone hear her? She made a mental inventory of what she had that could serve as a weapon, but came up empty. On the bar, she saw a long handled knife used to chop up fruit, but it was too far out of reach.

Tony turned and hid his face behind an arm. Melanie heard something snap and pictured two long fangs extending in his mouth.

"I vant to suck your blood," Tony said jumping up, his hands curled and poised to strike.

Melanie gasped, then saw pieces of the red plastic cocktail sword sticking out of his mouth like a walrus with a crooked grin.

"And maybe something else." Tony tried to bare his fangs and one of the plastic teeth fell to the ground.

"You jerk!" Melanie laughed and shook her head. She couldn't believe she had let Lucas's delusions get to her so much.

"Ow!" Tony yelped and pulled the other piece of the plastic sword out of his mouth. "Damn thing cut my gums."

"Was it worth it?" Melanie asked, her muscles relaxing.

"Totally." He leaned in as if he was about to bite her neck.

She shrieked and playfully pushed him away. Maybe she could crash at his place for a few days. Bartenders made great boyfriends. They slept all day, worked all night, and had access to free booze. Plus they usually came home horny and with a ton of cash in their pockets.

"What the fuck?" Lucas stood on the bottom of the stairs watching them, a bouquet of lilacs in his hand.

Melanie's face went slack, and she stood up, moving away from Tony. "Lucas."

He threw down the flowers and headed back up the stairs.

"That the vampire?" Tony asked, but Melanie ignored him and chased after Lucas.

She caught him at the door. "Wait!"

Lucas stopped with his back to her.

"You brought me flowers?"

"I wanted to apologize. I sometimes get a little carried away..." his voice trailed off. "What a jackass I am, huh?"

Carried away? Melanie liked that. Lucas had feelings for her, even if he was too much of a boy to say anything. "No, of course not." She wanted to tell him that she found herself believing him more and more, despite her better judgment, but couldn't. She wasn't good with apologies. Instead she took Lucas's hand and kissed his ear, soft and wet, and whispered, "Let's take the night off, huh? Go back to your place so I can apologize properly?"

Lucas smiled a wide, stupid grin. *Men are so easy.* Tomorrow she'd pick out a shirt for him. *He'll look good in something with a collar; powder blue maybe.*

They headed out the door, holding hands but Melanie stopped suddenly. "Hold on a sec." She ran back inside. A moment later she emerged, holding the flowers. "They're beautiful," she said, and rested her head on Lucas's shoulders.

Blood and Sunlight   Jamie Wasserman

Ten minutes later, they stumbled through the door of Lucas's apartment and crashed together on his bed. Melanie pulled his shirt off and kissed and nipped at his neck and chest. She kissed her way down, yanking off his pants and underwear in one tug. His pubic hair was thin and blonde and soft. Melanie dug her nails into his thighs and took all of him in her mouth. Lucas however, didn't respond like she had hoped.

She looked up. "What's wrong?"

"Not like this," he said. He pulled her to him, kissed her dryly on the mouth and then pushed her back on the bed. He roughly yanked off her pants and underwear then pushed up her shirt. Two kisses on her belly and then he was leaning above her. Melanie could feel him, hard and assured, now pressing at her. She opened her legs wide because she wasn't that wet yet. And then he was inside her. Lucas mistook Melanie's whimpers of pain and thrust harder. She struggled to take off her shirt and bra. She wanted to feel her chest against his, but Lucas didn't move, and the shirt sat bunched awkwardly around her neck like a noose.

When her body finally began to respond, she opened her eyes. Lucas was pushed away from her, balancing his weight on his elbows, his eyes set firmly on his cock moving in and out of her. She wrapped her arms around his head, tried to pull him to her for a kiss, for eye contact, for any acknowledgment that she was there, but Lucas only pulled out and tried to turn her over.

"I don't want to do it like that, Lucas," she said. She didn't find it degrading, just too far removed from the action. It made her feel like she was being nailed to a cross.

"Just for a few minutes," Lucas said in a ragged breath and then came almost immediately.

When he was done, he collapsed on top of Melanie, breathing hard. She could feel him softening, slipping away from her. After a moment, Lucas rolled off and stood up. "I'm going to take a shower," he said, lightly touching her shoulder before stumbling out of the room.

She thought of the coroner comforting her after her mother died. That kind of obligatory, empty comfort only reminded her that she was in this alone.

She wished just one thing would come easily for her. She felt close to tears, angry; not stretched out, filled, and spent like she'd hoped.

When Lucas returned, she pretended to be asleep and, after a few hours of staring at the widening moon out the window, she finally was.

Chapter 12

It took Melanie a moment to realize where she was. The sun was not yet up, and the room was filled with the gray half-light of dawn. She rolled on her back and looked up — someone had tacked a target practice sheet to the ceiling. She was in Lucas's bed. She closed her eyes and tried to imagine Bryan asleep next to her, gasping for air as he fought off his early-morning sleep apnea. She never thought she'd miss his snoring. The peaceful image did not last long.

"Did you take anything outta here?"

Melanie looked up. Lucas sat on the dresser, fully dressed in a black commando outfit, the small red purse in his hands.

"Uh, good morning?"

Lucas stood up and held the purse in his fist. "Tell me!"

Melanie wondered why everything was so difficult. *Did Prince Charming remind Sleeping Beauty to wipe her feet before entering the castle? Did Belle fuss about all the hair on the carpets and furniture? That's the part of the fairytale nobody ever tells you about. What happens after they lived happily ever after — they made adjustments, sacrifices, they fought, they cheated. They changed. And, in the end, it was always the same — they died.*

Melanie pulled the covers up. Suddenly, she was very aware that she was naked. "I thought I needed a tampon," she said. "I didn't think you'd care."

"Don't touch my things!" he shouted, punctuating each word with a fist against the dresser mirror.

Melanie just nodded her head.

Lucas smoothed the purse carefully and tucked it away in a drawer. It may as well have been a prayer cloth for all the attention he gave it. When he was done, he stormed out, slammed the bedroom door behind him, shattered something in the vicinity of the kitchen, then stomped out the front door. A few moments later, she could hear Lucas's car squealing out of the parking lot. *God help anyone on the road.*

Melanie slumped back on the bed. She had envisioned a morning of feeding each other fresh fruit and reading the paper on the deck, maybe even morning sex. Bad sex was better than none at all. Now it looked like it'd be stale corn muffins at work and trying to tune out Sasha's incessant gum chewing.

She felt a twinge of guilt that she did not feel the same level of protectiveness about Bryan's memory as Lucas seemed to about Leah's. Maybe he believed Leah would return after all. And what would Lucas do then? Cut out her heart and burn it, like Melanie had read in one of his books? Or would he keep her locked up in his bathroom, feeding her his own blood until he could find a cure? Or maybe that was what he wanted Melanie for. She wished she had some Vicodin left over from her root canal. Anything to dull her senses. She had an over-active imagination, and if she followed any train of thought long enough, it usually ended with her being mutilated in some ingenious way.

Melanie shook her head and rummaged through Lucas's room to see if she could find more cab money. *Screw him, and screw his stupid rules.*

As she ransacked his underwear drawer for the second time in as many days, she decided this simply wasn't worth it. Lucas had saved her life, and she slept with him. *Debt paid. And,* she reasoned, *there must be at least one man out there who wasn't interested in playing dress-up or hanging me on the end of a supernatural hook.*

She packed up all of her stuff and threw it hastily into her bag. She could walk to Bryan's apartment from here and borrow his car for a while — that is, if his greedy mother hadn't gotten to it. First thing in the morning she would reapply to art school.

* * * * *

By the time she got to Bryan's, she was winded and sweating. She decided she would reapply to art school *and* quit smoking.

Blood and Sunlight   Jamie Wasserman

Parked in front of Bryan's run-down apartment complex was his pride and joy — a 1970 Cadillac Fleetwood hearse done up in bright purple. Melanie had painted flowers above the taillights. The car reminded Melanie of Bryan — creepy but practical, and a terrific ride.

She felt under the thick metal bumper and found the spare hide-a-key. She actually drove the car more than Bryan did. While he slept his days away, she took the car to work, did errands, then picked him up after he had 'risen.' The next day she'd walk the half a mile back to his place and do it all over. The car, she reasoned, was practically hers anyway, so it wasn't exactly stealing, although she was sure her old Sunday school teacher would disagree.

She thought about going up to his apartment to see if she had left anything important behind, but decided, *Screw it. Opening that door would be like opening the coffin of a fresh grave — you could never be sure what state things were in, and nothing could ever prepare you for what you might find.*

She tossed her bag on the passenger side and found Bryan's emergency cigarette taped to the back of the sun visor. She fumbled through her bag for matches, since the hearse's lighter mysteriously dripped some kind of strange liquid and hadn't burned for years. The first thing she grabbed, however, was Leah's license.

She looked at it more closely — the picture was from a few years ago, maybe even when Leah was sixteen and had just passed her driving test. She had soft blue eyes and a wide grin on her face.

A butterfly fluttered inside the car through the open window. Melanie tried to imagine how the squat and meaty caterpillar turned into something so light and airy. Even the chrysalis was grotesque — it looked like cat poop. The butterfly drifted back out the window, and she lost track of it in the sun.

She decided then and there that she'd call in sick to work. Tips sucked on Tuesdays anyway.

Maybe a butterfly could emerge unscathed from a dark ugly cocoon, but not people. Dead is dead. Nobody ever came back, no matter how much you begged, bargained, or cried.

And quite frankly, she'd had enough talk about vampires to last three lifetimes. Lucas and Bryan had left a lasting impression on her. As long as some doubt remained, no matter how faint, she would always be looking over her shoulder, wondering when the next ghost would come floating through her window.

She pumped the gas three times, revved the engine, and the car sputtered to life. She forced herself not to look back one last time at Bryan's apartment, and drove purposefully as she headed towards Leah's house.

* * * * *

Leah lived in one of the newer hillside townhomes that overlooked the city, built on the leveled grounds of an old church. Like so many other streets in this town, they kept the names — Church Road, Davis Springs, Pike's Orchard — but did away with all remnants of the former occupants.

Leah's townhouse was an end-unit, situated right off the main road. Melanie sat in her car and fiddled with Leah's key ring. She realized a purple hearse might not be the optimal getaway car for breaking and entering. If she were going to go inside, it would have to be now.

She walked across the parking lot on stiff legs and stood in front of the house. The windows were boarded up solidly, just like in the trailer. This was a common sight in downtown Baltimore, and Melanie almost preferred the heavy plywood planks in the city to whatever ruin and filth awaited the unsuspecting inside, but here in her backyard, the effect was unsettling. This was a house that had something to hide. She wondered if the boards were there to keep people out, or to keep something terrible contained inside.

She touched the sturdy wood door, hoping it could communicate something — a warning, a signal to run — but as usual there was no telltale omen, no magical lamp to light the path to safety.

She slipped the key in the lock and let it rest there. She would have given anything at that moment for the key to not work, to be able to go back to her car and say, 'Oh well, I tried.' She realized she was sweating and her hands were shaking. She felt like she was being watched, despite the house being sealed and blank as a stopped clock.

The key turned and, before Melanie could stop it, the door swung back and slammed against the wall, essentially announcing her presence to the neighborhood and certainly anyone — or anything — that might be inside.

The first thing she noticed was the smell. Like rotting fruit. Alternately sweet and sickly. It made her nauseous and a little dizzy. She braced herself for a swarm of flies to descend on her, but the air was still, and the room looked undisturbed.

The house opened to a large living room that might have been bright and airy once — certainly the floral drapes and teak furniture gave it the appearance it had enjoyed countless hours in the afternoon sun. But now heavy plywood planks sealed off all light. Strands of tape lined the edges of the board, ensuring that the room remained sealed in a timeless dark. The curtains were carefully drawn on top of that, in a feeble attempt to make the room still look homey.

In the back was a small kitchen with a sliding glass door that must have led to a porch, but the glass was painted over in black, and a sheet was haphazardly nailed to the wall, covering it in fits. Melanie imagined that from the deck you could see train tracks winding their way to California or Seattle, places built more on hope than on endless graveyards and dead religions.

Someone had gone to great lengths to ensure not a spot of daylight could seep in. *Lucas,* Melanie figured, and shook her head. She could just imagine him bringing her here, showing her the house, which had been locked down like a vault, and saying, 'See?' There was a logical explanation for everything. Maybe the police did it to keep would-be looters away.

She opened the fridge and was hit with the stench of rotten food. It wasn't the same smell that filled the house, though the scent of both mingled and made her gag.

In the back of the kitchen, a heavy wood staircase led into even darker gloom.

Melanie paused at the bottom. In her hyper-alert state, she half expected to hear the creaking of floorboards or a door quickly shutting, maybe even a tortured wail. Instead, a slight breeze disrupted her hair, and she imagined she felt the entire house shudder and sigh.

If she left now, she reasoned, she would have lost a whole days' pay for nothing. She was here to face the bogeyman head-on, instead of waiting for him to creep into her dreams or lurk in her soft shadows. She wanted to put an end to this ridiculous nonsense once and for all. If Lucas was right, there was a vampire upstairs sleeping peacefully on its home soil, perhaps hanging upside-down like a bat, or sleeping in a blood-soaked bathtub. Maybe she would even find one of Carl's rings or — she gulped — his desiccated corpse.

If Lucas was wrong, the house would be empty, and she could go home and sleep by herself for a long time. Loneliness was something she would get used to. This fear was something new that made her stomach churn and stuck in her throat like dust.

When she reached the top of the stairs, she noted with a great deal of dismay that all of the doors were soundly shut. It felt like a gigantic 'Keep Out' sign, with a skull and crossbones on top, surrounded by barbed wire.

She screwed up her courage and opened the first door. It was a bathroom, far darker than the rest of the house, if that were possible. The shower curtain fluttered a little with the force of the door, and Melanie gasped and stumbled back.

Stupid.

She took one step in and quickly pushed the shower curtain back. She kept her other foot on the carpet, as if that might keep her safe from whatever waited inside. *Empty. Only gleaming white tiles.* She could vaguely make out butterflies on the curtains.

She turned back to the rest of the hall. There were two remaining doors, one on each side.

"Let's see what's behind door number two, Melanie," she whispered and noticed for the first time how dry her lips were. If she'd had enough courage, she would have run back to the bathroom and lapped up water straight from the sink. Instead, she pressed her ear to the door and gripped the handle. The only thing she heard was her own ragged breath and the dull rush of blood in her ears. She had an image of fish guts being tossed into the black, shark infested Atlantic.

The door swung in and collided against something hard. Melanie actually shrieked and backed into the hall, nearly colliding with a painting of two people embraced in a kiss so passionate, their faces lost all definition.

The room seemed to serve as a small office, with a wood desk carved with flowers — the kind left over from a spoiled childhood — a computer, and once again, a solidly boarded window. The door had collided against an uncomfortable-looking wood chair. This room was brighter than the rest of the house because the computer was still on, the dull swirls of a screensaver endlessly spinning in wide arcs. This was the first comforting thing Melanie had found. She thought vaguely about checking her email or updating her Facebook status — 'Melanie is hunting vampires.'

With a little more courage now, she walked to the third room. She didn't give herself a second to hesitate, and pushed it open. The stench here was overpowering — mushrooms, formaldehyde, standing brackish water. Based on the smell, this room should have been covered in mold and crowded with rotten timbers and termites, but it was neat and clean and appeared undisturbed. Melanie covered her nose and mouth with her hand.

It was a well-kept bedroom. On a simple teak dresser sat a jewelry box and small crystal knick-knacks. A queen-sized bed sat below two more boarded windows. A picture of Leah and her friends doing an imitation of a chorus line was taped to the dresser mirror. Above the bed hung a print of a dog sleeping in the afternoon sun. More pictures sat on the nightstand — Leah parasailing, Leah swimming next to a dolphin, and several more pictures of the girl in the photo from Leah's wallet. *No pictures, though,* Melanie noted, *of Leah and Lucas, or any evidence really that he had ever touched her life. As though he never mattered, or the room had been deliberately scrubbed clean of his existence.* But things like that only happened in bad murder mysteries.

A large TV sat in the corner with a box of DVD's overflowing underneath it. Next to that was a small, partially opened closet. In short it was an ordinary bedroom in an ordinary town where the only weird things that ever occurred were in the heads of those who had been trapped there for too long.

She felt terribly relieved. Her muscles relaxed as the adrenalin vacated her system. She thought about investigating Leah's jewelry box, maybe even borrowing some of her clothes. She looked forward to giving Lucas a big 'I told you so,' then taking a nap. She could re-piece everything that happened into something that made sense and just move on.

She sighed and laughed to herself, and got up to leave — when the sound of the closet door screeching back on old caster wheels sent a cold, creeping sensation straight up her spine.

Melanie didn't stop to look back and took the stairs two at a time. She was covered in sweat by the time she hit the street and the breezeless, Maryland afternoon. She didn't even bother to shut the door.

She stood catching her breath on the sidewalk, feeling dizzy and nauseous, but relieved, maybe even a little silly. It was probably nothing — a tree branch scraping the window, something falling from a top shelf in the closet ... the product of an overactive imagination and a steady diet of hallucinogens.

She laughed and walked quickly back to the car. If she hurried, she could still make her shift, and she'd only be an hour late, not that anyone at work bothered to track her time. *Christ, would they even notice if I disappeared?*

Behind her she heard a car pull slowly into the small parking lot. Not wanting to look suspicious, she kept her head down as she fiddled with the lock, then climbed into the hearse.

So there were no monsters, no bogeymen. Everything bad that happens, we do to ourselves. She could understand Bryan and Lucas a little better now. *It would almost be comforting to think that our suffering isn't just everyday, that's-life, screw-you pain, but the result of some malevolent force out to get you.* She had to admit some sick part of her was even a little disappointed to find it wasn't true; that being alive meant being in constant pain, at the random whims of the cruel universe.

Or maybe she had simply been overly optimistic about what she'd find in Leah's house. *It wasn't like walking into the Wizard of Oz's palace — you weren't going to discover a gigantic floating head to announce where you were.* Maybe she should have given the floorboards a rap or two, checked the bookcase for a secret passageway.

Dummy. This is probably how Lucas got started on his witch hunt. Let just one of those silly thoughts go, and the rest start flying out of your head like a cluster of balloons. She was an idiot for having even gone to Leah's place to begin with. But at least now she could say goodbye to Bryan, goodbye to Lucas, and Carl, and even Leah. *Goodbye to all of the creatures of the night. It was time to start living in reality. Wash the black eyeliner off and maybe get a real job, move to the city, buy a Labradoodle.*

There was still time to make it into work. She still didn't know what she was going to do afterwards, if she could even bring herself to go back to her apartment. But that was eight hours away. Right now, she only had to worry about clearing tables and serving stale muffins. And that was doable. Everything else would fall into place. It always did.

She took a deep breath and exhaled. Her lungs felt raw, like she'd been swimming for hours. She reached for Bryan's emergency cigarette behind the sun visor, then remembered she'd taken it down earlier. It wasn't on the passenger seat. She scooted forward and felt behind her, but it wasn't on her seat either.

She pressed her head against the window and looked in the space between the seat and door. She could just make out the top of the cigarette.

She wedged her hand down, grasping for it, but only succeeded in knocking it back further.

"Shit." She freed her hand and reached between her legs underneath her seat. The tip of her fingers brushed something that might be a cigarette. "Almost ... got it..." she said, extending her arm as far as she could.

She had just managed to brush the cigarette a little closer and was about to reach in and pick it up, when a shadow passed over her and remained there.

She gasped and sat up, knocking the cigarette into the recesses of the car.

Lucas stood at her door, the sun coming down behind him, darkening and twisting his features.

Crap.

She rolled down her window, but only a crack.

"They found Leah's body."

"What?"

"A few days ago apparently. My dad just called. She was at the bottom of Bloody Fingers."

Bloody Fingers was the local hot spot for weekend climbers. The wall was a hundred feet tall with vicious outpourings of limestone, making climbing extremely difficult and painful. It was the one area Melanie hadn't used to smoke weed. Just looking up to the top was dizzying for her.

"They say she fell."

"I'm sorry, Lucas." And she was. Not just because Leah's death was real now, but his hopes of a vampire being responsible were also dead. Now he had to deal with the sad realization that the world was an ugly place, the imaginary monsters pale in comparison to the real-life ones. She knew first-hand that lesson did not come easily.

"They had to identify her by dental records. That's why it took so long. There was nothing but bone. Can you roll down the window?"

That meant Leah was probably dead at least a few months. That's how long it took a deer carcass to get picked apart in the woods until all that remained was a thin, fragile skeleton.

Melanie hesitated, then opened the window a little further. She felt bad for Lucas, but in her mind, she was already on a new path that didn't include him, and she wasn't interested in backtracking. Backtracking meant admitting she had gone the wrong way to begin with.

"How'd you know I was here? Did you follow me again?"

Lucas shook his head. "I went to throw away her stuff after I heard. Couldn't quite bring myself to do it before. Then I noticed the keys were gone, and her license. I sorta figured you'd be here." Lucas paused and looked Melanie hard in the eyes, "Anything else?"

"No," she shook her head dumbly.

Lucas stuck his open hand inside the car through the crack in the window. She flinched at first, then realized he just wanted her things back.

She fiddled through her bag and quickly found them and dropped them in his waiting palm.

"Thanks."

As soon as his hand was back out, Melanie rolled the window up another inch.

Lucas glanced in the backseat. "That your bag?"

Melanie nodded.

Lucas bit at his thumbnail. "I guess if I find anything else of yours, I'll just leave it at your door." He tapped his hand on the roof of the car. "See ya around, I guess."

Melanie didn't expect to run into Lucas here, but her worst-case scenario brain had at least touched on what might happen if he found out about her trip. There was far more yelling and glass breaking in her imagination, but Lucas was resolute and seemed at least genuinely contrite.

He took a few steps back and smiled with half of his mouth. As he did, the sun hit him from the side so Melanie could see him better.

His hair was darker, the piercings gone from his eyebrow and ears. And he was wearing — *gasp* — a blue polo shirt and a pair of tan pants. The dark hair gave his face more definition, made him seem less boyish. His eyes looked dull and listless; less frantic, hungry. For a second, she pictured herself on his arm, laughing, and kissing him on the cheek.

Maybe his change in appearance marked a turning point for him.

"Lucas, wait!" she called, rolling the window down half way.

Lucas stood in place and raised his eyebrows.

"Did you do something different with ... um..." She didn't know where to begin. It seemed like everything about him had changed.

He rubbed the back of his head. "Yeah, this is actually closer to my natural color. Took out the piercings, too."

"I like your shirt." *God, Melanie. Is that the best you can come up with?*

Lucas laughed and tugged at the lapels. "It's the only outfit I've got left. I used to wear it to church. I took everything else to Goodwill."

"Why?" Melanie rolled down her window the rest of the way and leaned on the door.

"I got rid of everything."

"So no more...?"

"Nah," Lucas shook his head. "Seems kinda silly now."

They stared at each other for a long moment. Lucas had arrived at the same place as she had. They were both deep in the woods and lost, but lost on the same trail, and that was kind of comforting.

"I've gotta go. I've got a car full of library books I need to return." He nodded to his left where his car was parked — it was packed ceiling to floor. "The fine is going to kill my allowance for the month. I might have to get a job."

Melanie smiled, and so did Lucas.

He took a step towards his car then stopped. "Hey, when I get back, if it's okay, I thought I'd swing by your apartment and fix your door."

"You don't have to do that." Melanie dropped her hand to the door handle but couldn't quite bring herself to open it.

"Least I can do."

"Thanks."

Lucas kicked at a rock on the ground, and Melanie slumped back in her seat. A moment ago, if she had gotten out of the car, Lucas might've rushed to her and taken her in his arms, but that moment had passed. All that was left was awkward silence.

"Okay..." Lucas tried to smile but it came out as a grimace. Neither one of them was ready to make the first move.

Lucas got in his jeep, backed quickly out of the space, then stopped. Melanie watched his car idle a few feet from hers. *Not too late,* she told herself, but she still couldn't get her hand to move.

A second later, Lucas emerged back at her window. "Hey."

"Hi," Melanie smiled as she looked up at him.

"For what it's worth, I had fun. You know, in between the other stuff. Maybe if I get my head on straight, who knows, I could call you, or something?"

"I'd like that." To Melanie, that sounded perfect. Normal, healthy, slow. No more diving in headfirst into everything. There was something to be said for wading in at the shallow end.

Melanie's door opened suddenly. Lucas slipped in and knelt down in front of her. "How about tonight?"

"Tonight?" Melanie asked confused. They hadn't even put Leah in the ground yet.

"Dinner. Crescent Manor?"

Melanie looked surprised. That was the most expensive restaurant in town. She'd always wanted to go, but even the cheapest entrees cost more than she made in a day's work. The waiters there must make a killing.

"Maybe we can help straighten each other's heads out."

"Um..."

"That sounded weird. Forget I said that. Let's keep our heads where they belong. Can I just take you to dinner?"

"Yeah, I guess so." After all, Bryan was gone, and he was never coming back; and even that didn't matter. Anyway, it wasn't even him that she missed. It was the idea of him. She knew she would never go back to school. And she would never leave this town. She would have to find happiness wherever she could, because this was all there would ever be. Lucas was here right now, and that was enough. Still, she felt a buzzing in the back of her head. A tiny voice of doubt. But that was something she had learned to ignore years ago, silenced by pills and alcohol. Two days of sobriety had allowed that creeping voice to return, but it was all just white noise now. Easy to ignore.

Lucas kissed her passionately on the mouth, and she kissed him back but there was nothing behind it. She may not have understood men, but she did understand need. It was an empty spot in her chest that seemed impossible to fill. Not with cigarettes or drugs or drinking or sex or art. But that hunger could be quelled, if only for a little while. And maybe that was the best she could hope for. Her prince had not died fighting for her against the evil dragon after all; he had simply failed to show. And worse yet, he was never coming. There would never be a happily ever after in her story, just blank page after blank page, until there was truly nothing left.

Chapter 13

Crescent Manor was a stately old house that sat in the thickly wooded, unclaimed area that connected Ellicott City to Catonsville and Baltimore beyond. The sign for the restaurant was always lit up with soft fluorescent floodlights, even in the middle of the night when it was closed; even in the middle of the day when the sun rendered the floodlights useless.

Though they were only half a mile outside town, the woods felt claustrophobic and lifeless. Driving there in the last of the afternoon sun, Melanie had the impression of an old-washed out painting done in muted grays and browns. Nothing moved.

The all-wood old manor home, painted rich white, was accentuated by heavy stone columns and flickering gaslight. One half expected to see a horse-driven carriage come clomping up the driveway.

Inside, little had been done in the way of modernization. The dining rooms were small with low ceilings and, apart from the tables and dessert carts, appeared probably as they did a couple hundred years ago.

Melanie had managed to stifle whatever little concerns might have remained about Lucas and found herself actually excited about her date. She was, after all, dressed in a brand new blue silk dress that Lucas paid for, and eating at a restaurant she could never afford. This was the prom she never made it to, the homecoming she missed when her boyfriend at the time decided he'd rather throw rocks at rats down by the dump. That nagging voice was not, she told herself, sounding an alarm; it was merely doubt leftover from dozens of toxic relationships. There could be something here if she could only stop her brain from getting in the way.

They ate dinner in one of the smallest rooms, probably a child's nursery or servant's quarters back in the day. From the window, Melanie watched the strained half-light of dusk settle, first on the treetops, then on the graveled driveway. Fewer and fewer cars passed. By the time Lucas insisted

Melanie order dessert to cap off a dinner of thick clam chowder, a water cress salad, and roasted duck, dark had settled gentle as a body rolling off to sleep.

The waiter brought two servings of lemon gelatos, but Lucas didn't touch his. He seemed content to watch Melanie enjoy the sweet dessert.

"What?" she said, smiling. "You're making me nervous."

Lucas had his head propped up on one hand. "Nothing. I was just thinking."

Melanie took another bite, then reluctantly put her spoon down, concerned. "About what?"

"About how beautiful you are." Lucas held out his hand.

Melanie took it and looked shyly at the table.

"We should've toasted." Lucas stroked the back of her hand with his thumb.

"To what?"

"A fresh start."

"Now that sounds good." *Finally, a partner. Someone on equal footing, where we can take on challenges together.*

The waiter brought the check, and Melanie snuck a look at the bill — $140. She gasped a little and then made an empty gesture of going through her purse. She didn't have any money in there, and her credit card was maxed.

"What are you doing?" Lucas asked as he slapped down two hundred-dollar bills.

"Chipping in." She pulled out a tampon, frowned, then shoved it back down.

"When's the last time you went on a real date?"

Melanie thought for a moment. Did driving to St. Mary's to do grave etchings count?

"C'mon." Lucas stood up and pulled Melanie's chair back.

"Don't you want your change?"

"Nah, this night was perfect. Let's go for a walk."

"A walk?" This wasn't an area you walked around in. It was a place you used to get from one spot to another, and even then reluctantly and quickly.

"It's beautiful out. We'll walk off dinner."

"Okay." Melanie was vaguely worried she had eaten too much. She patted her stomach.

They walked out the front door and headed back in the direction of Main Street. There were no sidewalks here, so they kept as close to the woods as they could. If a car passed, it would be a very tight fit. But the road was empty, and only the night pressed nearer.

Lucas held Melanie's hand, and they walked in silence for some time. Melanie remembered a stupid cartoon she had taped on her mirror as a girl, that proclaimed, 'Love is ... being together in perfect silence.' Now, it didn't seem quite so silly.

Lucas paused along a particularly deserted patch of the road. The remains of the old Legionnaire's Hall was on the left, an empty shell that no one bothered to knock down and clear away. Nothing more urgent was needed for this spot. The river could be heard rushing somewhere beyond the trees, and beyond that, the faint whisper of cars returning to the city.

"Do you know where we are?"

Melanie paused. She was more concerned with how far Lucas wanted to walk. She didn't want to kill the mood, but she wasn't used to heels and certainly wasn't prepared for a hike.

"Sure. Frederick Road. Keep following it, and you'll end up in Catonsville. It goes all the way to Baltimore."

"Right, of course that wasn't built till much later. But you can take the road back the other way, and we're on Main Street."

Melanie shuddered. *But first you have to go under that horrible bridge.*

"And that road there..." Lucas pointed at a narrow stretch of asphalt that dropped off into the woods. "That's Thistle Road. It goes to Hell House."

That was about the last place she wanted to hear about.

"More than that, it's the first road they built here. Of course, it was all dirt back then. It connected the mill to town."

Melanie nodded. Lucas had an odd tone in his voice, and she didn't want to lose the romance of the evening. "Look how big the moon is tonight. And red. What is it they say? Red sky in the morning, sailors take warning. Red sky at night—"

"The road used to run up there into the hills." Lucas continued, seemingly not hearing her. "That's where the foreman and the mill owners used to live. They literally looked down on everyone."

There was a road there, Melanie noticed, but she didn't ever remember seeing it before.

"A few of the old houses still stand, but it's mostly just woods and rock now. They keep moving the highway further away."

Melanie shivered. "Can we head back now? It's kind of chilly." She rubbed herself with her free arm.

Lucas's hand tightened slightly around Melanie's, not enough to hurt, but enough to let her know they were no longer holding hands, he was holding her. "The land doesn't forget though. This area here is the first crossroads. Do you know what that means?"

She had a vague recollection about a blues musician who supposedly sold his soul to the devil at the crossroads. Bryan had a poster of him in his bedroom.

Lucas tightened his grip even further, and Melanie winced. "They used to bury suicides at the crossroads. Drove a stake through their hearts to ensure they couldn't leave. You see, they believed that a suicide would return as a vampire. You were never supposed to travel there at night, or their spirits would get you. Drink your blood dry."

She tried to pull her hand free, but Lucas held tight. "What are you doing?" Her stomach fluttered. Something was wrong.

"This was the first spot on the map, Melanie."

"You're squeezing my hand too hard."

"I didn't mean to hurt her. Not at first, at least."

A small gasp escaped Melanie's lips. "Leah?" She barely breathed.

Lucas nodded. "She called me some horrible things that night. She was fucking the bartender, and who knows how many others. Oh she denied it, but I knew. She wasn't so innocent after all."

The headlights of a car crested over the hill towards them. Melanie tried to run towards it, but Lucas yanked her back. She watched sadly as the lights cut a wide arc across the road as the car turned down a side road.

"But you said they found Leah's bones. She must've been dead for months."

"That doesn't prove anything. Rapid decomposition. Maybe they don't turn to dust right away, maybe... Shut up!"

"Lucas, please. You need some help. Let me go. I promise I won't say anything."

"This is bigger than just you." He pulled Melanie closer to the woods. The darkness under the trees was much thicker and colder.

"When I was done, I dragged her over here." He kicked at a rotting clump of leaves that had somehow survived the summer.

"He seemed to come out of nowhere, but I think now he was watching us from the woods the whole time. Waiting."

Melanie narrowed her eyes and stared into the dark. She couldn't see beyond the first few trees, but she knew there was nothing out there. No salvation whatsoever.

"He only hit me a few times, but it was enough. Three of my ribs punctured my lung. My chest caved-in, and I was bleeding internally. That's what they told me at the hospital. I told them I crashed my car into a tree and was thrown. Dad, of course, didn't believe me."

Melanie remembered her conversation at the café with Officer Tyler. She'd give anything if he were here now.

Lucas grabbed her arm and twisted it behind her back, and she yelped.

"He thought I was out cold, but I was smart. I watched everything. That's how I knew."

Melanie tried to shout, but Lucas hit her on the back of the head with something hard and then wrapped his arm around her throat. Her eyes teared up so she could no longer see clearly. "Please," she sputtered.

Lucas's demeanor never changed — he was calm and detached, methodical, as if he had planned this all along.

"He picked her up like she was made of feathers and set her down in his lap. Right over there." Lucas pointed, and even through her teary eyes, Melanie could see the long hunting knife glimmering in his hands.

She struggled some more, but it was no use — Lucas was too strong for her.

"I saw him bite open a wound on his wrist and dropped his own blood in her mouth. Not long after, her eyes opened." Lucas spit onto the ground.

"The blood summoned him. It's all my fault, you see. That's why I have to stop this."

Lucas relaxed his grip enough that Melanie could move her head more freely. Without thinking, she bit down on his forearm and then threw her elbow into his stomach. He stumbled back, and she took off into the trees.

"Melanie!" he roared behind her.

She couldn't run fast. The trees were too thick, the ground too overgrown. She pressed forward, branches and thickets pulling at her clothes, tearing at her arms and face. At some point, she lost her shoes.

She constantly had to double back, turn. The sound of her heavy breathing overwhelmed all else.

"I didn't want to do it like this!" Lucas shouted. Melanie couldn't tell if she had put any distance between them — his voice seemed to echo all around her.

"You just wouldn't cooperate. We would've found him eventually, but you have no patience. No faith. Get out here, you whore!" Lucas screamed.

Melanie stumbled but righted herself. A clearer path opened in front of her, letting her move more quickly through the trees. She pushed through dying brush and stumbled free, right back onto the road. "No," she cried, but the tears did not come.

The voice in her head returned, clearer now. *Isn't this what you've been asking for, all along?*

Lucas stood only a few feet away, waiting for her, the knife held at his side. He lunged forward and grabbed her by the hair.

"I'm ready for him this time," he whispered, and kissed Melanie on the cheek. "I truly am sorry."

She whimpered and closed her eyes tightly.

"The hard part is over," Lucas said. "He'll be dead soon, and I'll be three thousand miles away. A fresh start. Look at it this way. You're doing some good here, Mel."

Lucas pulled her head back and held the pointed end of the knife at her throat. "Come out, come out wherever you are," he shouted to the night.

Only the distant highway made a soft hissing sound. Melanie struggled to breath. The knife cut deep into her throat. She felt her skin separate, something warm on her chest.

"She's going to die!" he shouted, but there was only more silence. "I'll do it, I swear."

"Fuck!" he threw Melanie to the ground. "Fuck, fuck fuck!" Lucas punctuated each word with a kick to her ribs.

Melanie sucked in a deep gasp of air, as if she was drowning. She was having trouble opening her eyes. She groaned and collapsed flat on the ground. Her arms and legs were numb.

"She's going to die. She's going to die because of you." Lucas drove a final kick into her side.

Something in her chest gave way. She thought she should be in more pain than she was. She felt light and airy, and was only vaguely aware of Lucas standing over her. He seemed to be shouting something, but she couldn't hear him, only the slow rush of air escaping. She wondered if she was falling.

In Sunday school, her teacher used to describe how God would come to take you home — descending on a celestial staircase, ready to carry you off like Rhett Butler in Gone with the Wind. Melanie added a gold hat and cane for effect. She imagined a harp and hosannas and a terrible sense of excitement, like the moment before orgasm.

But she didn't feel anything. She had no sense of where she was, could no longer move or feel her own body. The rush of air in her ears dimmed, and her lips parted with an involuntary sigh. She especially didn't feel anything when Lucas finally drove the knife straight through her heart.

PART II

Rise

Chapter 14

"Once upon a time—"

"Daddy!"

"Yes, dear." The man looked down at the little girl in his lap. Her eyes were wide. She had no intention of going to sleep until the story was over. He liked her stubbornness. It would serve her well later in life when things became difficult. When nothing went as planned.

"You already said that part."

"Yes, I know, honey. The story starts over here."

"But the first one didn't end."

"In a way, it did."

"No it didn't," the little girl insisted, frowning. "Fairytales aren't supposed to end like that."

"This is more of a real-life fairytale. You don't get pretty endings in real life."

"But you said there were monsters."

"There are."

"Monsters aren't real life."

The man pinched the bridge of his nose. Only his daughter could talk him into a corner. "Maybe not the kind of monsters you're thinking of." The man absently tugged at his shirt so the silver buttons caught the glare from an outside streetlight. "I can protect you from *these* monsters," he lied, hoping she wouldn't ask about her brother, why he hadn't been able to protect him.

"Okay," the girl nuzzled against her father's arm.

"And, Daddy?"

"Yes, honey?" the man asked, grateful for the interruption. He couldn't remember how the second part of the story went. The happy part. With all the love and discovery. Maybe because he knew it would all come crashing down, making the retelling of the good parts so difficult. It would be neater, less painful, to simply end the story here.

"Does the princess come back?"

"Yes," the man said sadly. That was really the only part of the story that belonged in a fairytale. In real life, you didn't get second chances. In real life, you made mistakes, and then had to spend a lifetime dealing with the consequences.

"Daddy?"

"Yes, my love."

"Are you going to finish?"

"Sorry." The man had been staring out the darkened window. He should still be out there, searching. Stopping the real-life monsters before they got too close to his real-life family. Before they took what little was left. "Where was I?" he said finally.

"Once upon a time..." The little girl fidgeted.

"Right," the man continued. "Once upon a time, long ago, there lived a handsome prince..."

Chapter 15

Melanie woke suddenly, alert and rested, like she had never truly slept before. Out of habit, she half-stretched on the bed and smacked her lips together, expecting that mossy and acrid taste that greeted every morning, but her mouth felt clean, her breath sweet.

Her alarm clock blinked 7:12 pm. Sundown.

She had slept the whole day.

She rubbed her empty stomach. Of course, she was hungry. She had dozed right through breakfast, lunch and dinner.

She felt blindly for the phone to call Bryan, but realized she did not even know what day it was. If it was the weekend, she'd meet him at the Old Monk. Maybe she'd arrive a little early and get some sketches done. Undoubtedly, he'd want to make another trip out to Hell House. She groaned and thought about what she might wear; maybe the almost new, almost silk top she bought in Canton. But only if the sky looked clear, and the weather held out.

She leaned over and pushed back the bedroom curtains, then furrowed her brow — someone had boarded up her window just like in ... just like in ... but her thoughts remained elusive as a butterfly. Bits of color, an unexpected flutter, and then nothing.

The motion of sitting up made her feel dizzy. She felt as though she should throw up, but her body was being remarkably uncooperative. *I must still be drunk or high from last night,* she figured, though she couldn't seem to remember what she had taken or done, let alone where she would have gotten the hammer, nails and plywood, or why she would have boarded up her windows to begin with.

She sunk back onto the bed and kneaded her temples with her fists, wondering if she should just go back to sleep.

"Pity. I had hoped to kiss you awake." A man appeared in the doorway. Though the apartment was dark, she could see him quite clearly, as if he radiated his own light. He wore a simple black shirt and a pair of well-worn jeans.

Melanie gasped and sat up straight on the bed, childishly yanking the covers to her neck. "Who are you? Get out! Get out of here!"

"You're confused. That's to be expected." The man had a bemused expression on his face, which relaxed Melanie a little. Besides, it wouldn't have been the first time she woke up with a strange guy in her apartment. But ever since Bryan, she had been more or less monogamous.

Melanie shook her head, trying to remember how he got here, but her brain felt clouded, with vague shapes occasionally appeared in the mist, only to disappear again. Briefly, she pictured Carl balancing precariously on a metal chair outside the Old Monk.

"How did you get in here?" Melanie eased her death-grip on the sheets a bit.

"Key," the man said, holding up her key ring.

"Oh." Melanie felt more than a little ashamed. She'd blacked out while drinking, but she had never lost an entire day before.

"I'm terribly sorry. I thought you'd be more comfortable waking up in your own bed."

She looked more closely at the man. There were far worse people she could have woken up with. His hair was darker than anything she had ever seen, and it fell around his face in loose curls. His eyes were green and bright, but not glassy — they seemed to pull in all available light in the room. He was, in a word, beautiful. Not the adjective she'd ordinarily use for a man, but nothing else seemed to fit. Still, she had a boyfriend. Bryan. And as she thought of him, she saw herself running through the woods breathless, though she didn't why.

"Do I know you?" Melanie asked. "I mean, did we meet before..." *Before whatever the hell happened last night,* she silently finished in her thoughts. Her stomach grumbled loudly.

"You're hungry." The man laughed.

She placed a hand over her belly and blushed. *This wasn't good.*

Blood and Sunlight   Jamie Wasserman

Enough small talk with the handsome stranger, she scolded herself. *You need to get him out of here in case Bryan shows up.*

"Thanks for getting me home ... um..."

"Keenan."

What a nice name... Stop it, Melanie! "Thanks for getting me home, Keenan, but I really need to get dressed for work," she lied.

He didn't move. Not a single muscle. She could only barely make out the slight rise of his shoulders as he breathed. The stillness was disconcerting.

"Keenan?" Melanie asked, hoping she hadn't pissed him off. She didn't want a scene. This was always easier when she woke up at the guy's place.

"I'm sorry," Keenan muttered. "I was just waiting." He looked a little puzzled.

"For?" Melanie asked with growing impatience. *Gorgeous or not, he was beginning to wear out his welcome.*

Melanie caught sight of the poster of The Lady of Shalot she had tacked up next to her dresser. She couldn't remember the colors being quite as vivid, the lines so well-defined. At least not from this far away. Even the drab white plaster walls looked brighter.

"Get dressed. I'll be waiting for you in the living room."

"Now hold on just a minute—" Melanie snapped her attention back to Keenan, but he was already gone. "Unreal," she muttered to herself.

In the next room, he switched on the TV. A nature show by the sound of it.

"Make yourself at home!" Melanie shouted. She shook her head and bit at her lower lip. *Maybe I should just get dressed and leave. It's not like I own anything valuable. Hopefully he'll just get bored and go home before I get back.*

Gingerly she made an attempt to stand up. She put her feet on the hard wood floor — it was cool to the touch, though she didn't shrink from it as she expected.

The TV got a little louder.

"Deaf boy."

She got up and rummaged through her closet and found her favorite pair of jeans and a flimsy top. She didn't want Keenan's last image of her to be bedraggled and surly. *Who knows, if things don't work out with Bryan...* She smiled to herself.

She got dressed, quickly tearing off the baggy sweatshirt and boxers she was wearing. Not her usual sleepwear, but she was glad she had the foresight to put on anything at all.

In the other room, the TV went up another octave. It sounded like a thousand crickets had invaded her living room.

"Hey!" Melanie called out. "Can you turn that down? I've got neighbors."

But Keenan didn't reply.

She quickly buttoned up her jeans and padded barefoot out to the living room. "I said, turn that down!"

She rounded the corner of her bedroom and stopped short. Keenan was leaning against the edge of the couch, studying a framed picture of her as a little girl at Halloween. In it, she sat crying on the stoop of her parent's house, wearing a Cinderella costume. She wanted to go as Chewbacca, but her dad insisted that was unladylike. She kept it around as a reminder to herself — head up, shoulders back, be ladylike, demure. The picture represented the closest she could get to fatherly advice anymore.

"This you?" Keenan asked, fixated on the picture.

Melanie snatched the photo and set it back on the coffee table. "Do you mind?"

"You were lovely. Still are." His voice had a lilt to it that she hadn't noticed before, a faint trace of an Irish or British accent. Keenan's lips rose at the corners and Melanie saw flecks of gold shimmering in his eyes. She was transfixed.

"Yes, that's me" she said, snapping back to attention, the anger gone. She couldn't work herself back up to her earlier fury. "Could you please turn down the TV?"

Keenan nodded in the direction of the television. It was off, but the loud thrum continued, and was growing progressively louder.

She could make out other noises now. Chirping, the wind, a heavy crunching sound.

"Where is that coming from?" Melanie stuck her fingers in her ears and walked around the apartment. Her radio was unplugged, and her CD player remained stuck, forever sealing away her favorite Tori Amos CD.

The noise seemed to spring up all around her. She figured it must be coming from the apartment below, but had a hard time imagining the Gothels, a geriatric couple who slept all day, going this crazy with their sound system.

She stomped her foot on the floor, and the entire apartment shook. An empty vase sitting on her coffee table teetered, then crashed to the floor, shattering in pieces.

"Make it stop!" she screamed, and was surprised at her sudden level of anger.

Keenan appeared next to Melanie and pulled her hands away from her ears.

"Listen." he whispered, but she heard him as clearly as if he had shouted it, even over the growing din.

"I can't," Melanie whined. "It hurts. Let me go." She tried to pull her hands away, but he held fast with a powerful grip.

"Listen," he said again more gently. "Outside. What do you hear?"

"Get off me."

"Please." He rested his hand on her shoulder, and the noises faded slightly. The tension that had been building in her shoulders fell away. The fear, however, remained just as strong, a terrible wailing that reverberated throughout her head.

"In the woods, beyond the river. What do you hear?"

And then the tumult disappeared completely, and she did hear it ... the wind disrupting the trees, and a few leaves, still green with summer, dropping slowly to the ground. Beyond that, the Patapsco dipped and rushed over grey rock. A deer sipped water near the bank, then raised his head. His pulse suddenly quickened with fear.

She remembered Bryan's words, *Listen to them, the children of the night. What music they make.* She felt her cheeks flush and burn.

"It's a bit like a radio tuner. You just have to learn to control the frequency and the volume."

"What did you do to me?" Melanie breathed heavily, sucking in tight fists of air. She felt disoriented, her mind focused in a hundred different directions at once.

He must have drugged her. That's why she couldn't remember last night. That would explain the hallucinations. She looked around the apartment for an escape.

"It'd be best if we wait until you can remember for yourself." Keenan pulled gently at her hand, trying to lead her towards the couch. "Sit. Please."

"Get away from me!" she shrieked, and yanked her hand away.

"It's just, well, you've stepped in some glass."

Melanie looked down at her feet. Bits of the broken vase surrounded her. She lifted one foot slowly — a large shard was sticking right out of the soft spot of her foot. She hadn't felt a thing.

"Oh, Jesus. Oh, Jesus." She grabbed hold of the glass, clenched her eyes shut, and yanked the shard out. Then she stumbled backwards with another crunch, and sprinted for the door, praying it wasn't bolted. She imagined a blood-stained set of footprints marking her escape route, leading this psycho right to her. She'd need every second to get out safely.

Just as she was about to reach for the door knob, Keenan stepped casually in front of her, blocking the only way out. He was as threatening as a brick wall but appeared just as impenetrable as he urged, "Please. Try to calm down."

She looked back to the spot where he was standing just a second ago, half expecting to see him still there. Nobody could move that fast. She shook her head. He must've slipped by her, that's all.

The loft. My phone is there. All I need to do is dial 9-1-1. I should have them on speed dial by now. They'll come even if he can grab the phone before I can talk.

She turned and ran for the stairs and made it without a problem, exhilarated, grateful that her brain was working more rationally now. She

Blood and Sunlight Jamie Wasserman

fought the urge to look back to see if he was following, and kept her head down.

When she got to the top of the stairs, Keenan was already there, leaning over the rail that overlooked the apartment.

"I didn't have the heart to board up the skylight."

Melanie looked slowly up. Out the window she saw more stars than she ever thought possible; she could spend three lifetimes just trying to wish on each one.

She gasped and put her hand instinctively over her heart, imitating a gesture her mother did anytime she was shocked or disgusted. It took her a moment to find her heartbeat and, when she did, she was surprised to see just how slow and dull it was.

"Spectacular, isn't it? I don't think that view will ever get old. Of course, if you stay here, I'll have to board it up before dawn."

"What are you?" She backed away, never taking her eyes off Keenan.

He straightened up and watched her, an odd smirk on his face, "Melanie, you already know."

She looked searchingly into Keenan's face, but it was smooth and expressionless, revealing nothing. *Grandmother, what pale skin you have.*

She looked at the thin line of his mouth and watched as his lips parted, revealing an impossibly white set of teeth. When she looked into his green eyes, they flashed white, then yellow, catlike. And she did remember.

She remembered her father holding her bike steady as she squealed with delight, riding up and down her driveway. She remembered trying on makeup and jewelry with her mom. She remembered the way the light came down through the trees in the woods behind her home. She remembered almost drowning in the frigid pond behind her house, her father's strong hands pulling her free of the ice. She remembered the day her dad lost his job. Her first taste of alcohol. Losing her virginity in the basement and the blood that forever stained the old couch. Smoking cigarettes behind her school. She remembered the day the police brought her home for shoplifting, and the gutted look on her dad's face. She remembered telling him 'I hate you' a thousand different times. She remembered his funeral and the day her mom stumbled home drunk for the first time. She remembered the fire that ravaged her old house and burned away the last memories of her father. She saw herself throwing rocks at the trailer she had to move into. She saw the faces of dozens of boyfriends; long hair and sticky, anxious hands reaching out to her. She saw her mom dead in her favorite chair, a bottle of Melanie's grain alcohol in her hand. She saw Bryan in his goofy Halloween teeth pushing her protectively behind him.

She saw Carl's body and Bryan crumpled at her feet.

She saw herself in the woods, standing in front of Lucas, the knife held steadily at his side. And there she stood, oh so calmly in front of him, ready for everything to finally be over.

And she knew it had all been leading to this.

Finally, she saw herself lying on the ground, the moon casting its one bleary eye above, the dark woods all around maintaining a silent vigil. And then ... Keenan, appearing out of nowhere, like he had been lying in wait all along, two white fangs gleaming in the dark, carrying her nearly lifeless body out of the dark, taking her away from everything she had known.

She remembered.

It took her a moment to realize that the terrible screaming she heard was coming from her own lips. Keenan scooped her up in his arms like a child and set her gently in his lap on the mattress underneath countless glittering stars.

She continued screaming until her voice cracked and broke with exhaustion. Not even the sweet, cedar smell emanating from Keenan's cool skin could calm her, or his soft fingers delicately tracing the lines of her face.

She wasn't screaming for the memory of the pain Lucas had inflicted, or for the sudden shift in her reality. She was screaming because the future, even in its bleakness, had always been carefully laid out for her. It was miserable, but it was safe, and it was hers. Now that had all been taken away, and she was left, alone again, like a child, in her first room, in that first dark, wondering what terrors the world had in store for her next.

Chapter 16

Melanie cried for what felt like hours until her voice cracked and squeaked. She cried until she was sure there was nothing left.

For his part, Keenan never moved, not to vainly wipe away her tears, or push her away when she rubbed her snotty nose on his shirt. He was so still, she had to look up a few times just to ensure he was still there. He didn't tell her 'it was going to be okay' or come up with some way to fix things. He simply lay there, one hand firmly on her back. Melanie decided even if she lived for a thousand years, she would never be able to repay him for that kindness. And then she wondered if she would indeed live that long, if everything Lucas and Bryan had imagined was really true.

"You were cold before," Melanie croaked into his lap. His body had felt good against her flush cheeks.

"You'll get used to it."

She wondered if he meant she would get used to his cold body, which wouldn't be the worst thing in the world, or if she had changed, too. She didn't feel any different. "You're warm now."

"You've been lying on top of me for some time."

"I'm sorry." Melanie sat up, feeling very self-conscious.

"You didn't have to move." Keenan opened his arms for her to sit back against him. After lying in one position for so long, Melanie wondered why he didn't want to get up and stretch, or kick out his sleeping legs.

She sank back into his lap, and he stroked her face with the back of his hand. His skin was as soft as a child's. She felt very comfortable with Keenan, but she didn't trust that feeling. Nothing ever came easily to her. Why should this be any different? Maybe he was just fattening her up for a snack.

"I like the way you smell," Melanie whispered.

He chuckled. "What do I smell like?"

"Like the woods. Like fall."

"My favorite season." Keenan rested his head against the wall and closed his eyes.

She watched him for some time. His skin was white and ageless, unblemished. The skin of a newborn or an airbrushed Vogue model. His lips were red and full and wet. Melanie remembered a line from Snow White; the real Snow White, not the watered down Disney version. "If only I had a child as white as snow, as red as blood, and as black as the wood in this frame."

"What are you?" Melanie asked so quietly, she wasn't even sure she had spoken aloud.

Keenan opened his eyes, and his face lit up with a big smile. "What do you think I am?"

Embarrassed, she buried her head in his lap. "I don't ... I'm not sure. My ... *friend*," she said, spitting out the last word because she didn't want to say Lucas's name and didn't know any other way to describe him, "seemed to think you were a ... that you are a..."

"Yes?"

Melanie took a big gulp of air. "A vampire." She looked up at the skylight. With clouds rolling in now, she hoped for a well-timed bolt of lightning, but was disappointed again.

"If that helps you."

"Am I...?" her voice trailed off.

"There was no other way." His eyes looked cloudy and darker than before.

She tried to remember everything she had heard about vampires. Sunlight and garlic and crosses. Sleeping in coffins. Turning into bats. Lucas's core legends. *Um, fire, water, ice. No, fire, earth, and...* She couldn't remember the last one.

The thought of 'becoming' did not repulse her as much as it should have. Her mind was being remarkably accepting of her suddenly very unusual circumstances, like it had secretly been preparing for this day for years.

"So, is Lucas—" she clenched her teeth.

"I'm sorry..."

Melanie let out a breath. She pictured Lucas as a dried out husk, bits of him flaking off until there was nothing left to prove he had ever existed.

"Who is Lucas?"

Melanie frowned. "The boy who hurt me."

"He'll live." Keenan mumbled.

"He'll live?"

"There are far worse things than dying, Melanie."

"Like what?" Her brow furrowed. Dying was *it* unless Keenan believed in eternal damnation.

"Like having to live every day with your failures. Realizing you are not in control of your world, and you are far from the strongest thing in it."

Melanie shook her head lightly. *Big freaking deal. I do that anyway. What good is being a vampire if the worst you can inflict is guilt?*

She looked down at her arms and body, then pressed weakly on her ribs, but there was no pain, nothing broken or on the mend. "So what, you just showed up and carried me home?"

"Something like that." Keenan smiled and stroked her cheek.

"How did you know where I live? How do you know my name?"

"Driver's license."

Right, he found my purse. *It isn't enough to be rescued by a supernatural creature, you want him to be clairvoyant too.*

"How long was I—"

"Three days. And while you look beautiful when you're asleep, I was beginning to wonder if you'd ever wake up."

Christ rose in three days, Melanie thought ignoring Keenan's compliment, then felt ashamed for thinking it.

She pictured a caped vampire shrinking from the cross. *An abomination,* that's what her mother would say. But she didn't feel any different. Wasn't a vampire supposed to be a soulless, evil creature; the antithesis to everything that was good and pure? If indeed her soul had vacated her body, it had not left an empty space behind. She felt whole, intact, and frustratingly the same.

Only one way to find out.

"I need to check something," Melanie reluctantly pulled herself away from Keenan, brushed her hair back and walked downstairs.

He was lounging against her bedroom door waiting for her.

"Show off."

Keenan winked at her and moved aside so she could go in.

Melanie walked to her nightstand and opened the top drawer, revealing a tiny brown Bible that Bryan had stolen from a Motel 6 in Ocean City. She kept it more out of habit than anything else.

She paused with her hands inches above the book and glanced at Keenan to gage his reaction. His face was calm, unreadable. Frustrated that he was giving no clues, she grabbed hold of the book.

She expected steam to rise and to drop the Bible screeching in pain, but nothing happened. She flipped it over, hefted it in her hands. It felt like a Bible. It smelled like a Bible. She turned to the first page and read in neat gold print, 'Placed by the Gideons.' *Goddamn busybodies.*

The Catholic schoolgirl in her was more than a little relieved. She could still go to Mass, get married in a church, eat the host without screeching in pain. Even her mother would have struggled to find fault.

Keenan was next to her now. He took the book from her and held it above his head like an old time preacher, "For the life of a creature is in the blood, and I have given it to you to make atonement for yourselves on the altar. Leviticus 17:11."

"Enough of that." Melanie snatched the book out of Keenan's hand and threw it back in the drawer. It was bad enough being read scripture by her mother. Vampires should be quoting Byron or Keats and whispering lewd but perfectly agreeable suggestions to their companions.

She stood in front of her full-length bedroom mirror and looked closely at herself. "I have a reflection," she announced, sighing with a little relief and laughing to herself. There was something reassuring about seeing the same old face looking back at her from the mirror. She pulled down the corners of her eyes and tugged at her ears, looking for a trace of something different.

Keenan stepped behind her. "As do I." He opened his mouth and

133

stuck his jaw forward.

His warm breath on her neck sent a delightful shiver down her back and made her hairs stand on end. Even that did not fit. Vampires were dead. Or undead. They didn't breathe or sigh. And their touch certainly didn't send warm, syrupy sensations straight to one's groin.

Melanie took a deep breath and collected herself. There was only one thing left to check. She turned around and found herself only inches from Keenan's face. "Hi," she said and rested a hand on his chest, lightly preventing him from getting any closer.

"Hello."

"Don't bite me, okay?"

Keenan cocked his head to the side, but otherwise didn't move.

She reached up slowly and touched his cheeks, ran her fingers along his lips. Keenan closed his eyes and opened his mouth as she ran a finger along a very ordinary set of teeth. His mouth was soft and warm, a stark contrast to his cool skin. He must be a terrific kisser.

"You don't have fangs," she said, frowning. Reluctantly, she pulled herself away from him and stuck a finger deep in her own mouth. Nothing felt different. "This is stupid. I'm still asleep and dreaming."

In the mirror, Melanie could see Keenan press something into the palm of his hand. She saw him wince and hide his fist behind his back. Then something sweet filled the room, thick and delicate as incense. She closed her eyes, sniffed the air, and opened her mouth, hungrily taking it all in.

"Now look," he whispered in her ear.

She opened her eyes. Two long fangs descended where her incisors should be. She touched a thumb to the edge of one and a small trickle of blood bubbled to the surface of her skin.

She laughed at her own reflection and remembered Bryan with his goofy, over-sized fake teeth. Comparatively, these looked sleek, deadly — a newly sharpened machete held next to a Boy Scout pocketknife.

She clamped her teeth down a few times. This was nothing like her first pair of braces, that ill-fitting hunk of metal that made chewing anything next to impossible. No, this was like ... this was like finding the perfect jeans, the missing glass slipper. She felt instantly transformed, diaphanous.

Melanie twirled in front of the mirror. She felt lighter on her feet, but sturdy, as if gravity lessened its impact just for her. She was a little disappointed to see that she was not pale and drawn like the vampires on TV — her arms were still bronze from afternoons spent sunning on her balcony. She could even smell the sun still baked into her skin.

The small scar on her forehead that she got when she fell off her bike as a kid was gone. So too, the summer freckles that showed up around her cheeks and nose. She felt beautiful, infused with a strange sense of confidence that she was unused to. *Who's the fairest of them all now, bitch?*

When Melanie looked up, Keenan was staring at her, an impossibly wide smile on his face. It made her feel self-conscious. "Why are you so happy?" A grinning vampire usually meant he had just killed someone or was about to. At least that's the way it was in the movies.

Keenan took her hand in his. "I'm just glad you're up."

"I'm up. Was there a worry?" she asked, wondering. She couldn't believe her luck — she had been given a whole new life with a standing prince. "Oh!" she yanked her hand away and clenched her stomach.

"What's wrong?"

"I'm hungry," she said, and doubled over. "Oh God, I'm starving." She waited for the latest pang to finish rippling through her belly before slowly straightening up. "I need food. Now," she said flatly and headed straight for the kitchen.

"Where are you going?"

She turned, ready to shout back to Keenan, but he was already in the living room. She didn't think she would ever get used to that.

"I'm going to make dinner. Do you want anything to eat?"

"Uh, Melanie?" He watched her clatter through her cupboards from the safety of the couch.

She found a few slices of bread and some greasy slices of turkey. She added a bag of potato chips, leftover pizza, a tub of vanilla ice cream, a brown banana, and a quart of orange juice to the pile on the counter. A small chipped plate was stacked precariously on top.

"Melanie," he called out again, but she was too involved in the kitchen to take notice.

"Never mind," Keenan mumbled. "You'll figure it out soon enough."

"Mm-hmm," she said ripping open the bag of potato chips and dumping them on the pile.

Keenan sniffed the air and lightly touched a dark spot on the carpet. "Melanie," he called out. "What happened here?"

"Bryan," she answered, her hands full of more food. "My boyfriend."

"Dead?" Keenan asked as casually as if he were asking about the weather.

Melanie nodded without turning around. She piled handfuls of turkey on the bread, dumped the contents of the ice cream next to it.

"He was with you at St. Xavier's?"

She grunted a 'yes' as she inhaled the sweet aroma from the vanilla ice cream. Everything smelled so good, and her stomach felt emptied and desperate to be filled.

Keenan mumbled to himself, "That was careless."

More and more food piled on the kitchen bar.

"I'm sorry," Keenan said louder. "Leah was my responsibility, and she slipped away from me. It won't happen again. Your other friend—"

"Carl," Melanie muttered as she ripped open the brown banana. If she didn't know any better, she could almost smell ozone and rain and mud.

"I buried him proper on the grounds." Keenan paced around the spot a few times and rubbed the back of his neck. He mumbled something and lightly touched the brown stain. "I wish I could undo what happened."

But at the moment, Melanie didn't care. She could see Bryan's face clearly, but it was flat and colorless, like an old yearbook photograph. She could not remember the way his lips tasted or the smell of his hair. The only thing that mattered was hunger, and everything else, everything human, fell away. She briefly hoped it was not lost forever.

Her stomach growled and heaved. She sat down at the bar and tore into her sandwich, then immediately spit it out. The meat must have gone bad. It tasted rancid, mealy. She tried to wash away the taste with some juice, but it was just as foul. She sniffed the carton, but there was only the scent of oranges and sugar and water. She inhaled again and almost smelled wet earth and Brazilian rain, mangoes and kiwi, sweat from sun-baked hands. Her head was dizzy with a million scents. She popped two potato chips absently in her mouth. They were as dry and tasteless as paper.

She swept everything onto the floor and cried. "I'm hungry!"

Keenan was standing in front of her now. "I can still remember how my nan's stew tasted. Sometimes I'll cook a pot just so I can smell the garlic and carrots, onions, thyme and basil."

"Garlic?" Melanie asked, wiping away a tear.

"It's almost cruel isn't it? You can discern every ingredient, even the smell of the soil the food was grown in, but you can taste nothing but rot."

Melanie gripped her belly and sobbed — she felt completely emptied, a thin fabric of skin wrapped around a hollow drum.

"You've forgotten the most important myth. The only one that really matters." He held up his palm, revealing a deep gash in the skin.

"Blood," she whimpered. The color was dark like cabernet, and though already starting to clot and heal, it was still wet and warm. *How natural it would be to just take a taste.* Every cell in her body seemed to demand it.

"Come." He offered his good hand as if he were helping her across a rickety bridge.

She looked at it for a moment. She wasn't sure this was a bridge she wanted to cross. Below, the waters crashed against jagged rocks, and dark shapes swirled below the current. It was a long fall.

"Please," Keenan said. A mist rolled in over the water, obscuring everything but the wooden bridge, the twisted rope handles.

"Where are we going?"

"You need to eat."

"But I have a million questions."

"You've got all the time in the world."

She took his hand, and he squeezed tight.

None of this was fair. She wanted her old life back. No matter how miserable it was, there was a routine she could count on. There were no surprises. She wanted her monsters tucked safely away in books. But most of all though, she wanted Lucas to be as scared and lost as she felt at this moment.

Chapter 17

"You look nervous."

Yes, well duh. Melanie was doing her best not to think about what 'getting a bite to eat' with Keenan entailed. She knew it sure as hell didn't involve a late night visit to the Taco Bell drive-thru. All she could manage was a nod.

Keenan held her hand as they walked through the dense woods surrounding the town, and that did lessen some of her anxiety, but she would have loved some of Carl's homegrown weed about now.

Everything was wet from a recent rain, and the grass and trees sparkled as if crystals grew from their branches and stems.

"Don't be. You'll make the right choice."

"Choice?" She looked up at Keenan, but his smiling face still revealed nothing. Nonetheless, now that she knew she had some say in what was happening, whatever that might be, she felt more relaxed. Finally she had some control over her own destiny.

As they walked, Keenan whistled a tune that Melanie had never heard. The melody was complicated and, if she closed her eyes, she would have sworn she was listening to a prelude played on the flute. "What is that?" she asked, reluctantly interrupting him.

"It's a song about Liban the Sea Woman. Would you like to hear the story?"

Melanie was finding it increasingly difficult to concentrate. Her hearing fluctuated to different patches of the surrounding woods — she caught the rustling of wings, nails clawing into tree bark, hooves digging deep into the soft muddied ground. It made any sort of discussion difficult as her concentration was pulled from one place to another.

It didn't help either that, as she walked a half-step behind Keenan, he gave off a sweet woodsy, fragrance, and wisps of cold drifted from his skin.

Blood and Sunlight   Jamie Wasserman

She wanted to bury her head in his neck, to wrap herself inside his arms, to shut away the rest of the world. "Please." She was desperate for a singular thing she could focus on to slow her racing thoughts.

"Liban was the daughter of a king. When a sacred well in her village overflowed, she was buried under the water. The entire village was killed, but Liban survived in a sea cave. She prayed to the Goddess Diana to transform her into a salmon so she could swim more easily among the other sea creatures. Instead, Diana cursed her and changed her into a mermaid."

They reached the wrought iron fence that separated the woods from the tracks. It was easily thirty feet tall, rusted blood-dark, and foreboding, designed to keep the daring and the suicidal away from the trains.

"Watch," Keenan said, and he let go of Melanie's hand. He crouched low, balancing on the tips of his toes, then sprang up into the air, sailing easily over the high fence. He landed lightly on his feet on the other side.

"Your turn." He motioned for her to follow.

"Yeah, right."

"Stop over-thinking it. Just relax and let your new body do the work."

Melanie hesitated. The fence was tall enough that she had to crane her neck backwards to take it all in. She had spent a lifetime avoiding high places, particularly ledges. Even standing on the edge of a tall curb was enough to make her feel light-headed and dizzy.

She knew she should be scared now, but her stomach, save for the hunger, was remarkably calm. Perhaps along with her old life, she had outgrown all of her old fears, shed them like a second skin.

She did her best to shut away the tumultuous night, then bounced on the tips of her toes like Keenan had. She felt a strength in her legs that she had not felt before. Her muscles stretched taut, pulsated with energy. It was like revving the engine of a Maserati.

One more bounce, and she threw herself into the air, much higher than she expected, but not quite high enough. She caught herself at the top of the fence and held on for dear life.

"Just let go," Keenan said.

"Are you kidding? I'll break a leg." She hadn't outgrown anything —

she was still a child alone in the dark, afraid of the shadows on her walls. She closed her eyes and gritted her teeth.

"Let go, Melanie."

"No. Get me down!"

"Melanie," Keenan called out calmly, his voice velvet and rich. "Look at me."

Melanie got a better hold on the fence and managed to open one eye. He was further away than she had pictured in her head, and she slipped a bit at the top.

"Do you want to hear the rest of the story?" His eyes glittered, though the moon was safely tucked away behind dark clouds. Melanie couldn't look away, no matter how badly she wanted to shut her eyes and pretend she wasn't there. She nodded, her hands shaking as bits of the ancient gate flaked off under her skin.

"After one hundred years, Liban came upon a holy man who was fishing in the water." Keenan paused. "Can you climb over to the other side of the fence?"

Melanie shook her head furiously.

"The holy man took Liban back to his church and gave her a choice — three hundred more years of life as a mermaid, or baptism and instant ascension. Death. She chose death."

After a long moment of silence, Melanie asked, "Is that it?"

"That's it. It goes against all of our being to let go of life. To trust enough that something more exists on the other side. I don't have it in me."

Melanie hid her head in her arms. "Maybe she was just tired of being a fish."

"Huh. I hadn't thought of that. You're very clever."

Melanie could hear the smile in Keenan's voice and peeked over at him just enough to make sure he wasn't making fun of her. He had a bemused expression on his face, but his eye crinkled with worry. "Melanie," he called out.

"What?" A cold creeping sweat was working its way down her back.

"You can jump down now."

Melanie opened her eyes. Somehow she had climbed over the arched points of the iron fence.

"Let go," he whispered. "I won't let you get hurt again."

She wasn't ready to completely trust Keenan, but she wanted to, more than anything. She took a deep breath, then released her death-grip, resigned to whatever abuse the ground offered.

As she fell, her body twisted and turned, and she came to an abrupt landing crouched on the ground like a cat. Her eyes widened. Keenan helped her to her feet and brushed some imaginary dirt from her shirt. "Are you alright?"

Melanie's cheeks felt warm, her whole body pulsed with energy. "What else can I do?"

Keenan laughed deep and wrapped an arm around her. He kissed her hair and led her down the tracks.

She stole a last glance back just to make sure the fence was real, that she had really jumped it on her own. For the first time, she felt ready for whatever else the night might bring.

* * * * *

They walked onto the train bridge that spanned Main Street. Melanie was surprised how quickly they had reached this point. She paused here, enjoying the view of the city lit up. So much life nestled between so much rock. For the first time, she found herself thinking about her hometown without imagining some sort of escape route.

She listened to the sound of cars winding in a hundred different directions, a woman laughing, and the clink of pint glasses. There was music here, far different from that of the woods, but distinct and beautiful. The scent and smells were intoxicating — she could have remained here all night, but Keenan's gentle pressure on her hands reminded her that they had somewhere else to be. "Where are we going?"

"Familiar territory."

"How familiar?" After the excitement of leaping over tall buildings in a single bound had worn off, Melanie was filled with a growing sense of anxiety that she couldn't quite place.

"Come." Keenan gestured for her to follow down the wooded tracks that led outside of town. Reluctantly, she left the bridge and obeyed.

She stepped along the treacherous path easily — her feet did not catch in the rocks, nor did she stumble over dead wood or sudden dips in the trail. When they passed a set of deer remains, Melanie imagined picking her teeth with the bones.

They passed the abandoned switch house where the giant turkey buzzard made its nest. The sound of that bird's wings beating the air used to send chills up her spine. Now it stirred something within her. Her heart beat harder in her chest. The large bird looked down on Melanie from its nest on the remains of the roof. Its ivory beak glinted in the moonlight like a newly sharpened axe handle. The bird lowered its head and stretched its dark wings. When they passed the switch house, the buzzard took flight, circling above them, waiting.

Finally, they made it to the mouth of the old train tunnel, that dark space that seemed to swallow a piece of Melanie every time she passed through. Now the tunnel glowed softly, but clear as foxfire. Tonight, the entrance seemed more like a keyhole than the great yawning chasm she remembered.

She stepped inside and felt an instant cooling, but her body quickly warmed to compensate. Lucas was wrong about that. Melanie was no lizard. Her skin seemed to adjust to any temperature. She'd never need to wear her ugly yellow parka again.

She admired the large rough-hewn bricks that made up the walls. The glint of broken glass and old nails on the tunnel floor shone like trapped stars. Water dripped from the ceiling; rain from a century ago just now finding its way through the rock. She could smell coal and soot and steel. A thousand eyes watched them from above as they passed — a colony of bats clinging stubbornly to the smooth stone — and she saw an entire world that had once been invisible to her.

Finally, they walked into a clearing. Melanie felt some disappointment.

Blood and Sunlight   Jamie Wasserman

The ancient dark had elevated her senses even further, awakened something primal within her. She imagined fire pits and hollow drums and soft earth.

Keenan continued quickly towards the worn path that led to only one place. Hell House.

"Whoah. Where are we going?" She stopped short. She should have noticed before — all night they had been retracing Bryan's off-the-wall detour to Hell House, but everything appeared so different, so new, it was like she was seeing the world for the first time.

"These grounds are special."

"Not for me they aren't." Melanie crossed her arms and planted her feet on the ground. Only bad things had happened here — Carl was killed, Bryan was attacked, and worst of all, she had met Lucas here. She began to wonder now if there was a nugget of truth behind some of the more sinister stories concerning Hell House.

Keenan sighed, picked up a stick, and drew a line on the ground. "The stream attracts a variety of animals." He added a hilltop and a thick cluster of surrounding trees. The drawing wasn't half bad. "The house tends to bring people. Usually outsiders who are curious. In small groups. We're insulated from the town by the woods, so no one can hear any ... well, screams."

"Screams?" Melanie asked and remembered the sight of Leah snapping at Bryan's neck like a pit bull.

"Before the mill, this was sacred hunting ground."

"Oh," Melanie said, finally connecting the dots. *We are here to hunt,* she realized. *Animals and —* she swallowed hard — *people. For their blood.* Still, she couldn't imagine herself as the source of anyone's screams of terror. Disdain, yes. Anger or indifference, frequently. But never fear.

Her stomach rumbled and clenched tight like a fist. She grunted and doubled over.

"It gets easier," Keenan whispered, rubbing her back until the pain subsided.

Melanie slowly straightened up. "Okay, now what?"

"We wait." Keenan sat on the soft, wet grass and motioned for her to sit down.

"For what?"

"You'll know."

Melanie patted the ground, looking for a slightly less damp place to sit. "Can't you just tell me, and cut this cryptic vampire cr—" She turned to face him, but he was gone.

"Hey," she called. "Keenan, I know you can hear me." She paused but heard only a lone owl hooting from the safety of the trees. "Keenan!" she shouted.

"Nice," Melanie said to herself. She picked up a large rock and hurled it against a tree. It shattered in a cloud of dirt and dust.

All around her, she heard small creatures scurrying away, clearing the area, quieting the woods. *You better run, you little bastards.*

* * * * *

Not more than an hour had passed. The forest noises cautiously returned with a soft cacophony of chirping, cawing, and scratching. Melanie was bored as hell. This wasn't any more exciting than sitting in the dank basement of the Orange Brewery, waiting for a vampire to show up. At least there she had a dry place to sit. She could already feel the wet ground creeping into her favorite jeans.

She tried to draw a map in the mud the way Keenan had, but found she couldn't match his delicate touch. Her finger kept sticking deep into the ground. She was like a kid practicing with her first crayon.

Unconsciously, she raised her head.

Something else had entered the woods and was getting closer. Larger than the raccoons that occasionally ambled by — these had a very human presence. She could smell musk and dander; she could hear the brush of fur against bark. She heard their heartbeats thump slow and calm, long before she saw them. And there was that energy again, pulsing through her veins, calling her to action. She was on her feet before she realized it, following the scent.

At the base of the hill nearest the stone steps that led up to Hell

House, two deer emerged, drawn to the wild milkweed that grew there. She could hear their blood churning over like an ocean wave crashing on a sandy shore. She wanted to bathe in it.

She circled silently around them, weighing and judging the two creatures like Goldilocks. This one was too lean, this one was just right. Her eyes instinctively focused on the animal's jugular, his center.

You are mine.

Her entire body tensed, and she felt poised, ready to snap its neck open. Then a smaller deer stepped into the clearing on shaky legs. He looked up and met Melanie's eyes. She saw the fawn take a step back and heard it make a terrible bleating noise. *Mother, mother* the deer seemed to be calling, the way all young children do when something scares them in the dark.

She saw herself, sweat-drenched, tangled in her sheets, yelling for her dad after a nightmare. But her dad was dead, and no one ever came to comfort her.

"No!" Melanie shook her head then looked away, hoping the deer would leave before she changed her mind.

Her muscles relaxed as she heard the deer turn and trot off into the safety of the woods. She felt like she had failed an important test. She could not be the monster in the closet waiting for the parents to shut out the lights. Overhead, the vulture keened and flew off in search of a fresh kill.

"It's not as easy as it looks."

Melanie wasn't surprised to hear Keenan's voice. Though she still couldn't see him, she replied, "No. I'm sorry."

"For what?" He dropped out of one of the taller oaks just in front of her.

"I should go home." *Maybe I'll get lucky and a bear will eat me,* she thought, sighing.

Keenan blocked her path, "What are you sorry for?"

She looked away, ashamed. *I was a failure as a human, now I'm a failure as a vampire. I'll starve to death.*

"Melanie," he whispered and held a finger under her chin so she was forced to look him in the eyes. "There are alternatives."

He wrapped his arms around her and pulled her close. As if reading her mind, he added, "You'll find a balance. Something you can live with because you're going to be living with it for a very long time."

He held her tight, not moving a muscle. Hesitantly, Melanie leaned against his shoulder and hugged him back.

In her head, she counted, *One Mississippi, two Mississippi, three Mississippi,* a habit she had picked up as a little girl. In happier times, she had once asked her mom how she knew that her dad was 'the one.' Her mother replied, "Because when your father held me, he was never the first to let go." Ever since, Melanie kept tabs on her various boyfriends' embraces. She had never counted past three before. The shorter the hug — damn it if her mother wasn't right — the shorter the relationship.

Still wrapped in Keenan's arms, Melanie stopped counting when she got to thirty. Keenan hadn't moved, hadn't lessened his grip, didn't push her awkwardly away, didn't look around embarrassed, afraid of what other people might think. His eyes remained closed, and she heard a soft sigh escape his lips. She thought it was the most wonderful sound in the world. He was with her, and nowhere else. She knew then that he would hold her like this for an eternity. She had only to ask.

"Keenan," she said into his chest.

"Yes?" he ran his fingers through her hair.

"You can kiss me now. If you want to."

Keenan lightly pushed Melanie back at arm's length and studied her face. She creased her brow, worried that she had overstepped some cardinal vampire rule or, worse, had misinterpreted his kindness.

Instead, he stroked her cheek and lightly brushed her lips with his fingers. "I thought you'd never ask." He pressed his forehead against hers. His breath was warm, and she could feel her own breathing accelerate, her heart speeding up to a more human rate. He lingered there, tracing the curves of her face with his hand, his closeness warming her cheeks.

She opened her mouth and leaned in to kiss him. She had never wanted anything so much in her life, but Keenan pulled back. "Slow. There's no rush." He drew back the hair from her ears and kissed her forehead, her eyes, her cheeks.

Melanie's hands trembled as she ran her fingers through Keenan's hair. She wanted his lips on hers, but tried to focus instead on his soft locks, his smooth skin. When Keenan nuzzled her ear and whispered her name, she moaned audibly.

She took his face in her hands and stared into his eyes until she saw only her own reflection looking back. When he finally did kiss her, she had completely forgotten who she was or where they were. His mouth fit perfectly onto hers, his tongue found hers easily. When he finally pulled away, Melanie staggered a step. She had left her body, and the return to earth was not a smooth one.

She rushed at him, hungry for more but he held her back. "We should go."

"Why?" There was a desperation in her voice.

Keenan laced his fingers into hers and kissed the back of her hand. "You need to eat, and the sun will be up soon."

"The sun?" Lucas was right about that, too. *Damn him.*

She realized she would never get to tan on her deck again. She would never drink another Long Island iced tea or shiver when the cold water dripped from the glass onto her bare skin. She would never fall asleep in the warm July afternoon.

"Melanie," Keenan said, interrupting her thoughts. "Let's go, I want you to see something. I think you'll like it."

He kissed her again. His lips tasted sweet like mangoes or peach. Her skin raised with goose bumps. *To heck with it. I'll also never have tan lines or need to rub aloe on my skin to ease a burn. I'll never have to try on another bathing suit again.*

Keenan tugged Melanie's hand to get her walking. Her head still buzzed from his kiss. "What did you want to show me?"

"A surprise."

"Can I turn into a bat?"

Keenan chuckled. "No."

"Wolf?"

"Afraid not."

"Can I fly?"

"Do you have wings?"

"No." Melanie frowned.

"Then, no."

Too bad. Flying would have been a pretty cool trick. That is, if she could get over her knee-shattering fear of heights.

They entered the mouth of the train tunnel again. Even as a vampire, she felt the tunnel dictating silence. Like entering a library or church. No, a cemetery. That kind of reverence for something unseen but still tangible.

This time Melanie held Keenan's hand confidently. She was thinking if kissing Keenan was that good, just imagine...

He froze in place and raised a hand, motioning for her to stop.

"What is it?"

"Not a sound."

In a flash, Keenan had Melanie pressed flat against the wall.

He kissed her hard on the lips. Her spine tingled from her lower back straight to her neck. Every kiss was like the first one.

She pushed back on Keenan's chest. "Not here," she whispered. She wanted Keenan in a bed, stretched out where she could kiss and taste every part of him, not in a dank tunnel, being ogled by bats. *Oh to hell with it,* she said to herself, and wrapped her hands behind his neck. She surrendered everything to the kiss and found herself grabbing at Keenan's hair and pulling at his shirt.

Though he kissed her back, his enthusiasm did not match hers.

"What's wrong?" She pulled back the few inches his hold would allow.

"Just keep looking at me."

Melanie raised her eyebrows. *Why would I want to look anywhere else?* She stroked his cheek to reassure him, and then tensed up. She heard awkward footsteps further along the tracks. Giggling.

Keenan must have felt her body stiffen, because he pressed her harder into the wall and kissed her again, but with more fervor. But this time she could not be distracted.

Blood and Sunlight   Jamie Wasserman

A pulsing sound played off the walls of the tunnel, accompanied by a heavenly scent.

She heard a man say, "I thought you were going to bring the flashlight."

"You can hold my hand if you're scared," a familiar voice teased.

"Ha!"

Two people stood at the mouth of the tunnel now, visible, even without vampiric eyes. A man and a woman walking close to one another. Melanie could smell peach schnapps. Grape bubble gum. Cigarettes. Cologne. Perfume. Very cheap perfume. And something sweeter than all the rest put together.

"Look at me!" Keenan said through gritted teeth, but his voice, ordinarily so clear, sounded muted, as if spoken underwater.

"Are you sure this is the right way?" the man asked wearily.

"Yes. This girl at work goes here all the time."

It was Sasha. That miserable little gum chomping, tip stealing...

Melanie's fangs extracted, and she felt a low growl tickle the back of her throat.

"Come here," the man said.

"Why?" Sasha pouted and started to walk away, but the man grabbed her hand and pulled her to him.

"Naughty boy," she said, and he kissed her hard on the mouth.

"Ow, hey!"

"What's wrong?"

"Sorry. You grabbed me right on the cut on my arm," the man whimpered.

"Is it still bleeding?"

"No, just stings."

"Well, maybe later I'll kiss it and make it all better," Sasha cooed.

"How about now?"

Melanie heard Sasha's pulse quicken, her muscles contract, then relax. She could hear her blood quicken to her cheeks and hands, to her groin.

If the deer's blood was like an ocean, this was like a tidal wave pulling Melanie down into the sand. But she didn't fight it. Instead she swam faster, straight to the bottom. The deer scent was meaty, tempered with oil and fat. This new aroma was sweeter and warm. Melanie's stomach flipped excitedly with the smell — this was what her body wanted. No, this was what her body demanded.

She tried to push away from Keenan, but he was too strong. She snarled, and the animal sound coming from her throat startled her, brought her momentarily back to reality.

"What the hell was that?" the man asked.

"Maybe we should go back."

Melanie tried to lunge forward, but there was no give in Keenan's grip.

"You don't want to do this," he whispered in Melanie's ear, his lips fluttering against her hair.

She let out a pained cry. "She's getting away," she whined and felt the first tears brush her cheeks. She had never needed anything so immediately.

"Bite me."

"What?"

"You need blood now. Bite my neck."

"No." *Not when that skank Sasha was right there. If anyone deserved to die...*

Keenan's wrist went to his mouth.

Melanie struggled feebly and sobbed as Sasha disappeared the way she had come ... like a little kid watching helplessly as her balloon drifted off into the stratosphere.

And then her nostrils flared as something sweet filled the tunnel. *Nectar.* Melanie sniffed. *Like honeysuckle, but richer.* The scent did not call to her like Sasha's blood had; the aroma was weaker, strained like watered-down coffee. The smell did not demand her attention, but it was living and warm, and her stomach growled in anticipation.

She stopped struggling. Keenan loosened his grip. She turned to face him. Blood dripped from a puncture wound on his wrist.

This was the final piece. Forget the incredible sight, the newfound hearing or power. Once she drank blood, Melanie realized, she would never be able to deny what she was. There was no going back.

Keenan touched her lips and whispered, "Drink."

And maybe, if he remained by her, that wasn't such a terrible thing.

She lowered her head to the newly opened cut and sucked at the blood until her stomach relaxed, until the pulsing grew quiet and the angry waves calmed to a soft grey.

Chapter 18

"This is where you live?" Melanie stood outside a looming, white-faced house with turrets jutting from the roof like a castle tower. It was the same house she had tried to find so many times but always came up empty.

"Among others. But mostly here."

No wonder the house had been so elusive — it sat teetering dangerously on a high outcropping of rock. Below ran the Patapsco and a stretch of the old B&O line. There was no road, paved or otherwise, to connect the house to the street, so it had the appearance of springing out of the ground like a magic pumpkin. The dark woods leaned close to the roof but held their distance out of respect, fear, or simple awe. It was a house that a medieval warlord would have been proud to own.

Melanie's heart lifted. It was almost a storybook ending. Saved by the handsome stranger and whisked away to his palace in the woods. Though some small part of her secretly wished she had dropped a trail of breadcrumbs in case something tried to drag her away.

"Did you build this?" She looked at him in awe.

Keenan laughed. "I guess you've never taken any of the local ghost tours."

Melanie shook her head.

"This was a French castle that was brought brick by brick to the New World by one of the early rail barons. Supposedly it's haunted."

"Is it?"

Keenan frowned glumly, "Only by me. Do you like it?"

"Yes." She bit at her tongue.

"Hmm." He creased his lips together.

"What?"

"Nothing. I just thought you'd be more excited."

Melanie wondered briefly how Keenan knew this house was special to her, but put it down to simple deduction. *It's a castle, for God's sake. Of course I should be excited.* But still, something had been troubling her ever since they left the tunnel. "I'm sorry. I was just ... no, forget it."

Keenan stepped in front of her. "Tell me. No secrets between us."

She looked up into his face. His eyes were dark and focused intently on her.

"Will I always be like that around people?"

"Ah. You mean will you always want to..."

"Yes."

"It's worse when you're hungry and worse when there's open blood like that. But yes. Always. You'll just learn to control it better."

Melanie frowned and stared at the ground.

"I'm sorry. I shouldn't be so blunt."

"No!" She took Keenan's hand. "Thank you." *Better the truth, better to be prepared. If there's a monster in the closet, then warn the kid before she goes to pick out her pajamas. If there isn't, then just open the damn door for her.*

Keenan nodded and produced an ordinary set of keys out of the folds of his coat.

Melanie felt a tug of disappointment. Dracula didn't have a home alarm system; he had wolves to guard the door.

"How long have you lived here?" she asked, trying to head off her natural inclination towards pessimism.

He held the door for her. "Hard to say..." His voice trailed off.

She involuntarily held her breath, half expecting the same rotten stench like back in Leah's townhouse, but the air was a mixture of airiness with just a hint of must, like a new library filled with ancient books.

The door opened to a small foyer and a heavy wood staircase that led upstairs. Beyond, Melanie could see a kitchen that certainly pre-dated Better Homes and Gardens. The wood floor was warped and buckled, and a heavy layer of dust covered a well-worn table. It made sense of course. Why would a vampire need to cook? Not exactly Prince Charming's Mansion. More like Sleeping Beauty's Palace after a hundred years of sleep and nightmares. But it wasn't without its charm.

Melanie wanted to say, 'You have a lovely home,' but it seemed like a vast understatement, and the time for small talk had long been chucked out the window. Instead, she blurted out, "It doesn't stink in here."

"Thank you. I guess." Keenan furrowed his brow.

Melanie's cheeks pinked. "I just meant, Leah's house. I went in there and..."

"Ah." Keenan kicked at the floor. "It happens sometimes."

"What do you mean?"

"The change-over isn't always clean."

Melanie waited until she was sure Keenan wasn't looking, to sniff her arms. She didn't smell anything offensive, but then wondered if maybe she was just used to it. And would Keenan be the type to say anything? But then he did hug her out in the woods. Would he have done that if she smelled like hot garbage?

"How old are you anyway?" she asked, abruptly changing the subject. She knew she wasn't getting anywhere with that kind of thinking.

"Twenty-seven."

"No, I mean how old are you really?"

Keenan grinned. "How old do you think I am?"

"Fifty?" she guessed and immediately hated herself for it.

Keenan walked past the staircase into a comfortable living room. "What year is it?"

The furniture there was threadbare and worn like something one would find in one's grandmother's house, but nonetheless comfortable. An old marble fireplace sat against the far wall. New ashes filled the hearth.

The interior did not meet her expectations. There was no grand library covered floor to ceiling in ancient manuscripts. There was no spiral staircase or dripping stone walls. Instead of a cavernous fortress, she found the house simple, warm, and homey. She was surprised but not disappointed.

"You don't know what year it is?" She sat on a couch thrown somewhat haphazardly in the middle of the room and noticed for the first time a fat calico cat wheezing happily in its sleep on the next cushion.

"The whole world does not center round its cradle and its trappings."

"Huh?" Melanie looked up. She was edging as far away from the cat as space would allow. Just a whiff of cat dander was enough to make her eyes puffy and itchy.

"I measure years a little differently." He pulled a small black case from the fireplace mantle. It was about the size of a shaving kit. "Don't you like cats?"

She was vainly trying to push the cat away, but it only snuggled closer to her in its sleep. "They don't like me."

"I find that hard to believe."

Melanie reluctantly pet the creature. It amounted to nothing more than bonking his small head with the palm of her hand, but the cat snuggled more, undeterred. Her allergies seemed to have been cured along with her case of near-death. "What year were you born?" she asked.

"1810, I think." Keenan sat down on the floor in front of her.

"You think?" She feverishly brushed strands of cat hair from her pants.

"My birth wasn't worth noting, apparently."

It felt like a frivolous thought, but all Melanie could think was that he had gone two hundred years without a birthday present.

"Will I live forever?" The cat woke and stared at her with a wary eye, then stretched out on the couch. This was the first cat that didn't instantly try to claw her ankle or attack her shoes. It didn't make her any more trusting of felines.

"Not if you starve yourself. You have to eat."

She'd been too preoccupied with the house to notice, but her stomach had started to rumble. "Again? But I just ate."

"Are you hungry?"

"Yes."

"Then yes, again. You'll eat when you're hungry. You'll sleep when you're tired. That hasn't changed."

Yeah, except now I'm drinking blood for dinner and sleeping ... where am I sleeping? Melanie wondered. *Do I go home and find a night job and continue paying my car insurance and utilities, or do I move in with Keenan? Are we bound together now through some sort of blood tie? If that's the case, it would have been nice to have been asked. Maybe even get a promise ring or at least a nice necklace as a token gesture, a sign of commitment.*

Her eyes roamed to the staircase. Hopefully, the upstairs was in better condition. She imagined satin sheets, dripping black candles, opium incense...

Keenan opened the black case and pulled out a hypodermic needle.

"What's that? Heroin?"

Keenan regarded Melanie for a moment. "So many questions."

Her faced turned red. "I'm sorry. This is new to me." There was more she wanted to ask, but since most of her questions went along the lines of 'Do vampires get insomnia?' she bit her lip.

"It's fine. In time, this all will seem ordinary."

Melanie fidgeted. She wasn't sure she ever wanted to reach a place in her life — or unlife — where hanging out with a two-hundred-year-old vampire became as dull and commonplace as watching Wheel of Fortune reruns.

"C'mere, Tristan." Keenan picked up the cat and set him down in his lap. He scratched the back of his neck, and the cat purred, raising his head in response.

Melanie closed her eyes. The purring sound filled the room and had an oddly calming effect on her. When she opened her eyes, Keenan had inserted the needle into the cat's neck and was drawing blood.

"What are you doing?"

He pulled the needle out and rubbed behind Tristan's ear.

"You eat cats?"

"I don't eat them, I drink their blood. In exchange, I keep them well-fed and well-loved."

Melanie twisted her mouth up.

He added, "A cat's heart pumps three times as fast as a human. They're able to produce enough blood for two."

Melanie flinched at the way Keenan said *human*. Like it was an 'other,' an entirely separate species. She did not feel that different. She still worried about breaking a nail or split ends. She still didn't think she could sleep in a room if the closet door was open even a crack. She was certainly not a creature who went around noshing on felines.

The cat purred and nuzzled his hand as he stroked its neck. "I try not to kill anything," he added defensively. He took out a small silver shot glass from the case and filled it with the blood from the syringe and offered it to Melanie.

"Is that silver? You're not supposed to touch silver."

"Just drink," Keenan said, the strain showing in his voice.

"Can't I just..." She pointed to his wrist. She liked the closeness of drinking from him, the small sigh that escaped his lips as she sucked away the blood, how he absently stroked her hair, and the rich, honey taste of his blood.

"No." Keenan's smooth voice was gaining a rough edge.

"Why?" she heard herself whining, but was feeling too powerless, too lost to care. She hadn't asked for any of this. Drinking blood from a cat — of all creatures, and from a glass — made her all too painfully aware of what she was doing. When she stopped to think about it, it was actually quite revolting.

"My blood won't stave off your hunger for long." He offered her the glass. "Please. It's the only way."

Melanie took the cup, braced herself, shut her eyes, and knocked back the shot. She expected to wince or gag, but the blood warmed her throat like whisky. She set down the glass and smacked her lips together. The taste was tepid, watered down despite the burning in her chest. The real thing must be amazing. She closed her eyes for a moment, wondering if she could still hear Sasha stumbling through the woods.

"Thank you." Keenan sat back down on the floor in front of her. "Animal blood is weaker than..." He struggled to finish his thought and bit at his lower lip. "You may need to drink often."

"Or what?"

"There is no telling what you would be capable of."

Melanie saw something dark and frightening behind Keenan's usually serene countenance, something that he was fighting to hold back. It made her afraid, not of what Keenan might do to her, but because she worried something even worse might be lurking inside her.

"And if you still remain un-sated, you will rot away from the inside, and eventually you will die."

"So we're not immortal."

He chuckled. "Let's just get through tonight first."

"I just—"

"No." Keenan shook his head. "Forget immortality. There are a million ways for you to die. There is only one way for you to live." He carefully cleaned and put away the needle into his bag with the practiced hands of a physician.

"Forget everything. Forget crosses and holy water. Forget garlic. There are no silver bullets. Do you understand?"

"Yes," Melanie said, though she didn't. Yesterday vampires were pretend, but even then, they came with a distinct set of rules. Now she was learning the rules for both pretend and real vampires were a lie.

"Good. Your senses and strength are poisoned. Forget those too. Everything you think or do will be driven by hunger and addiction." Keenan glanced to the boarded windows. "There are only two things to remember. Remember the blood and remember the sunlight."

"What does the sunlight do?"

"Let's just say it's one of the worst ways to go."

'One' of the worst, Melanie repeated inside her head. Joy. She looked at the shot glass in her hand and then tilted it back, catching the last few remaining drops. Secretly, she wanted more, to open the cat's neck like an egg and suck out the insides.

"You're lucky," Keenan added. "There was no one to teach me."

She did not feel lucky. She felt like someone newly sightless being told by a doctor that her other senses would heighten. She was in that same world of darkness, feeling blindly for something familiar, something she could hold onto.

This was Lucas's fault. She closed her eyes again and listened to the night. Perhaps those footsteps she heard lightly stepping along the cobbled path of Tiber Alley were his. Or maybe it was him slamming his car door outside The Old Monk. She vowed then and there, she would drink Lucas dry. even if it was the last thing she did.

Chapter 19

They sat together in silence. Keenan took her hand, though Melanie barely noticed. She watched a spider drop from the ceiling and scurry into the fireplace. She listened to the ancient room, hoping to learn its secrets, but she could only hear paint flaking and floorboards sagging under the weight of generations. Even the rock the house was built on groaned and shifted. All around her was decay.

"So now what? she finally asked after the novelty of literally listening to paint dry had worn off.

Keenan looked slightly startled, as if he had forgotten she was there. "How do you mean?"

"I've eaten. Now what do we do?"

He shrugged his shoulders. To Melanie it seemed a very human gesture and completely out of place for him. Like having a dog wink at you.

"The rest of the night. For fun. What do we do?" She imagined sweeping across cobbled streets in a dark cape ... hiding from angry villagers wielding pitchforks and torches ... whisking away virgins into the night ... rolling around on silky sheets.

"What did you have in mind?"

Melanie blushed, but Keenan's face was expressionless and smooth. Clearly they weren't imagining the same activities. "I don't know. I just thought there'd be a little more to do."

"I survived another day. I count myself fortunate and ask nothing else."

"But that's all you've done!"

"And what else would you have us do? Go out dancing or to the cinema? You can't be around people. You've seen that. I still struggle with it. And if you are discovered, if anyone should find out what you are ... try to imagine the reaction."

Blood and Sunlight

Melanie took her own initial fears and multiplied them by ten. Keenan was right, of course; she would be torn to pieces by an angry mob or end up dissected on an operating table. Still, it didn't make the prospects of an eternity locked up in a house with a bunch of cats any easier.

"It's another cruelty, I'm afraid. Your sight has improved, but all you can do is sit back and watch the world and everyone in it grow old."

"So this is it?"

Keenan's lips curled into a sly smile. "For tonight." He leaned his head back against the wall and shut his eyes.

Melanie glared at him. She didn't like ending an evening so early or so sober. She sighed and stood up and brushed cat hair from her clothes. Keenan did not budge. *Great. So I won't die of a stake through the heart or starvation or burn up in divine conflagration in the sun. I'll suffer slow death by boredom.*

"Don't you ever want to go anywhere else?" she persisted. "The Grand Canyon? Niagara Falls? Paris?" she asked hopefully.

"No. This is my home." Keenan opened his eyes and stretched underneath the boarded window. He would have looked romantic if the moon poured in through the glass, but there was only hastily nailed plywood boards and dust.

Melanie wondered why anyone would want to live here in Ellicott City in the first place, let alone a two-hundred-year-old vampire. He should be locked away in an abandoned abbey in England, or roaming the halls of a crumbling castle in Transylvania — anywhere but this dead-end town whose last claim to fame was the railroad. *Christ, did anyone even take the train anymore?*

"What do you mean? You were born here?"

"In a manner of speaking."

"Oh."

He leaned back against the wall and shut his eyes.

Melanie was used to men who poured out their souls, given the slightest invitation. If a first date didn't end with the man sobbing in her lap, she counted it a wasted evening. She was getting tired of asking all the questions. "What happened ... I mean how did you end up like ... turned?" Melanie racked her brain — what the hell was the proper verb? They certainly didn't cover this in Freshman English.

Keenan sighed and took a deep breath. After a few moments, Melanie wondered if he was asleep. Just as she began pondering the etiquette concerning poking a vampire with a stick, he finally spoke. "Do you really want to know?"

There was something ominous in his tone, but she ignored it and replied, "Yes."

"It would be easier if I showed you. Will you look at me?"

"Okay." Weird request, but sure. She shifted so that she now sat in front of him.

"What do you see?"

The most perfect, kissable set of lips...

"Melanie."

Caught. She looked up into his eyes.

"What do you see?"

"Nothing." She looked down, embarrassed.

Keenan lifted her chin with one finger. "What do you see?"

She met his gaze. His green eyes seemed lighter, watery. Flecks of yellow spun slowly through his irises, like gold leaf in a bottle of Goldschläger.

"Let me show you," he urged. "Would that be alright?"

Melanie nodded her head slowly.

Keenan moved his face close to hers. He stroked her hair and whispered, "Will you follow me?"

"Anywhere," she breathed, and reached to take his hand, but he didn't move.

Keenan locked eyes with her and spoke softly. "No matter how quickly I run, will you follow me?"

"Yes," she insisted.

"No matter how terrible the places I go, will you follow me?"

She nodded again, her gaze never leaving his.

Blood and Sunlight   Jamie Wasserman

His eyes brightened to absolute white, and Melanie soon found herself lost in its brilliance.

Follow me, she heard Keenan say, but this time it wasn't out loud, it was in her head, it was all around her.

Follow me...

The ground under her gave way, but she hovered weightless in the air. She was alone now with only her memories for comfort, but one by one they too fell away. She reached out desperately to hold on to something, but there was nothing there. Nothing. She whimpered and hid her face behind her hands.

Open your eyes, she heard a voice say. It was silky, comforting. And more than that, it was something. She did as the voice commanded.

The ground had returned. Definite, unyielding, and she kicked her foot at the earth for reassurance. Her memories returned as well. A startling assault of colors, sounds, smells and thoughts. She saw a wizened old woman knitting by a fire. She smelled lime and sulfur, heard a prayer recited in Latin. They weren't her memories, but she didn't know any better. She was just relieved to be away from the nothingness.

Above her, an impossibly blue sky arched over a green expanse of grass and low rock walls. Everything glistened from a recent rain. She heard the bleating of sheep and then a sharp voice calling, "Keenan! Get back here now!"

She rubbed her face — it stung sharply. *Next time,* she thought, *I won't let you get away with that. Hit me with your fists. Don't ever use the Bible again.*

Turning, she saw a small ramshackle house and a hawk-faced woman brandishing a small book like a club, leaning out the window. *It's not home. It never will be.*

A sudden flash and pop like an old time camera made everything whiten and gradually reform. Now she stood before an open hearth. Flames spit outside the stone, licking their way up the walls. Her body was caked with ashes and sweat. Every bone ached.

A big man stood in a doorway, putting up a poster. Melanie could only read one word, 'America.'

Flash. Pop.

The ship was crowded, but Melanie managed to find a place on deck. She watched her small island fade away to nothing, and she felt a sense of freedom she never imagined possible. She would be completely happy, if not for the searing pain in her gut.

Flash. Pop.

A crowded flat. The room stunk of sweat and grime, cigars, grain alcohol. Fifteen men crowded here. Playing cards, arguing, yelling in the same tongue of home. Melanie felt trapped. She escaped nothing.

Flash. Pop.

She stood along a freshly dug set of railroad tracks. Men loaded heavy chunks of granite onto a cart. A large black man carried a granite sill on his shoulder. The other workers stood back in awe. As he walked past, he asked, "How you holding up?"

"My hands are shaking."

"Don't let the foreman see you. And get out of the sun. You're burning up."

Melanie nodded. "Gotta get the cart loaded first."

"I'll take care of it, friend."

"Thanks Preira."

Flash. Pop.

It was evening. The sky was blue, but darkening quickly. Yellow lanterns lined the track. Melanie felt dizzy and smoked a cigarette under a tree. Another man approached from the direction of town. He had an angular face and sunken gums. Melanie could hear him talking to the foreman. He wanted work. The hairs on the back of Melanie's neck stood up. She was worried that the flux was worsening. Soon she wouldn't be able to work. She wouldn't be able to afford even her tiny bedsit. She'd lose everything.

Flash. Pop.

The sun was bright and hung in a cloudless sky. The rest of the men were shirtless and drenched in sweat. Melanie shivered, barely managing to lift the cart. Her throat was dry and burned, but she knew even water wouldn't stay down. Preira stood with the foreman next to what was left of a large rock. He'd been trying to break it for six days. Today it was nothing more than rubble and sand.

"You do this?"

Preira shook his head. "Stavros," he said and scratched at his beard.

"Impossible."

Flash. Pop.

Evening again, but there was no need for the lanterns. The moon was full and impossibly large. It lit the campsite with a cool glow. Melanie leaned next to Preira against a tree, using a pick-axe to support her weight. They both watched Stavros lift and carry a granite sill over each shoulder.

Preira stared in awe as Stavros strode past. She heard him mutter, "Legba."

Flash. Pop.

All was dark, but Melanie heard shouting, someone calling her name. She was too weak to open her eyes. She felt a set of hands lift her into the air.

Flash. Pop.

White sheets. A black robe paced next to the bed. A large, cavernous room that was otherwise empty.

Flash. Pop.

There were others here now. She heard them wheeze and struggle for breath. One man cried pitifully.

Flash. Pop.

The priests had stopped coming. The room was silent. "Keenan!" a ragged voice called. It was Preira but something was not right. She heard him gurgle before the room fell into a deathly silence again.

Flash. Pop.

A hand pushed open Melanie's eyes. She had to struggle to focus, to see the utterly white face in front of her. Stavros. He pushed her head back, and she felt something sharp dig into her throat. She wanted to scream, but it felt like the air was being sucked out of her. Just when she thought her lungs would explode, the pain stopped. She did not want to die. One lifetime was not enough.

Stavros was in front of her again. A thick black liquid dripped from his lips. He smiled, revealing a set of deadly fangs, and then the lips parted and moved towards her mouth. She screamed.

Melanie.

Something grabbed her shirt. She thrashed and tried to push it away. Everything was dark again.

Melanie!

Two hands wrapped around her waist. She smelled something sweet. She screamed again, louder, and it carried throughout the room.

"Melanie!"

Something soft and wet touched her lips. Two hands held her steady. It took her a moment to realize that it wasn't Stavros, that the lips were only kissing. She kissed back.

"Are you okay?" The lips stopped kissing but lingered in front of her.

"Keenan?"

"I'm here."

"What the hell did you do to me?"

He laughed, relieved, and kissed her forehead. "You're okay."

Melanie's head was literally buzzing. She felt very tired and wrapped her arms around his neck. *Explain that one away, Lucas,* she thought.

He held her tightly and stroked her back.

"So you're Catholic?"

He laughed again into her hair, then pulled out a silver cross dangling from a chain around his neck. "Glory be to the Father, and to the Son, and to the Holy Spirit. As it was in the beginning, it is now, and ever shall be, a world without end. Amen."

"Amen," Melanie added automatically, and then wondered which version of the Bible Keenan's mother used to hit him. She preferred the King James; it was thinner and left fewer welts.

"So Stavros—"

"Yes."

"And everyone else, all the other workers ... Preira?"

"Gone."

She touched his neck — a thick, knotted white scar like a little fist covered his jugular. There was nothing neat about this cut, nothing like the simple pinpricks she had seen in movies.

"Why do you stay here?" *Why remain where every day is a reminder of the terrible things that happened?* She wondered if Lucas had been right about that part, if there was something more powerful at work keeping Keenan here, binding him to his home soil.

"This is as close to a home as I've had."

"Oh." She frowned. She'd probably feel the same way, too, if she ever found somewhere she belonged.

"Is Stavros even still alive?" she asked.

"Does it matter?"

"I guess not. Are there more?" Melanie asked hopefully. If there were, it would be like gaining a whole new family; the Manson family, but a family nonetheless.

"Sometimes, I think I can hear others. But mostly it's quiet."

But beyond Ellicott City, he seemed to be implying, there were. "What about Leah?" She felt a twinge of sympathy for her now. They had both met the same fate at the hands of Lucas. She would be the closest thing she ever had to a sister.

"Gone."

"What do you mean, *gone?*"

"It's not important." He moved closer to her and stroked her face.

She stiffened and something clicked in her brain. Of course, Lucas was right, just as he had been right about so many other things. He had warned Melanie, but she didn't realize it until now. The entire night she had been retracing Leah's steps, from the woods to Hell House — the vampire's hunting grounds.

"She killed the deer," she mumbled to herself.

"Pardon?"

"You took her into the woods by Hell House, just like me, but she killed the deer. It was a test, wasn't it?" She felt her dull heartbeat lurch and quicken.

"I don't follow."

"What would have happened if I had killed the deer back in the woods?" She studied Keenan's plaster face, searching for some hint of betrayal.

"Nothing."

"The fawn. Did you summon her? Use some kind of secret telepathy to bring her to me?"

"Summon a deer?" Keenan chuckled and covered his mouth with the back of his hand. "You're being serious?"

Melanie's eyes darted around the room. Would he let her go, or was she bound to the same fate as Leah?

Keenan reached out to touch Melanie's shoulder, but she got up and backed away in fear.

He stopped and cocked his head to the side. "You are being serious. I'm sorry."

"What happened to Leah?"

He tugged his ear and sat cross-legged on the floor. "Most who come over, don't last. Their bodies burn up like candle wax. She was fine, at first. A natural hunter. I think she enjoyed her newfound power. But my poison was too much. Her brain was the first to go. That was the creature you saw. Nothing left of her real self. Just a hellacious beast driven by instinct alone. The rest was mercifully quick. She lasted longer than most."

"Poison?" *Well, that put things in to perspective. And the smell of rot inside Leah's house, that was what? Leah's body decomposing from the inside out?* Melanie shuddered.

Keenan ran his fingers through his thick hair. "Sadly, you are the exception and not the rule."

"How many?"

"What?"

"How many others have there been?"

Keenan rubbed the back of his neck. "Too many to remember."

Melanie crossed herself. It was such an automatic response to hearing about death, that she didn't even think about it.

"I didn't kill them, if that's what you think. The others, they were dead without me. If it wasn't flood or fire or a bear, it was your friend Lucas with his little knife. I gave them all a chance for just a little more. But you were different."

"Different? Right. How the hell did you know?" Melanie paced back and forth. She wondered how many others the well-meaning vampire had doomed. "You're no better than Lucas. Or Stavros!" Keenan's trial and error process of turning people had killed Bryan and Carl and Lord knows how many others. She felt a low growl tickle the back of her throat.

"Wait. Please," he said holding up his hands. "Can I show you something?"

Melanie stopped, still stiff, still guarded.

With deliberate slowness he leaned over towards the chest that served as his table and opened it up. From inside, he produced Melanie's missing backpack.

"My bag!"

She grabbed it and rummaged through its contents. Everything was there — her car keys with its tangled knot of key chains, her favorite lipstick, Officer Tyler's business card, gum. Everything except for her sketchbook. When she looked up, Keenan held it in his hands.

"We see the world the same. You already understand this life better than anyone. I thought we might be able to help each other."

And my sketchbook was what convinced you I would cross-over successfully? Melanie's forehead creased. But she had lost her book days before Lucas tried to kill her. She wondered if Keenan had been following her, and if so, for how long.

When he opened the cover, her face blanched, and she gasped. She took a step and reached for the book, then dropped her hand. She realized he had already seen everything in it. Her sketchbook was the closest thing to a diary she had, and he had witnessed every page, every secret.

He studied her face and stroked the first page reverently. A self portrait she did of herself looking in the mirror. She felt as if it were her own cheek he was stroking, and she closed her eyes, anger falling away from her like ash.

He turned the page, and Melanie's stomach fluttered. There was a charcoal drawing of a galaxy crowded with stars, and the towering spire of Keenan's house penciled above a thick tree cover. Even the scarred network of Bryan's wrists were represented, hastily done in cigarette ash. She was surprised at how resilient even the sketched scars were. They had not faded one bit.

To her surprise, she did not feel raw or exposed as Keenan continued to look at her work, something she had never shared with anyone. Instead, she felt completed. The book needed a reader. The princess needed a happily ever after. Otherwise, what good was storming the castle, tackling the dragon?

But Keenan had taken a tremendous gamble with her life. He didn't know what would happen to her after he changed her. Wouldn't it have been better to simply step off the curb into the truck's path than to live a half-life like Leah or Bryan?

Keenan knew about as much as Lucas did of vampires — a knowledge that was based partly on deduction, partly on observation, but mostly on hope. And hope was never a guarantee. No one knew that better than Melanie.

But was his gamble any worse than the one she had taken every day of her careless life? Every time she took a pill without knowing what it was. Every time she drove herself home drunk or high. Or picked up a stranger, or broke into abandoned buildings in the middle of the night. It was Melanie who sought out Lucas, after all, then stood before him without fear when he came for her with the knife. Wasn't she ready to die long before Keenan came along?

"You didn't just happen upon me when Lucas attacked me, did you? You'd been following me."

Keenan lowered his head.

"So you didn't have the balls to do it yourself. You just waited for Lucas to attack me, is that it?" She gritted her teeth, already knowing the answer. Keenan had already seen Lucas kill Leah; he knew what he was capable of. The rest was just a matter of time, biding his time until Lucas did the same thing to Melanie. What a perfect opportunity to change her without fear of guilt if things didn't work out.

"For that I am sorry."

She remembered Keenan's words on the way to Hell House, *I won't let you get hurt again.*

Her shoulders sank. "You watched me die. You could've stopped all this. Why?"

"I thought that maybe this life was something you wanted. That this life was something we could share." He looked up at her expectantly.

There it was. Two hundred years to perfect the human existence, and loneliness still remained. What hope did anyone have?

Melanie paced around the room, feeling conflicted. She had gotten her wish after all. Keenan had opened his soul for her. But would she have been better off not knowing? *No.* Nothing scared her more than the unknown. And would her life really be any different had Keenan swooped down from the trees like a great bat and carried Lucas into the woods? Not for her. That's not to say there wasn't someone else out there who did need saving from Lucas.

She chewed at her lower lip. Keenan sat motionless on the floor, waiting for some kind of reassurance from her. She wanted to keep him in suspense, anxious, off-balance the same way she had felt every step of this night. That would be something to see, but Melanie knew Keenan could wait, in fact, forever.

"I don't care."

"What?"

"I don't care," she said with growing conviction. What really had she lost? Family. Dead and gone. Friends. Bryan and Carl were just one more diversion before the next one came along. Not even a pet. Nothing depended on her because Melanie reminded herself nothing could depend on her. She was alone and that was fine.

But not anymore. She was part of someone else, and he was part of her. They were chapters in the same book, bound together forever.

Keenan opened his arms to her, and she curled against him. She

172

wanted to taste his lips, to feel his body against hers, but she knew now there would be plenty of time. She no longer had to be in a rush to get somewhere else — she was exactly where she was meant to be.

"Thank you," Keenan whispered, and kissed her hair.

Tristan planted his head in Melanie's lap and looked up at her expectantly. This time she didn't push him away. She absently stroked his back and closed her eyes, letting her mind wander from the surrounding woods, to the river, and on to the road and Main Street. The murmur of the human and animal world combined to make a strange cacophony of sounds. Her place, she suspected, was somewhere in between both.

When she opened her eyes, Keenan was studying her intently.

"There is good in this, isn't there?" He wanted reassurance.

"I guess so," Melanie muttered.

She looked at the boarded window and somehow knew dawn was nearing, just like her mom knew when it was going to rain — she felt it like an ache in her bones.

"Shouldn't we go to sleep or something?" She imagined an exquisite coffin lined with velvet in the bowels of the house.

"Are you tired?"

"No." She yawned and nestled into the crook of Keenan's arm.

This had been the longest, strangest, most awful and wonderful night of her life. And now the night would never end.

Chapter 20

In Melanie's dream, a fine mist drifted over the old stone pier in Fells Point. Black water slapped against the dock, lit occasionally by the sudden flare from gaslights lining the harbor. She heard heavy footsteps approaching on the cobbled street and the high-pitched squeal of a bat zeroing in on her prey.

The bat, Melanie realized, was her, transformed. Even the mist seemed an extension of her body, the soft tendrils of fog sinking the dock into nothingness. She followed the footsteps into an alley that wound away from the water.

A man in a tilted Victorian top hat walked at a steady pace, his hands tucked away in the folds of his long black coat. Melanie could feel the man's heat, his fear, as his heartbeat raced and he hastened his steps. Melanie glided in the dark, narrowly focused on her prey, aware and enjoying the fact that she could take him anytime she wanted. She fluttered to the ground and instantly transformed back into human form, a sheer white dress billowing inexplicably around her otherwise naked body.

The man stopped, sensing perhaps Melanie's sudden manifestation. He turned slowly. Though his face was weathered and the eyes looked red and haunted, Melanie recognized him right away.

"Hello Lucas," she purred.

Lucas's eyes widened.

"Come here."

Lucas obeyed, stepping forward seemingly hypnotized.

"That's it." Melanie wrapped her arms around his neck and opened her mouth wide. Two perfect white teeth glistened in the moonlight.

She brought her hungry lips to his neck, but before her teeth could find purpose, Lucas's hand shot forward, catching her in the chest. She stumbled backwards, a wooden stake buried deep in her heart. Before she could disintegrate into a cloud of dust, Melanie woke.

She had to catch her breath. She didn't usually dream — or if she did, she certainly never remembered them. She wondered if this was something else she would have to get used to — the animal part of her brain continuing to scheme and plot while the rest of her body had shut down.

She looked for meaning in the dream, but aside from 'Don't play with your food.' its message eluded her. She wouldn't make the same mistake when she killed Lucas.

She looked around and was a little disappointed to see that she was on a very ordinary mattress in a very ordinary room. A house this old should have a dirt-floor basement or a wine cellar carved out of rock. She should be encased in a glass coffin covered in lilies.

She was only a little surprised when she saw that she was now wearing a nightgown. Before, Melanie had never been a sound sleeper. All it took was the slightest drip of a faucet or the air conditioner kicking in to wake her. She couldn't understand why suddenly she slept like a coma patient. It made her feel vulnerable, helpless.

"Damn it, Keenan!" she shouted at the closed door. "Stop moving me around while I'm sleeping. And stop dressing me. I'm not a doll."

The door opened, and Keenan stood there smiling, several boxes tucked under his arm. He was wearing a faded pair of jeans and a tight white tee shirt. No shoes. No piercings or rings. No hair gel to tame his curls. No black eyeliner. Nobody else could look this good, wearing so little.

"I'd argue that."

For someone who did not get out much, Keenan was a natural flirt. She thought about pulling the covers back, a silent invitation to join her, but didn't want to rush him. He seemed to have a distinct timetable of when and how things should happen, and she wanted to make sure she didn't miss any of them.

A fluffy white cat bounded into the room.

"Oh look, breakfast in bed."

Keenan protectively scooped the cat up and shooed her out the door.

"How many of them are there?"

"Just the two."

"Meals on wheels."

Keenan scowled and narrowed his eyes.

"Jeez, I was only kidding."

"The cats are important to me." He glared at her. The gold flecks in his eyes darkened to orange and red.

"Okay. I'm sorry," Melanie said and tried to change the subject. She had obviously struck a nerve. "Did you bring me something?"

Keenan set his boxes down on the bed, and Melanie examined them. There was Scrabble, Monopoly, Chutes and Ladders, and Clue.

"You seemed bored last night. I thought maybe later we could—"

"You've got to be kidding." Melanie opened the Chutes and Ladders box. The board was frayed and coming apart at the seams. The dice were missing, and the little cardboard children game pieces had endured unimaginable horrors. "Where did you even get this stuff?"

Keenan smiled. "I have my ways."

"No, seriously." Vampires shouldn't do mundane things like go to the store to buy light bulbs or try on new pants at the Gap. And they sure as hell shouldn't be shopping for board games.

"The dump." The smile from his face vanished, and he looked a little ashamed.

"I see." This was Ellicott City, she reminded herself, not gas-lit turn of the century New Orleans. There were no late night rendezvous in above-ground cemeteries. No drunken salon girls and jazz music. Only Tiddlywinks and ruin. She'd have to keep pressing Keenan for a visit to Paris, or at least a train trip to New York. If Keenan had found a way to peacefully live here, surely he could go anywhere.

"And that's where this tasteful frock came from?" She lifted a frilly sleeve of her nightgown. It was salmon colored and done up with a recurring floral pattern. She felt like a walking pillowcase.

"Unattended clothesline."

"Nice." She made a mental note to pick up some clothes from her apartment, then stopped short. What exactly was the living situation here?

They had kissed, they just hadn't gotten around to doing the deed, what with drinking blood and jumping over fences and nearly attacking people. Were they boyfriend and girlfriend? Was this just a short learning period before he kicked her out to fend for herself? There were too many questions. She decided to test the waters. "Keenan?"

He looked up woefully from the stack of board games, dejected. "Yes, love."

Love, Melanie repeated inside her head. *That's a good start.* "I was thinking of going back to my apartment."

"Oh?" he asked. His face was smooth and blank as a sheet.

"Maybe get some clothes. Some personal stuff."

Keenan stared back at her, revealing nothing.

"Would that be okay?"

"Why wouldn't it?" He sat on the bed next to her.

Melanie gnashed her teeth together. Nice to see guys remained just as oblivious and unobservant no matter how many centuries they've lived. She wasn't ready to give up yet, though. "This is a big house."

"Do you think?" Keenan fidgeted with the stack of games.

"Maybe even too big for just one person?" *Don't make me ask,* she silently pleaded.

"Undoubtedly," he added distracted. "You know, there is something else I like to do for fun." His face brightened, and he pushed aside the games.

"Yes?" she cooed and wondered briefly if she had shaved her legs and then if she still needed to.

He stood up and pulled out an old fashioned pocket watch from his pocket. "Hmm. We'll have to leave now, if we're going to make it."

"What are you, the white rabbit?" Melanie teased.

"Alice in Wonderland. One of my favorites."

"*One* of your favorites?" She tried to imagine the vampire curled up with a good book by the fireplace.

"I love reading."

"Where are we going?" She decided to drop the subject. If Keenan told her he had a library card, she'd probably lose it. Best to leave some of the mystery in place.

"We'll have to run if we're going to make it. Think you can keep up?" He beamed.

"Yeah, I guess—"

She looked up, but he was gone. "Keenan!" she shouted, then remembered she didn't need to.

"Downstairs. Hurry. There isn't much time."

She could hear his voice as easily as if it were whispered in her ear. "I'm not dressed."

"You're gorgeous. Now keep up."

She heard the door open, and Keenan pacing on the stone steps outside.

This was not her usual wake-up routine. Generally, she would lie in bed as long as she could, cradling her head and swearing off whatever she had taken the night before. She wasn't used to feeling so alert, and so she resisted as long as she could.

"Melanie."

Damn it. "I'm coming."

She sighed and got out of bed and stretched. She scrunched up her face, trying to get her fangs to extend, but they held fast.

"What'd you do with my shoes?"

"You don't need them."

To go running? Of course I need shoes. Then she remembered stepping on glass back at her apartment. She looked down at the soles of her feet. The cut had healed. Still, she didn't like to get dirty.

"Do we need to take some dirt with us?"

"Dirt?" Keenan deliberated on this for a moment. "No, there'll be dirt where we're going."

"No, I just meant do we have to..." but now that she'd said it out loud, she realized just how stupid it sounded. *Bound to carry a pocketful of mud wherever you went? Ha!* "Never mind." *Core legends, my ass.*

"Tick tock, tick tock."

"I said I'm coming!" she growled and walked to the top of the landing.

"Jump."

Melanie peered over the railing. It was a good drop to the floor, but definitely not higher than the rail fence had been. She visualized herself vaulting over and landing lightly on the ground below, but her stomach sank and the old fears returned. She ran quickly down the steps to Keenan.

Ever the gentleman, he did not say a word about it.

She arrived on the porch feeling frumpy and disheveled.

"That's how you're going dressed?" he raised a disapproving eye.

Melanie fumed, "You said—"

"I'm kidding. You couldn't be lovelier." He leaned over and kissed her on the lips.

"Ha ha."

"I'm serious." He held her by the waist, searching her face until she looked up at him. "I wish you could see yourself as I do."

Melanie nuzzled against his shoulder. "You know, I'd be just as happy going back upstairs..."

In the next instance, Melanie's arms were empty, and she staggered forward. Keenan stood about twenty feet from the house, grinning impishly. "Catch me if you can."

"Wait..." she begged, but he was already a blur as he turned and sprinted into the woods.

"I really don't want to do this." She took a few steps towards the woods. A late night run had all the appeal of elective dentistry, but her heart felt a tug as she watched him slip away from her.

"Wait up," she called and started trudging into the woods, gingerly at first, not used to the feel of her bare feet on the grass, or anywhere near Mother Nature for that matter. To her surprise, the rough, pine-laden ground felt silky and cool. "I can do this." She worked herself up to a slow trot.

As she entered the woods, the night clamored for her attention from a thousand different directions, but she practiced focusing just on the sound of Keenan's light steps, and everything else faded to a dull thrum. When his movement was no longer discernible, Melanie found she could pick out his sweet scent even among the mélange of rotting leaves, mud, animal musk, and dried out pine. She ran faster until the trees and rocks blurred past her. When she came to a fallen oak blocking her path, she leapt in the air and hit the ground running on the other side.

"Well, that was cool!" She hadn't seen the oak until the last second, but she had sensed that it was there, something large and immovable, and her body knew to jump out of the way. She decided to test a little further and darted off the path into the thick covering of trees and brush. She ducked, jumped, and spun her way through, not catching so much as a bur or thorn on her sleeves. She only slowed temporarily when she heard a high-pitch trill then realized it was coming from her own mouth. She was giggling.

Keenan appeared next to her, laughing also. He took her hand, and they ran even faster until they exploded through the trees and fell together on an empty stretch of railroad tracks. They clung to each other, rolling like children back and forth on the ground, their laughter growing louder and louder.

"This is much more fun with you here." He nuzzled her neck.

"You, too," she whispered.

"Oh." Keenan pulled suddenly away from Melanie and looked down the tracks. "We've missed it."

She could just make out the low metallic rumbling of a train headed north. "We could just stay here." She lingered above him, her mouth inches from his.

"We could." He ran his hand down her back and pulled her closer.

She let out a small gasp and kissed him once, softly, and then pulled back. Just a tease. She wanted him to come to her, to need her as immediately as she needed him. She wanted him to be the one to get carried away for once. She could feel him press closer against her body, and his warm breath accelerated as he kissed her neck.

Ah, to hell with it. She pounced on him, running her hands down his chest, tugging at his shirt as she kissed his chin, his soft lips. He rolled on top of her and studied her face. *Yes, yes, yes!* She stretched her arms back.

"I know!" he said suddenly, and was on his feet before she could complain. He grabbed her hand and pulled her up. "Follow me!" He took off straight through the underbrush, with her in tow.

She didn't pay the trip much attention. This was the second time tonight she had tried to take things to the next level with Keenan, and the second time he had pulled away inexplicably. That kind of thing could really wreak havoc on a girl's confidence. "What are we doing?" she called out.

"Catching a train."

Surprised, she dropped back a few steps behind Keenan. She wondered if he was really going to take her to New York after all. She didn't even begin to consider how she'd react to the throng of warm bodies and even warmer blood mixing together on the sidewalk. That kind of temptation would probably be too much, even for someone as austere as Keenan. Instead, she pictured herself kissing him on top of the Statue of Liberty, the city and its denizens laid out insignificantly before her. Hell, they could even go to Philly or Detroit or Boston. She didn't care. It would be enough to leave Ellicott City and be with him.

"Don't look down," Keenan called out, disrupting her trip to the Liberty Bell.

"What?"

Before he could answer, the ground fell away from her, and a sudden rush of cold air stung her eyes and closed her throat.

Chapter 21

Melanie landed hard on the roof of a rocking train car and slipped as she scrambled for something to steady herself. There was nothing to hold onto. Out of nowhere, Keenan grabbed her arm and helped her to her feet. All around, the landscape escaped past them in a blur of black and green, faster than when she was running. Under her feet, a ribbon of silver stretched its way through the woods. A distinct whistle pierced the steady rhythm of wind, and a click-clacking noise pounded the air. She looked back to where she and Keenan had just jumped. There she saw the familiar overhanging rock and the sheer face of Bloody Fingers, the rocky overhang used by the local climbers.

"You jerk!" She punched Keenan in the shoulder, once she had her legs back. Gone was the usual panic that normally gripped her when confronted with even the tiniest heights. Instead, there was only fury.

He simply shrugged and put his hand around her waist. "Still afraid of heights?"

She found his voice, even above the rush of wind, then punched him again for good measure. "I was never afraid, and you're still a jerk." She shook her head, then laughed despite herself.

"Duck."

"What?"

"Duck!" Keenan shoved Melanie down, and she hit the train car roof with a metallic thunk. An enormous tree branch sped past them.

She heard the whistling again. "Keenan?"

"Yes?" He sat up on his knees.

"Why are we on top of the train?" She got up facing him.

He grinned from ear to ear. "It's quite the rush. What do you think? If we're lucky, it'll rain."

"Yeah." Melanie rolled her eyes. "Fingers crossed." She held up her hands.

There was a dark bank of clouds visible between the trees, and the air felt wet, scented, almost electric with some kind of possibility.

She shuddered. Keenan slipped behind her and wrapped his arms around her.

"Better?" he asked, and kissed her cheek.

"Actually, yeah." She sank back against his chest. "So this is what you do for fun?"

"What do you think?"

The trees thinned long enough that Melanie could make out innumerable stars. Their light brightened and dimmed in yellows and golds. Along the horizon, she could see the strained white light from the city. Away from the modern illumination, the sky itself was not the inky black she remembered. Rather it was a deep and varied shade of purple. Gray clouds stretched apart and re-gathered.

"Not bad. How far do you go?"

"Usually to the Catonsville line." Keenan rubbed Melanie's arm.

"I think you're right about the rain. I just felt a drop."

"Not yet," he said in a ragged whisper. His hand moved from her arms to her legs. "You'll know when it starts."

"So you've really never left Ellicott City?"

"Never."

Keenan's hands slipped underneath her nightgown and stroked her bare belly.

She squirmed, trying to keep her emotions in check.

"Which way are we headed?"

"North."

Baltimore would be the next stop. Then Philly, New Jersey, and New York. Then even further to Boston. Connecticut. She could be a suburban vampire with a white picket fence.

Keenan's hands grazed her breasts, and she clamped hold of his wrists from outside her shirt. "Keenan," she pleaded, turning to face him, "you have to stop. I'm going to lose it if—"

He grabbed the back of her head and pulled her to him, kissing her softly on the mouth. His lips tasted so sweet, she found it almost impossible to break away. She moaned, then pushed herself back. "Wait. Just wait." She tried to collect her thoughts, but they were all focused on ripping off his shirt with her teeth.

Keenan was breathing hard. His hands found hers, then they found her arms, her back...

"On top of a train. Really?" She searched his face. This was a new kind of kink. Even for her.

"Have you ever made love on top of a train before?" Keenan nibbled at her ear.

"No." Melanie frowned.

The nibbling became more frantic.

"Then yes. On a train. For the first time," he answered with another kiss, this one slow, lingering, even sweeter.

He wanted a virgin, she figured. He would be gentle with her, and she would have to pretend to be flattered by his caution, when all she wanted was someone to curl her toes and make her scream like she was on fire. Then Keenan ripped off her nightgown. *Or not.*

She watched the ragged cloth sail away as the train barreled forward. Her panties soon followed. She gasped and shivered as his hands found her nipples. She sank back against the cool metal of the car and stretched her arms behind her head.

He broke away for a moment as he struggled to take off his shirt and fumbled with his jeans. She sat up on her elbows and hungrily kissed his cheek, upset to lose his attention for even a second. And then he was naked, and they were on each other again.

The feel of Keenan's hands on her body was nothing compared to his chest pressed against hers. His skin was smooth, sculpted and surprisingly warm. She felt enveloped in his cedar scent, and it pressed around her like silken sheets.

Above, the trees thinned, then disappeared, revealing a dark expanse of sky. If it weren't for the rocketing of the train as it jolted back and forth on the tracks, Melanie could almost imagine herself completely alone in the universe with Keenan.

She tilted her head to the side, revealing her neck, then pulled him closer, willing him on, just as she had with Bryan only days ago. She wanted him to take from her, to drink like she had drunk from him. She wanted that same dizzy sensation when her middle school boyfriend sucked on her nipples for the first time.

She could feel his breath close on her skin and shut her eyes. This would be better than any awkward fumbling on a wobbly foosball table in a cluttered basement. *Yes!*

He bit her neck, and her body tensed, then relaxed. Her heart was racing hard, and Keenan must've felt it, because he pulled her closer and closer until he was finally inside her.

She moaned and clung to him desperately. She felt a pain as he moved deeper inside her, her body opening for him, just like it did the first time.

"Ow!"

The noise of the train fell away. There was only a dull rush of blood in her ears and the velvety comfort of Keenan's voice.

"Are you okay?" He stopped and smoothed her hair back.

"It hurts." She felt along her thighs where something warm and wet dripped. When she raised her hand it was smeared with blood.

Above, the sky swirled and darkened past twilight. The light of even the strongest of stars flickered, then waned under the approaching hour.

"Oh," she gasped. "Don't freak out, but I'm bleeding."

She felt Keenan inching away, but she grabbed his back and pulled him further inside.

"Do you want to stop? I don't want to hurt you." His brow was knitted in concern. Her blood didn't affect him at all. All of his attention was focused solely on her.

"No." She stroked his cheek. "It's a good hurt." Her body had healed. She was a virgin after all. She was being given a second chance. This time it would not be wasted.

She took Keenan's face in her hands, wanting to forever remember his kind green eyes, the part of his mouth, the way his curls fell and framed his perfect white face.

Slowly, he pushed himself inside, further than any man ever had. She closed her eyes and her body began to shake, but he didn't stop, grinding against her, until she thought she would explode from pleasure.

"Open your eyes."

Melanie's teeth were sunk deep into Keenan's shoulder. Embarrassed, she started to pull away, but he lifted her chin and kissed her.

"Keep looking at me." He took her hands in his. "I love you, Melanie."

"You do?"

She moaned as a new pressure started to build, first in her stomach, then her legs, and back. She felt like she was being pulled apart. Her nerves stretched taut as piano wire. Her pulse sang. She closed her eyes and gripped his hands tight.

"Keep your eyes open. Stay with me."

Her body glistened with sweat, and her legs began to shake as another orgasm rocketed through her. She had to concentrate to meet Keenan's gaze, to not let the next wave of pleasure take her away completely.

"I love you, Melanie."

Her body arched. Every single muscle tingled, her skin suddenly sensitive and delicate as a newborn. She scratched her nails down Keenan's back, struggling to hold on, and let out a scream.

"I love you," he whispered again in her ear. "Melanie," he murmured, repeating her name over and over, like he had forgotten every other word, and every time he said her name, it meant something different. She didn't want it to end. Not ever.

She could feel him releasing just as her body shook again. Finally, she felt his muscles relax and he buried his head in her neck and held her tight.

As he slipped away from her, she felt like she was drowning. She couldn't breathe, and she couldn't open her eyes. Keenan was gone.

There was another rush of blood in her ears and then ... nothing. Nothing. Just that terrible, contemplative moment after orgasm, where pleasure is replaced by uncertainty and doubt.

She reached blindly for Keenan, finding his neck, clutching him to her chest like a life preserver. She found his lips, and they kissed slowly, no longer desperate, content to simply taste each other's skin. There was no doubt, just bliss. She was still underwater, but he was there too, and she could see him clearly. She didn't think she had ever truly seen anyone before that.

"Keenan," Melanie breathed.

"I know," he gasped inches from her mouth.

The rhythm of the train returned, slower now, less frantic, or maybe it just seemed that way to Melanie. The soft edges of the night blurred back into being. All around, the horizon glowed as if dawn was approaching, but the light was cool and artificial.

They held each other in silence. Melanie wished she were back at Keenan's house, so she could fall asleep in his arms and, even more, wake up next to him. Only the unknown dread of what sunlight might do to her new body kept her awake and guarded and separated from total bliss.

And then the sky began to fall.

Chapter 22

Melanie had only a moment to react before what looked like a sheet of broken glass would collapse over the two of them. "Keenan, look out!" she shouted, then braced herself.

He raised his head, glanced to the sky, and grinned. "Beautiful isn't it?"

The first shards hit Keenan's back with a surprisingly soft patter. Then they began to fall faster, striking all around Melanie's body. She wondered how he could endure the pain. She wanted to turn him away from the onslaught, but he was pinned on top of her.

And then the first few pieces found her, striking her forehead, her mouth, around her tightly shut eyes. A cool, wet liquid dripped down her cheek.

"You can look," Keenan whispered. "It's okay."

Melanie opened one eye, then another. The shards were still falling, but she could see them more clearly now. They were teardrop-shaped, diaphanous, gathering not just the light from the moon and stars, but every color around them. As one struck the surface of the train, it exploded in a shower of sparks that glinted like crystal or broken diamonds. From the telephone poles and the bare-branched trees, more droplets fell and struck, clinging to every available surface before they too slipped to the ground, leaving a trail of light in their wake. It was the most beautiful thing Melanie had ever seen.

"If it rains any harder, it'll just look like gray. But I do love this time."

"Rain?" She sat up on her elbows. Drops fell down her arms and chest. Keenan slid behind Melanie and wrapped his arms around her. His body was slick and cool and felt wonderful against her skin. She felt another stirring between her legs, but fought it off. This was too amazing to be missed.

"Just ordinary rain?" she asked again, mouth open. A drop or two landed on her tongue. Though it felt cool, the taste was dry and wretched. An all too real reminder that this surreal view came at a tremendous price.

"What other kind is there?" Keenan lay back on the roof and rested his head in his arms. "I've forgotten what it looks like during the day. Is it even more spectacular?"

Melanie remembered the last time it rained. It was one, maybe two weeks ago. She was fighting a migraine and sat sullenly in her apartment, locked away in the bathroom so she wouldn't have to hear the incessant tapping on her skylight. She was bitter that it had ruined her evening plans to walk up to the Oella Gallery to see the new photography exhibit.

The rain was something to be avoided. Hidden from. She never once stopped to look at the shape of the droplets, or the way they sparkled when backlit by the sun. She never tried tasting the fresh water on her mouth, though she could smell the sweet ozone they carried with them now.

"I had no idea," she said flatly. Something so beautiful had been in front of her all along. If only she'd had the courage to open her eyes. All that time just wasted... What else had she missed? Lost out on? A tear welled up in the corner of her eyes, indistinguishable from the swell of rain that was falling harder now.

But Keenan seemed to sense her pain. He leaned in and kissed her shoulder. Again, he offered no empty words of comfort, just his presence. He understood better than anyone that what was lost was gone forever. But his company was enough to assure her — he would be there for her forever, steady, unyielding.

He wiped away a tear that no one else in the world would have known was there.

"I'm not usually this emotional."

"Too bad." He kissed her again, and they fell back together, lying side by side. "There's something to be said for getting carried away."

"Don't you ever get tired?"

"Not of this." He twined his fingers into her hair and kissed her hungrily.

This would take some getting used to. Bryan was never good for more than two times a night, and only with long breaks in between. Lucas was barely good for two minutes. She had a long history of boyfriends who rolled over and went to sleep the moment they were through. She had come to expect — and maybe even enjoy — the disappointment that followed. It gave her time to think, and something on which to focus her collective anger.

Melanie felt the train slow and lurch to an almost complete stop, and then pick up speed again. The movement was enough to jolt her out of her reverie. She noticed new smells here — diesel fumes, oil, stagnant water, cigarettes, rotting meat, sweat. Her stomach lurched. There was too much to take in. They weren't in Ellicott City anymore.

She felt Keenan's muscles stiffen, and he raised his head.

"Where are we?" he asked, and quickly shifted his body protectively above hers.

Melanie stretched her neck back. The landscape was bleak with burned out grass and smoking factories. In the distance, across a black expanse of choppy water, the Statue of Liberty rose benevolently in front of a throng of buildings and skyscrapers. "New York."

She had made it outside Ellicott City with Keenan after all. It wasn't Paris, but she was in a real city, with art galleries and colleges and intellectuals and artists and thieves and bums and hookers and... Her mind swam with all the possibilities, but still she couldn't help feeling a genuine sense of longing she couldn't name. The closest she could come was thinking she was homesick.

"It's okay," she added when she heard a low growl emanate from his throat. She realized to Keenan, who was used to the soft streetlights and intermittent phosphorescent glow from Ellicott City storefronts, New York must have seemed like an alien city. Back on Main Street with its cobbled streets and wood row houses, one could easily forget what century it was, but here with the bright New York skyline lit up like the mother ship, it was undeniable. Keenan looked puzzled and a little scared.

It was her turn now to be reassuring. "Really." She took his hand. "Trust me."

He stole another furtive glance around.

"I'd say we could go to a club or do some shopping in Times Square, but I don't think we'd meet the dress code." She didn't mind losing that horrible nightgown, but she was beginning to feel a little self-conscious, sitting completely nude on top of a train in the outskirts of one of the biggest cities in the world. "Maybe we should start heading back." The sky was a dim gray here, nearly obscuring the moon. It would be impossible to look up and tell what time it was, to know if daybreak was near.

"It's something."

"I know." Melanie scrunched up her nose. Popcorn, bird crap, rust. The smells were overwhelming. Not to mention the sounds. The screeching, flapping, shouting, crying, laughing. The sound of glass being smashed and dead leaves falling off dead branches. Decay. This was something she hadn't thought of — living in a city crowded with smells and possessing a powerful noise. This was nothing like the fragrant woods of home.

"I've never seen so many lights."

"Lights?"

She followed Keenan's gaze back to the skyline. Even with her improved sense of sight, the city did not look all that spectacular. True, the lights were more distinct than the postcards she had gotten, and the dark, gray buildings occupying the horizon could be seen in more detail, but they were still just dark, gray buildings; dead faces on a bleak landscape.

"They're spectacular." Keenan got to his feet. "I must see them."

"Um, sweetie." Melanie pulled at his arm and tugged herself upright. "You're naked."

"Hmm?" He tore his attention away from the landscape of neon. "Oh, right." He frowned and scratched his chest.

"Plus, we don't have anywhere to go during the day."

"There is that," Keenan said automatically, but his gaze never left the chirping lights.

Melanie tried to take a more direct tactic. "You know, there are a few more people here than in Ellicott City. I don't think I could—"

Keenan nodded and smiled weakly at her. "You're right, of course."

She briefly wondered how it had come to this — yesterday she was begging Keenan to let her see the world. Now, all she wanted was to have him all to herself, locked away in a house in Ellicott City for eternity. She was a kid with a new toy, and she didn't want to share. *Don't let yourself get carried away, Mel,* she scolded herself. *Men hate needy.*

Keenan sneaked a last glance at the skyline. "Another time, perhaps."

Maybe another century, Melanie thought, then laughed. She had centuries now. Centuries with just Keenan. She couldn't believe how quickly her luck had changed. "C'mon," she insisted, anxious to get him home. "I can hear another train coming the other way. We can hop it and take it back home."

Home, there was that word again. She repeated it to herself.

"The night is still young. Perhaps..."

"No. Let's go ... home." She said the word aloud again, and it tasted even better on her tongue. Like fresh-baked bread, and a fireplace, cinnamon, and sleep, and laughter, and everything else she had missed out on. And all of it would have been perfect, had it not been for the bogeyman lurking in the closet. Lucas was still out there, existing in his same comfortable world. He shouldn't have that luxury.

Oh, what the hell. "Keenan, now that you mention it, there is one thing I wouldn't mind doing."

"Anything." He put his hands on her hips and searched her face for a hint.

"Maybe we could stop for a midnight snack." She smiled, trying to keep it light. Perhaps if she didn't seem so hell-bent on vengeance, he'd go along with it. It would be nothing more than an errand, picking up some eggs on your way home from work. Killing off an ex-boyfriend before retiring to the ol' coffin.

"A snack?" Keenan cocked his head to the side and searched her face. After a moment, his forehead creased, and his eyes darkened. "You have to let this go."

Busted. "I was just kidding."

"No, you weren't."

She chewed on her lower lip. *Way to ruin the moment, Mel.* She knew she had buried herself, but wasn't content to just let it rest. She turned on Keenan, "Don't give me this holier than thou crap. What would you do if Stavros showed up here again?"

Keenan flinched at the sound of his maker's name. His voice was smooth but strained. "Lucas will not hurt anyone else. I promise. And he's not worth your hate. If anything, you should pity him."

"You're high." *That's it, Melanie. Keep poking the vampire.*

"Pardon?"

"You don't know him at all. What happens when he decides to stab the next girl? Do you swoop in and turn her, too? Add her to the harem?"

Keenan shook his head and closed his eyes. The gesture reminded Melanie of her mother. "You are different. I could never replace you."

"Yeah, you said that." She crossed her arms, feeling self-conscious. Arguments should never be done in the buff.

"You have no idea what I risked for you." He leaned in and kissed her shoulder. "Can you please just forget him?"

If she could stop herself from being so damned stubborn, forget about all her old baggage, she could be happy. Honestly and truly happy, forever and ever, amen. But she couldn't. She carried grudges around with her like other people kept pictures of their kids in their wallet. She shrugged away from Keenan. "I can't," she muttered through gritted teeth. Though she wanted to, more than anything. This wasn't just about Lucas. It was about everyone who had used or abused her. She was finally in a position to do something about it. To give a little back. How could she just walk away from that?

He turned his back on her and walked down the car a few steps. A southbound train could be seen rounding a corner and heading towards them.

"What's the appeal anyway? What is it about me that you think is so wonderful?"

Keenan watched the train approach. "You just seemed like someone worth saving."

Melanie scowled. As it turned out, she didn't want to be someone who needed saving. Not anymore.

He took a deep breath, turned, and wheeled on her. "Let's go then," he said taking her hand.

"Where?"

"You're getting what you want." Keenan clenched his fists. "We're going to go see Lucas."

Melanie opened her mouth to say something, but saw the warning in his eyes.

"And if you still want him to die after you see him, I'll kill him myself."

"Keenan."

"What?" he roared.

"Can we swing by the house and get some clothes first?"

Chapter 23

"You said we were going to go see Lucas. Where are we?"

"His father's house."

"Officer Tyler?" Melanie cringed. The thought of him still made her uncomfortable. And now, she realized, he was just as responsible as Lucas for everything that had happened. If he hadn't been covering up for his son, if he had been doing his freaking job to begin with...

"Take it easy."

Melanie realized her teeth were bared, and she was growling. Like a dog. *Very attractive, Mel.*

Officer Tyler owned a small row house on a side street situated between the old courthouse and Red's Tavern on Main Street. The thick granite walls and rusted metalwork of the courthouse loomed over the tiny home. He lived literally in the shadow of justice. Melanie did not appreciate irony.

"It's the middle of the night. No one is gonna be up."

"They're awake."

"I don't see what this has to do with—"

Keenan grabbed Melanie and kissed her desperately. After a few moments, he pulled back.

"Wow. What was that for?"

"Let's just leave. Please. Before everything changes."

His eyes looked watery in the harsh glow of the streetlights. Some idiot had installed the wrong bulb, and the light came down intensely white, almost surgical.

What could be so terrible inside that Keenan didn't want her to see? She conjured up the worst thing she could possibly imagine — Lucas smiling, his arm around another girl, another potential victim — but that only drove her resolve to see him even more.

She assumed Keenan was just trying to steer her away from his mistakes again, from hurting someone. Trying to spare her the guilt he carried on his head like a wreath of thorns. But Melanie would not be swayed. Guilt she could manage; it was a dull constant throbbing in her temples. The beginnings of a migraine. Easy to ignore. The trick was focus. And nothing made her focus like out and out rage.

She felt excited as they stood outside Lucas's house. Not nervous or frightened like she expected to be before killing. But then, she wasn't a 'someone' anymore — she was an 'other,' a creature of the night. She felt like she could rip apart the house with her bare hands. *I'll huff and I'll puff...*

No, she was born to be a vampire. Giving her fangs and immortality was like giving a shark an Uzi and malice. Complete and utter overkill.

She could hear labored breathing and someone pacing inside the house. Heartbeats sluggish with lazy blood. Something wet dripped down the corners of her mouth.

"You're drooling."

Again, Mel, like a dog. Now heel. Good girl. She smirked to herself.

"Try not to look so thrilled."

Bad girl! God, she was giddy. Her body tingled, and she could feel her muscles stretch and pulse. There was a power coursing through her veins, and it demanded an outlet. She shifted anxiously from one foot to the other.

"Second bedroom on the right." Keenan pointed up.

Just above the front door, a flat tin roof jutted outward, rusted and haphazardly tarred. From there, she would have a clear view into the rooms.

"Last chance." Keenan looked pleadingly into her eyes.

Melanie shrugged. "Sorry."

"Me too." He leaned over and kissed her forehead.

Christ, you'd think he was dying, and we were never going to see each other again. Leave the drama to the experts.

"After you." He waved her forward.

Melanie paced in front of the house, looking for a good jumping point. She gave up when she realized she had no idea what she was doing. She bounced on the tips of her toes and leapt up. It was a relatively short distance, and she landed with only a soft patter in the center of the roof. She was pleased with herself until she realized Keenan was already next to her, having made the trip quicker and more quietly.

"Go on." He pointed to the second window. "This is what you were looking for, isn't it?" He crossed his arms. She thought about asking Keenan to leave. Killing someone was private, something intimate between two people. Plus he was being a gigantic buzz-kill about this, but she could tell he wasn't budging.

She walked quietly to the small space between the two windows. With bright light streaming through both, it would be next to impossible to see out into the dark night.

Melanie stepped brazenly close to the right window. The room was tiny and cramped. An old single bed with a ship's wheel for a headboard was propped against the far wall. A child's desk took up most of the rest of the floor. There were pictures on the wall of Lucas as a kid in a scouting uniform, awards for track and field from high school, and a sun-faded Back Street Boys poster on the door. A picture of a pretty, smiling woman resting her hands on Lucas's head was placed on the desk, and all the papers and clutter had been reverently pushed away from it.

Lucas was lying on the small bed. Melanie could barely make out his face through the bruises, scrapes, bandages, and hospital equipment. Officer Tyler sat in a chair next to the bed with his back to the window. He had a small plastic bowl in his hand. The kind you might use to feed a baby his first solid food.

She gasped and went wide-eyed. He looked like he had picked a fight with a grizzly. Though she wouldn't put it past Lucas to take on a bear, she didn't think anything so natural had a hand in his abuse. "What happened to him?"

"He suffered significant trauma to his face and contusions to both eyes."

"I can see that—"

"Blunt force trauma to the abdomen, multiple rib fractures, and a non-penetrating blunt chest wall trauma. He has pulmonary contusions of the left and right lungs. A broken jaw and cheekbone, fractures of multiple ribs and his sternum. He has broken and cracked teeth. Both of his shoulders were dislocated, and he suffered a severe concussion. Doctors do not think he will regain sight in his right eye."

Melanie stared at him incredulously.

"I visited him in the hospital."

"I don't know what to say."

"It might have been worse, but you had lost a lot of blood. I didn't have much time with him." Keenan stared into the night.

Somehow, he had found the strength to tear himself away from Lucas's bloodied body in order to save her. Christ, she had struggled with just a few drops from a scraped elbow. She looked at him lovingly, but he would not meet her eyes. "Thank you."

He gnashed his teeth together. "You don't have to say that."

"I know that." Melanie shifted her gaze back and forth between Keenan and the window. Inside, Officer Tyler struggled to feed Lucas apple sauce through the tangle of bracing and hospital equipment. Apple sauce dribbled out of Lucas's mouth, onto his chin and shirt. Even from outside the window, Melanie could smell the sluggish, sour blood that ran through his veins. She'd sooner kick a wounded dog than finish him off.

"Damn it, c'mon Luke. Stop pushing the food out. You gotta eat."

Lucas mumbled incoherently. It sounded like his mouth was stuffed full of dirt.

"Never shoulda taken you out of the hospital." Officer Tyler threw the bowl down in disgust.

Melanie looked back at Keenan and smirked, but he wasn't sharing in her mirth. He wrung his hands together and clenched his eyes tight.

"What's wrong?"

Keenan shook his head.

Damn it. She could really be enjoying this, if it weren't for him. She mentally went through everything she had said or done that night, trying to figure out what had set him off.

Inside, Officer Tyler sat down heavily on a chair next to the bed and dug a prescription bottle from one of his pockets. "Think you can swallow the pill this time?"

Lucas managed a grunt.

He placed a tablet on his son's waiting, dry tongue. Lucas swallowed it with a wince.

"Attaboy."

Officer Tyler stood up and gently stroked his kid's cheek as best he could, then wiped his chin with his finger. "I'm gonna go check on your sister, okay? Love ya, buddy."

Melanie turned to Keenan, whose face looked even paler than usual. His eyes were wide open now and dark. "I had to stop him before... I didn't expect him to be so savage. You know that, right?"

"This is what you were trying to protect me from?" She didn't see the big deal. Heck, maybe if he had told her to begin with...

"No," Keenan whispered. He nodded towards the first window.

Melanie watched Officer Tyler walk into the other room and collapse in the middle of the floor. It looked like a little girl's bedroom done up in pink and butterflies and lace. He balled his fists up and pressed them into his eyes. When he looked up, she saw that he was crying. He held his arm to his mouth trying to muffle his sobs so his son wouldn't hear.

He whimpered and gurgled, low and animal-like. It was the same sound Melanie's bunny made after she accidentally ran over it with her bike. It was painful to hear. Melanie stepped back right into Keenan.

"I did that," he said mechanically. "Me."

She realized now why he was so upset at her. He was a good person — or vampire, or whatever. He was genuinely trying to atone for past mistakes. And because of her, he had nearly killed someone. Not only that, she had practically dragged him back here, forcing him to see the effects of what he'd done. But he wasn't to blame. He hadn't put the knife in Lucas's hand.

She wasn't used to someone with principles. Real principles. Keenan didn't wear his ideals on his sleeve like a badge or a collar. He simply went about his day, doing his damndest to stick to them. And she had screwed that up.

She wanted to apologize, beg his forgiveness, reassure him, but all she could manage was, "Lucas deserved what he got."

"Did his dad? Or his younger sister? She's afraid to go to sleep in case the 'bad man' comes for her." He rested a hand over his heart, searching perhaps for the almost human patter of its dull rhythm. "I know what you must think of me."

"Of you?" Melanie asked surprised. "You saved me." *Just who was he mad at here?*

Keenan looked at her. "It's almost stupid to pretend." The streetlight glinted red off his eyes, and his teeth extended. "This is who I really am."

"Stop this." She reached out to touch his shoulder, but he flinched and stepped back.

"Keenan ... don't ... I love you." Melanie didn't know she was going to speak those words until they came spilling out. She had said it before, of course. To Bryan after really good sex. To her psycho ex, who followed her while she was out on a date with another man. 'Of course I love you. And as soon as I get back from my date, I'll call you.' But she had never meant it before, hardly even understood its meaning. It was a practiced phrase in a foreign language that got her what she wanted, where she needed to go. *Où est la salle de bains?*

But now she understood those words, and she delivered them fluently, as if she'd been a native speaker all her life. She smiled, pleased at her own certainty, anxious to hear the words spoken back.

But Keenan only shook his head and took another step backwards. "I don't deserve it." One more step and he plunged off the roof, completely out of sight.

Melanie rushed to the edge, just in time to see a slight blur disappear past the courthouse.

"Shit." She stamped her foot, and the entire house shook.

The light in Lucas's room blinked off, and Melanie quickly flattened herself to the roof. She saw Officer Tyler press his face against the glass, back in Lucas's room now, searching the night.

"Must've been a squirrel," he said. "Night time, buddy. Pills gotta be kicking in by now." He rested a hand on Lucas's shin, one of the few places Keenan left intact. "Things'll be better in the morning."

Melanie waited until Officer Tyler gingerly shut the door behind him before standing. She looked at the frail, prone body before her. Lucas had been stronger than she'd been. He had manipulated and used her. But he was breakable after all. Given enough time, he would heal just as she had, over and over. But he would never be whole again. He would, just as Keenan had promised, have to live with his failures, while Melanie got a brand new start.

Lucas's one good eye, gummy and wet, went to the window. She could not tell if he saw her or not, but she did know her anger was gone. In its place was pity. Even if Lucas lived to be a thousand, he would never know the type of love she had now. He would always be alone, always fighting, struggling to make sense of the shadows on his wall. And less than a week ago, she'd been the same. "Goodbye, Lucas. Thanks for everything."

The eye blinked once, then twice.

Melanie turned and dropped from the roof and ran off in search of her boyfriend.

Chapter 24

It was damn near dawn before Melanie finally found him. The sky was milky gray, but brightening quickly. Her skin felt tender and itched like she was recovering from a sunburn. Or maybe it was just her imagination. She still didn't know what effect the sun would have on her, but that was all the more reason why she had wanted to find Keenan as soon as possible.

She checked the house first. It was empty, save for Tristan and Isolde sleeping in a furry heap near the door. They didn't even move when she entered. If someone had told her a week ago that she would fall in love with a man who owned cats, she would have laughed in their face ... perhaps only slightly less if she had been told that her future beau would also be a vampire.

Then she wandered down the deserted main street, wondering where the hell a vampire would go to do some soul searching, pondered briefly if vampires had souls, then gave up on the whole exercise altogether. Think Melanie, where would *Keenan* go?

From there, she ran up Frederick Road to Miller's farm, where she liked to sit sometimes and read on the stump of an ancient elm. She cut through the woods to Hell House and ripped through the rubble of the tunnels, then she followed Seminary Avenue, lined with new and expansive glass-front houses. Finally, she wound her way back to the center of town along the tracks that Keenan never got a chance to build.

Her skin was visibly red now, and a small blister rose on the back of her hands. Something in the animal part of her brain was screaming, 'Find shelter! Now!' but she couldn't. Not without Keenan. She needed to make this right. *Never go to bed angry, you never know when the other person might not wake up.*

She plopped on the ground where a disused patch of tracks came to an abrupt end in a small cluster of black-eyed Susans. If the sun was harmful, Keenan would show up in time to rescue her. He had promised he wouldn't let her get hurt again and, for once, she was a believer.

"Keenan," she said, head bent. To an outsider she might have appeared as if deep in prayer. "If you can hear me, I'm not going anywhere until you talk to me."

After a pause as long as a labored heartbeat, she heard, "You never listen."

"You didn't listen to me," she said, getting to her feet. "I said I love you, you big jerk."

She scoped the trees, but her vision was blurry. Maybe it was just the hot sun rising over the dry ground.

"And I said I don't deserve it. Now go home."

"Whose? Yours or mine?"

"You literally have minutes to find shelter."

Melanie lay back on the ground and put her hands behind her head. "I'm not going anywhere until you agree to listen to me."

"I said go!" he roared.

She sat up on her elbows and glanced at the treetops. She half expected a flock of birds to suddenly take flight.

"Are you coming with me?"

"I have shelter."

"Sorry. Nuh-uh. I'll wait."

Melanie could see the air begin to ripple with the coming heat. She felt dizzy. Again, the lizard part of her brain called out, and again she rested her head back on the ground.

She heard a growl from the tree line that grew louder and louder, and she smiled to herself. He was coming around. She could still make this right.

Her skin felt tight and dry, though, and she finally got to her feet. Panic was winning out.

Parallel to the tracks, she saw an ancient tree collapse to the ground. She vaguely remembered hoping there weren't any birds nesting in its branches before her skin began to crack along invisible seams. On the ground, she saw her shadow for the first time in a week. Like the groundhog, she suspected it contained an omen. She wanted to nail it to the ground, to hold it there forever, but the sun was brightening now, and soon even that would be lost.

"Keenan," she called, as the world somersaulted under her feet. "I think I'm in trouble."

* * * * *

"Oh, that's disgusting." Melanie spit the foul liquid on the ground, then wiped off her tongue with the back of her hand.

"We're in a cave. Our options are rather limited."

"What is it?"

"Bat."

"Yuck. Those things have rabies."

"That's the least of your problems right now."

Melanie looked at her arms — even through her blurred vision, she could see they were blistered and dried. Skin flaked off like chalk. A deep gash ran along both arms, disappearing into her clothes. She looked like an overcooked Thanksgiving turkey.

There was no pain though. Or rather, there was pain and its effect was almost narcotic. It was as though her body still hungered for the death it was originally denied.

Keenan offered her the bat again, but Melanie turned her head.

"Seriously, if you don't drink, those wounds will never heal."

"Would you still love me if I was all gross and disfigured?"

Keenan smirked. "You're fishing for compliments now?"

"I didn't hear an answer."

"Will you drink the blood?"

"Will you answer me?"

"Forever and ever."

"Amen." Melanie closed her eyes. "Now give me some more of that nasty stuff."

The bat no longer struggled in Keenan's hands. Either the poor thing realized it was pointless to fight, or his calming influence extended to the lower mammals as well.

Without his kit for drawing blood, Keenan had to nip at the animal with his teeth. He was delicate and precise as a surgeon, and Melanie was glad he had done the initial work for her. Otherwise, she'd probably end up like Ozzy Osbourne, with half a bat flailing from her mouth.

In an effort to distract her, Keenan explained that she now produced a kind of venom that prevented a wound from closing, so she had to be extra cautious when biting anything. That explained why Bryan damn near bled to death from the wound Leah inflicted.

"There," she said, struggling to sit up. "I drank it. Done." Her head felt clear, but she still felt weak. Exhausted actually. Her muscles simply refused to respond.

"Not by any stretch of the imagination." He gently pulled her back down so she was resting in his lap. "There's more here. You'll drink them all. As well as anything else I can find."

"Yummy." It wasn't chicken soup, but she supposed it would do. "So is this where you go to sulk? Or is this like your bat cave?"

"Stop talking and drink."

Another rush of rancid blood hit her mouth. "That is just awful," Melanie sputtered.

"It's their diet. Bugs mostly. Spiders, roaches—"

"You really don't have to tell me everything."

"Hang on." Keenan chuckled, slid back, and gently let Melanie's head rest on something soft. Given the strong cloying smell coming from her makeshift pillow, she figured it was his shirt.

A few moments later, he sat next to her. "Try this."

Melanie opened her mouth and tried to remember the taste of fresh strawberries.

"That's not bad." She sucked at her tongue. "What is it?"

"Roasted Duck with sautéed pears and baby potatoes."

"Keenan."

"Rat."

She coughed and sat up. "I'll make my own dinner."

"You're up," he said surprised.

"Whoopee." She twirled her finger in the air.

"No, I mean you're moving. You're recovering very quickly."

True enough, Melanie's arms felt looser, her muscles twitched and flexed. The long jagged cut running up and down her arms and legs like a zipper was bunched up, knotting together.

"I'll see if I can get something bigger."

"No, Keenan I really don't want—" but he was already moving into the darker passages of the cave.

She looked around. The cave was pretty much what she expected — low rock ceiling and packed earth for ground. Water dripped down the walls. She found herself wishing she'd known about this place before. It would have made a terrific place to get high.

She could see a faint orange glow at a sudden turn in the tunnel ahead. Daylight. She figured Keenan must have dragged her far enough in so that the sun could not reach them. She could easily understand the importance of having a back-up place to sleep. It just had never been a matter of life and death before.

She heard a yelp somewhere in a back chamber, and light footsteps dancing towards her.

"Veal parmesan?" Keenan appeared, holding a fox curled in his hands like a kitten. It licked his hands contentedly. He was like St. Frances or a Disney princess with animals. He set the critter in her lap and sat down.

Melanie frowned and stroked the creature's neck.

"What's wrong?" Keenan asked, inching closer to her.

"I'm sorry."

"What are you sorry for?" He leaned over and nipped at the fox's neck. It squeaked once in protest, then yawned and stretched out. "Lucas is..."

"Living with his failures."

"But living?"

"Yes."

Keenan half smiled. "Then you have nothing to be sorry about."

Melanie started to speak, but he lifted the creature to her lips. "Drink more."

When she was done, she let out a slow sigh and put her head down in his lap. The fox trotted off happily to the back of the cave.

"Amazing," he whispered, and ran a finger down her nearly unblemished arms. "You're so strong. It would take me ten times as much blood to recover. I'll see what else I can find."

He started to get up, but Melanie caught his hand. "I'm good." Better than good actually; she felt like she could run a marathon.

"Do you want to get up and stretch out?"

"No." She sighed and snuggled closer. "This is fine."

They lay there in silence for a moment. Melanie wanted to shut her eyes and go to sleep. The creeping rays of sunlight almost seemed to dictate that, but she couldn't shake the tension she felt around her. Keenan sat stiff, motionless. She screwed up her courage and blurted out, "I'm sorry for making you hurt Lucas."

"I don't understand." He frowned.

Melanie nuzzled her face into his lap. She hated apologizing, and he wasn't making it any easier by forcing her to explain herself. "I'm sorry for what you had to do to Lucas." She let out a long breath. "I know how hard you're trying to be good."

"Is that all?" Keenan smiled.

Jeez, he's milking this. "I think so," she added, but furrowed her brow, trying to remember if she had done anything else that might have offended him.

Keenan's hand went involuntarily to her cheek. She closed her eyes and pressed his fingers closer.

"And I was worried I had scared you off."

She opened her eyes. "Why would you have thought that?"

"Most girls wouldn't be quite so understanding about their boyfriend breaking their ex into pieces."

"Boyfriend?" Melanie grinned.

"You really are different."

And he said it like *different* was a good thing; no, like it was the best thing ever. She had never heard it like that before, so she pulled him closer and kissed him hard on the mouth.

Keenan touched her lips and slowly pulled back. "All this time I thought I was protecting you from the truth. I thought you'd take off if you saw the real me."

"Silly boy!" She wrapped her arms around his neck. "You ever fuck in a cave?" She licked his ear.

He grinned, then the corners of his mouth turned down.

"What's wrong?"

"I haven't been completely forthcoming."

"What do you mean?" She felt her heart speed up a notch as she mentally went through the list of responses she'd heard from a dozen failed relationships — *I'm gay, married, on work release, in the country illegally...*

"I may not be quite as moral as I've let on."

Definitely gay. "What are you saying?" She sat up on her knees and faced him.

"You have to understand, the choices I've made, the way I live, it's not..." he scrunched up his mouth and searched for the word. "Natural. Cat's blood is horse piss compared to the real thing."

That was the closest Melanie had heard Keenan come to cursing. It seemed a little silly on his lips. But it did make her wildly curious about the taste of human blood.

"I thought if you didn't know the difference ... if you didn't know the extent of what you were capable of, your choices would be easier than mine."

"Is that it?" *Over-protective beats gay, married, and ex-con any day.*

"No. I thought if you saw what I really was, what I had made you, that you'd hate me like I hate Stavros."

The future was still a huge question mark for Melanie. All of her old worries — bills, job, retirement, school were gone. Three days ago, that scared her more than anything. Now, the uncertainty remained, but the fear was gone — Keenan would be there with her, and that was enough. Still, the transformation had not made her any more expressive of her feelings. She shrugged her shoulders and casually tossed her head to the left, as if to say, 'No biggie.'

"So what's the real thing taste like?" she asked and reached up to stroke his neck.

"Do you like chocolate?"

Melanie nodded, then pouted — she would never get to eat chocolate again. No more truffles or nougat or covered strawberries...

"How about wine?"

Crap. No more peach wine or blush. No more zinfandel with its ticklish bubbles...

"Dark chocolates filled with praline and crème. Simmering, mulled wine tinged with nutmeg and cinnamon in a nearby pot."

"God, yeah."

"It's better."

Fuck wine and chocolate. "I want that," she said but her words came out mushy, since she was salivating so much.

"I do, too." Keenan sighed and leaned back against the wall of the cave.

"So...?" Melanie asked. *What the hell are we waiting for?*

"I need to show you."

"Okay." Melanie paused. "Show me what?"

"Why it's impossible."

"Okay."

Keenan raised his eyebrows.

"What, now?"

He nodded.

"Here in the cave?"

He nodded again.

"Okay, show me." Then Melanie's eyes widened in realization. "Oh, no way. Forget that."

Keenan smiled.

"Just tell me."

"Too difficult."

"I didn't need a creepy mind-meld to understand the story about Stavros."

"I may have been showing off a little earlier." He raised the corner of his mouth.

"And now?"

"Would you really believe me if you couldn't see if for yourself?"

"Keenan..."

"I want you to know everything. To see me as I really am. I want you to understand my choices and why I live the way I do. Most importantly, I want you to make peace with them."

"Are you going to show me how you do that brain thing?"

"Certainly."

"And the flitting?"

"Flitting?"

"You know, where you just appear out of nowhere and—" Melanie looked over to Keenan, but he was gone, and the cave was empty. "Keenan?" She turned completely around, but he was nowhere in sight. "Keenan!" she yelled, and was on the verge of convincing herself she had imagined him altogether.

Then someone tapped her shoulder from behind. "Like this?"

She wheeled around. He had his arms crossed and wore an impish grin.

"Especially that."

"Deal." He took both her hands and gestured for her to sit.

"Will you let me show you?" he asked, and raised his eyebrows.

"Stop." Melanie shook her hands free. "Can we do it without the creepy introduction?"

"Creepy?" Keenan frowned. "I guess I can try..."

"That's all I ask." She took his hands again, blinked a few times and stared deeply into his beautiful green eyes.

"Let me show you," he whispered in a heavy, monotone voice.

Melanie giggled at his theatrics and then bit her lip.

"Sorry, sorry. This is the way I've always done it."

She took a deep breath, stifled another giggle, and then sat up straight.

"Ready?" he asked, more than a little annoyed.

"Take me away, big boy."

"This isn't going to be fun."

"I'm done. Continue."

He leaned close to her, his soft lips inches from hers. Her mouth parted involuntarily, and a small sigh escaped her mouth. Quickly Keenan pulled away and looked into her face; his green eyes flashed once, then twice. *Cheap trick,* she thought, before the light brightened to oblivion.

✚

Chapter 25

After Stavros bit me, I awoke buried in a pit of dirt surrounded by the bodies of my fellow workmen. It took me days to claw my way out. When I finally emerged, I was half-mad with hunger.

Melanie heard someone singing, a man's voice tittering in a drunken falsetto. "And it's no, nay, never..."

She saw the unmistakable spire of a church, a gazebo covered in climbing lilacs, and a statue of the Virgin Mary turning an ear delicately towards heaven. She was at St. Xavier's, but it still stood new, bright with gleaming rock and stained glass that diffused the moonlight into a million colors.

She could smell the river and sweat and sun-baked skin, and something else, something sweet. Nothing she recognized, but she knew instantly what it was, and her stomach clenched. *Food.* She felt desperately hungry.

"No, nay, never no more..."

She stumbled down the hill and caught site of a man hobbling alone down the path that ran parallel to the Patapsco. She caught up to him. "Please," she said, twisting at her stomach.

The man stopped singing and squinted in the dark at her. "Colin?" he asked, then belched.

She took a few more steps on shaky legs. Her stomach heaved and ached. "Please," she groaned, "I'm starving."

The man was old with a week's worth of graying and patchy stubble on his face. He carried a few silvery trout over his shoulder. "Wachu want, boy-o?"

"I need some food, mister."

The man set down his fish and fumbled in his dirty pants for a pipe and matches. The sudden burst of bright flames blinded Melanie, and she winced and clenched her eyes tightly shut.

"What happened to you, lad?" The man exhaled a puff of smoke and licked his dry lips. He was nearly toothless and chewed and smacked each syllable with his tongue.

She grabbed the front of the man's shirt and pulled him close. She felt jittery, anxious, like she could claw her own face off. Her skin tingled and burned. "I need food!"

The man's breath was boozy and foul. Melanie could smell rot and the dead fish on the ground, and rank and dried sweat. She pushed the man aside, disgusted.

The man chuckled. "Ya look like ya fell down a well." He spit something terrible onto the ground.

"Don't laugh at me." She turned on the man, both fists clenched. She growled and then bent over in pain. She felt like the roof of her mouth had suddenly cracked in half.

"Take it easy, son." The man reached into another pocket and handed Melanie a stale hunk of bread with shaking hands. "Here ya go. Eat. It's not much, but you're welcome to it."

She snatched the bread and ripped off a tremendous piece with her teeth. She felt like a wild dog ripping apart a fresh kill.

"If I can get a fire going, we can eat these." The man kicked at the pile of fish on the ground with a grubby foot, then patted a hand on her shoulder.

Melanie spit the bread out and retched. It tasted dried out, mossy, and rotten. "What is this?" She hurled the hunk of bread to the ground.

"Why, you ungrateful prick." The man shoved her aside and picked the bread off the dirt path. "That's a week's worth of food. You shouldna done that."

Melanie felt dizzy and drunk. She dropped to her knees and banged her head against the ground until blood ran down her forehead. She looked up. The man was still talking, spit flying from his mouth, but Melanie couldn't hear anything except a slow pounding. The man pointed a crooked finger in her face and, without thinking, she clamped down on it with her teeth.

The blood hit her throat like whiskey warming its way straight to her belly. Her stomach relaxed, her vision cleared. She spit the man's finger to ground.

The old drunk was bent over, trying to stop the flow of blood, pressing his hand to his chest. Melanie cocked her head to the side — she didn't understand why the blood healed her, calmed her aching stomach, only that it did and she needed more.

Under the man's chin, she saw a blue vein throbbing and pulsating. Her body took over. It wasn't Melanie that knocked the old man to the ground. It wasn't Melanie who struck the man's face so hard his jaw snapped. And it wasn't Melanie who ripped the man's throat out with her teeth, lapping at the blood until there was nothing left.

That was the first. I felt nothing.

Melanie ran through the woods faster than she ever thought possible. All around her, small creatures turned on their heels and trembled under fallen trees or broken rocks. She ran for hours, never tiring, never sweating. Running because she felt like if she didn't, her heart might explode out of her chest.

She howled in ecstasy, charged with the animal power of the hunt, of being the most feared thing in the dark. Near where the Patapsco split and the river picked up speed, she brought down a deer and ripped it limb from limb. The warmth of the blood, the eyes dilated black with fear, and the engorged heart all excited her, but the blood itself tasted tepid, weak. It soured in her stomach and made her hungry for more of the real thing.

The blood is the life. You have no idea the power...

The sky was still that deep blue of twilight, but all around her, a white light began to creep over the horizon. It would be morning soon, and she began to tire. Melanie's skin prickled, and her muscles ached. She crawled under a rotting, over-turned tree on a hill overlooking Main Street, as if it was the most natural thing to do, and watched the last stars fade into dawn.

Now that the blood high was over, Melanie had some time to think about what happened. She did not know the word for what she had become, but she sensed that her problem could not be solved by doctors or leeches or magic elixirs. She wondered if perhaps the Bible finally held some answers for her.

Lazarus rose from his own grave. Jesus pushed back the stone to his tomb and emerged squinting into daylight, but the Bible was frustratingly vague about how he felt, what he looked like. Did he feast on blood as well?

Melanie imagined Lazarus stumbling barefoot from his grave, still wrapped in his shroud, open mouthed and wailing. He would have been hungry, confused. This is what passed for miracles. But Melanie did not think she had been blessed. Her gift came with a catch. To survive, she would have to kill. Which is what she had done. Murdered. One of the cardinal sins.

She remembered the old man's drained face, the withered hand reaching up to the sky for divine intervention as she bled him dry. The worst part though, was that she felt nothing. The man was simply a meal to her. Melanie realized she hadn't just taken someone's life, she too had lost something precious tonight. Her own humanity. She was an 'other,' and now she could never go home again.

Melanie then did something she had never done — not when her Jack Russell had run away, or her gran died. Not even when the flux first took her, and she knew she was as good as dead. She cried. She cried softly at first, then with deep pained sobs until her chest heaved with the strain of it. She cried until there was nothing left, and then finally she cried herself to sleep.

She knew the next time she woke, she would no longer be Melanie, but that thing every child fears, calling his name in the night, in the dark, waiting for his mother to leave the room, for the last flicker of candle to burn away. She would be the soft wailing heard in the distance, the creature skittering across the rooftop, dragging its nails on the bedroom window. She would bring misery wherever she went. And worse yet, she knew she would be very, very good at what she did.

But the power comes at a price.

The images came faster... An elderly couple in their bed. The husband's neck snapped like a broken doll. The wife ashen and dry. The wound on her neck secondary to the humiliations she had clearly endured. A hunter eviscerated with his own knife. Twin girls lying in a heap in Tiber Alley, clutching one another like a safety blanket.

Blood and Sunlight

Jamie Wasserman

There were more victims. Too many, in fact, to count, but they appeared so quickly now that Melanie could no longer discern their faces. Young, old, rich, poor. It did not matter.

It is all consuming. There is nothing you will not do to feed your hunger...

Melanie heard the distant charge of a rifle, voices whispering, and a drunken cheer. She retreated in the opposite direction, following the path along the river until she came to the half-finished iron train bridge on the edge of town. It was supposed to be a tremendous achievement, the first of its kind in the country. It was meant to put Ellicott City on the map. Instead, it sat, barely spanning more than a few feet across Main Street, a rusted, hulking mess. In a few hours, the first light of dawn would hit the bridge, giving it a bloodstained look; a sacrificial alter to an abandoned god.

On the bridge now, her feet dangling over the edge, Melanie nibbled on her fingernails, plotting her next move. It had been three nights since she fed. Before she changed, she could go a few weeks without food, maybe more if she had to. She wondered what kind of clock her body was on now. Already she felt drawn, fatigued.

She could hear the doors to Clancy's Saloon open and shut, a woman's laughter, and then a man's voice. Their pulse was slow, drowsy with liquor and approaching sleep. Melanie dropped from the bridge onto empty Main Street. If the couple heard, they didn't see a thing. She pressed herself flat against the nearest building.

The dirt road through town stretched about a mile into the hillside, where it stopped abruptly at the doorsteps of large manor homes and the Mills Farm. Here, lean-tos and row homes and the feed and hardware stores crowded both sides of Main Street.

Melanie followed the couple to the end of the street and up the steep path. They were wealthy if they lived here, well dressed and moving slow as fattened cows. She could hear nothing except the couple's voices and their blood churning thickly underneath privileged skin.

Ordinarily, she might have taken her time, severed the husband's artery and let him watch his wife get devoured while he bled to death. Fear, she found, excited the blood — it was a wonderful cocktail. But she needed to feed soon, to buy herself some time until she could figure out what to do next. There was nowhere she felt safe.

For the first time since she changed, Melanie felt fear. All it took was one person to see her sneak back into her shelter, and that would be it. She was powerless during the day. Moreover, new kills were becoming increasingly difficult to find, the patrols more regular, better armed. She was hungry and getting desperate.

The woman was big, and her steps were slow and pained. The husband kept one hand on her back while another held her arm, guiding her up the steep hill towards their home. Melanie decided she would feed on him first. She wouldn't get very far.

Melanie appeared out of nowhere and grabbed the man's neck from behind, slamming him to ground. The force knocked the wind out of him, and his wife gasped. Before he could scream, Melanie was on him, her teeth locked deep into his jugular.

"Millie," the man wheezed. "Run! Get home."

Melanie admired the man, thinking of his wife even as the color left his face.

The woman took a few difficult steps, then fell to her knees sobbing. Melanie smiled — planning was everything.

She pumped the man's chest several times, lifted his arms above his head. She wanted every drop. She saw the man's eyes roll back, and a final sigh parted his lips.

You will become careless....

"Hello, Millie." Melanie wiped her lips and walked towards the woman. She was no longer hungry. She simply wanted to see the woman suffer.

The woman panted, wrapped her arms around herself. "Please," she said and looked into Melanie's face. "I want to have my baby." She dropped her arms to reveal a round belly.

Melanie's eyes contracted and flashed. She heard the child's heartbeat quicken, driven by the adrenalin surging through his mother's veins.

Blood and Sunlight

She knelt besides Millie and reached a hand out towards her belly. Millie flinched. "May I?" she asked, then touched her stomach.

The woman cried, "Please, no."

Melanie listened as the baby turned in his mother's womb, gurgling happily in the amniotic sac. Flesh that had never seen daylight. Muscles that had never stretched. New blood coursing through the thinnest of veins.

"Please," Millie sobbed.

"The Lord giveth, and I taketh away." Melanie smiled broadly, revealing her fangs stained with blood.

"Oh God," Millie sobbed and covered her stomach, protecting the baby.

...and cruel.

The baby wailed, blind, red-faced and helpless in Melanie's arms. Millie lay dead at her feet, cracked open like a watermelon. She felt like she should have some connection to this child, that holding it should have woken a primal desire to protect, comfort, and love it. But she felt nothing for this squirming grey mass, other than a terrible desire to rip it to pieces. It was an affront, an abomination, a reminder of an all too helpless beginning which, even now, her brain was trying to forget.

Above her, a colony of bats crisscrossed the night sky. Melanie felt she shared more in common with them — they were hunters, survivors. The night belonged to them.

"For you my friends," she called to the bats as they landed on a nearby tree.

She raised the baby above her head, ready to dash it against the ground, but a sudden explosion shook the night, reverberated off the rocky hillside. Her knee ripped open, and she dropped to the ground, still clutching the baby.

"We have him!" a man shouted. And Melanie could make out more voices further out, moving closer.

A man stepped closer, watching Melanie with narrowed eyes over the blunt end of a rifle.

"Alonzo, careful!" another man said. "You might hit the baby."

Melanie rose to one knee, the baby held protectively over her heart. She was glad she had fed so much; her knee was already healing, knitting closed. *I'm invincible,* she thought, and then laughed.

"Don't move, mister," Alonzo said.

Melanie got to her feet. Though she felt light-headed, her strength was quickly returning. The baby was in hysterics and flailing his limbs; his clear vowels echoed throughout the woods.

"Hush now," she said, and slipped a bloody finger in its mouth. The baby suckled and quieted.

"Let him go, or I'll shoot. I swear it."

"Shhhh," Melanie whispered. She smiled and took several steps towards Alonzo.

"I don't want to do this." Alonzo cocked his rifle, then called over his shoulder to his friend, "Go get help."

The other man didn't need to be told twice.

Melanie shouted over Alonzo's shoulder, "Yes, go get help. Bring them all here."

"Put down the goddamn baby!" Alonzo's hands were visibly shaking.

"Relax, friend," she said and gently set the baby down in a soft spot of grass. "Just like Moses in the reeds." Melanie looked down at the child. "Now just sit there, yes?"

"You know, I can't do that." She took a few more steps closer.

"Please." Alonzo began to cry and lower his rifle.

"That's it," she said; her voice was silky, calming. "Why don't you set the rifle down so I can ... rip out your throat!"

She hurled herself towards Alonzo, but the man managed to get a shot off first. It caught Melanie in the shoulder. She grimaced in pain, but started to charge again. A second shot hit her in the gut, and she cried out, doubling over.

"I'll gouge out your eyes," she grunted, and tried to will herself to stand, but she was too weak. Blood rushed from her wounds. "You can't kill me." Melanie wobbled to her feet, and Alonzo let one more shot go. This one just grazed her shoulder, but it was enough to knock her flat on her back.

Blood and Sunlight Jamie Wasserman

Alonzo took the opportunity to get the hell out of there.

"Damn," Melanie said. Her vision blurred, and her ears filled with a rushing sound like a rising tide. The wounds had closed a little, but not enough to stop the blood.

Dogs were approaching with more men. She rolled herself over and staggered to her feet. In front of her, the woods rose up like a wall of thorns; dark, dangerous and impassable. The other way meant certain death.

Live, a voice commanded. Without thinking, she held her arms in front of her face and flung herself into the thick forest. Branches lashed her face, and the tangled bramble pulled at her clothes, weighing her down, attempting to drag her into the soft earth. She ran, and the blood poured out from her wounds like sand in an hourglass.

Just as she was about to give up, the woods suddenly parted, revealing a massive structure balanced precariously on a cliff ledge over the proposed rail line. She staggered towards it, desperate and hungry, like Hansel lurching toward a house made of gingerbread.

You will be hunted. Don't put your blind faith in your strength or your years. They do not rest, and they out-number you. They have generations. When one grows weary, three more will appear. You, however, will forever be running. And make no mistake — eventually they will catch you.

Above her, Melanie watched a spider spin a complicated web in a far corner of the root cellar. She had not realized just how delicate its silky lines were, and how much they shimmered. She wondered what other wonders she had missed in her mad rush for blood. *Too late now.*

Outside, a gunshot rang out. Melanie flinched and covered her ears. The sound was deafening and shook her splintered bones. The monstrous part of her, the one she had fed so freely over the last few months, spoke up. *Blood*, it said.

"Too much pain," she protested.

Blood, it demanded.

"I can't walk!" she whimpered.

Then you will die, it said simply.

Melanie lifted her hand — it was stained crimson. She hadn't noticed the pool of red spreading out from underneath her like a spring.

"Water, water everywhere," she croaked, "but nary a drop to drink." She chuckled to herself. "C'mon, where'd you go?"

But the voice did not reply. It left Melanie in silence. Death did not mean an end to the creature inside her, only to Melanie. Cruelty would always find purpose somewhere else. If she were to survive, she would have to do it on her own. But first, she just need to close her eyes and rest, if only for a second.

If salvation does come, it will be in unexpected places. Be open to it.

Melanie heard a soft murmur, like the clack of a train but muted. She opened her eyes, and two enormous green eyes looked back at her. She snapped her head back in surprise, and the eyes disappeared.

"Hello?" she called out.

Something brushed her shoulder. By the time she managed to move her arm, the thing darted over her leg. "Please," she said.

Something tapped tentatively at her hand. Keeping still, she lifted her head as much as she could. It was a cat, batting at her fingers like a toy.

Kill it, the voice demanded, returning. *Drink it dry.*

But Melanie knew where that path led. Already she saw herself tossing aside its emptied body and storming up the stairs into the main part of the house. She would move from room to room until everyone in it was dead. Until their strength was hers. And then she would return to the night.

How much longer though before another mistake? How many more would die? The end was written for her. It was only a question of when.

The cat rubbed against Melanie's hand, purring for more attention. Though every muscle movement hurt, she scratched its head and called it closer to her. "C'mere, baby," she cooed and then coughed. And the cat happily landed on her chest and curled in a ball.

"What's your name," she asked, pulling at the simple collar around her neck. "Juliet, huh? Well hullo Juliet. I must be Romeo."

The weight of its body on her made breathing difficult, but she continued to run her fingers through its fur. There wasn't enough blood to heal her completely. Melanie knew that. But if she took just a little, every day.

If she could coax the cat back, she would heal. Her hunger would be quelled, and the monster inside her would remain undisturbed.

The cat recoiled as Melanie suddenly grabbed it by the scruff of the neck and brought it closer towards her lips. Her fangs extended.

"No need to fear. Just enough, Juliet, love. No more."

Above Melanie, the timbered ceiling lit up like heaven itself was opening up for her. The light spread down the walls, underneath her, and then brightened to a single point.

"You can open your eyes now. If you want to," Keenan said.

Chapter 26

"Well, say something. Please."

Melanie was lying in Keenan's lap. The room spun on an uneven axis. "Give me a second." She felt as though she were trapped in a tilt-a-whirl — a thousand images jumped out of her subconscious, leaving ghost-like impressions on her retina. She wondered if she would get brain damage from too many prolonged sessions of Keenan's twisted version of home movies. She felt his muscles tightened underneath her. "Chill! Please." She needed to process, but Keenan wanted to talk it out, solve everything. *Typical boy.*

After a few moments of deep breathing, the room settled back into the muted color of reality. She shut her eyes and listened outside the cave. Children laughing. A car's tires squealing. Someone trying to coax an animal named Mr. Bubbles from out of the sewer. *Better,* she thought, and sat uneasily up.

Keenan had the same forlorn expression on his face as earlier, when they first stood outside Lucas's window.

Her head still spun from the journey. She started the conversation, small, harmless. "Tristan and Isolde?"

Keenan raised his eyebrows as if to say, 'Yes, and...?'

"Are they like vampire cats?"

"They're strays. I found them behind Orange Brewery, eating out of the garbage. I've always kept at least one. A stray or a feral. They're like my own St. Christopher medallions. I'd be lost without them."

"So no relation to Romeo?" She had an image in her head of Keenan as some kind of cat whisperer, raising and training generations of them.

"No." Keenan pursed his lips.

"So, animals can't become…"

"I have no idea! Why would I know that?"

"Sorry, just trying to get my head around all of this." She thought about the cellar. She could smell the mustiness, the acidic scent of ruined wine, feel the tangible layer of dust on the floor. There was something vaguely familiar about it — the curve of the room, the way the wood had aged maybe.

"That was the castle, wasn't it?" she asked.

"Yes." Keenan nodded vigorously, seemingly trying to urge Melanie on.

"What happened to the family that lived there?" she asked, and glanced at the floor. If he did go upstairs and kill them after all, that would almost feel like cheating. Especially after she had felt him cast aside his other self like a robe. Like going from the baptismal to the barroom, as her mother used to say.

"There wasn't a family. Just an old woman who lived alone. When she died — naturally — no one ever came to collect her things. I pay the taxes every year. I sweep the leaves off the porch."

Well, I guess someone has to. It wouldn't make an interesting movie to show Count Dracula pulling up weeds in the garden or watering the begonias. But then this was real life — you couldn't fast forward through the dull parts.

"Melanie."

"Sorry." She popped *Vlad's Gardening Tips* out of her mental DVD player and got to her feet. "I get it. You've got a past." Everyone had skeletons in their closets. Keenan's just had names and families as well. And besides, he was reformed. Demon, monster, vampire — whatever he was — there was more good in him than any man she had ever met. He wouldn't backslide; there was too much to lose. It wasn't just a single lifetime he would be risking.

So vampires weren't coldblooded after all — at least not any more than their human counterparts. Lucas was wrong about that, too.

"Do you understand why you can never have human blood?" Keenan asked.

"More or less." *Human blood is like heroin to a vampire. One taste, and you're hooked, and then you'd do anything to get more of it. More bitter irony, I suppose. The one thing that defines us, that makes us who we are, is the one thing we can't do if we wish to hold onto any of our humanity.*

"There is something terrible in us, Melanie."

"I got it." But cruelty wasn't the sole domain of the supernatural world. In fact, she was pretty sure mankind had the patent on it.

"Lucas—"

"—doesn't matter," she broke in. And he didn't. She would see Lucas die, but it would be on his terms. She would see him grow old, grow lonely and frail. She might even lay a flower on his grave. But she didn't need to have a hand in his death. She could simply sit back and watch him die a little each day.

"Do you understand what you're giving up?"

She understood firsthand the powerful need for blood. She'd felt it in the tunnel, like a starved man clutching at a piece of bread. There was nothing she wouldn't have done to get just a little taste. But seeing it through Keenan's eyes, seeing someone who had actually sated his thirst, she was surprised to see that the hunger hadn't diminished — it had actually grown, taken roots within his chest, grown teeth and claws, and then tried to take over.

She nodded.

He got to his feet, pulled her up, and wrapped his arms around her. "If things change—"

"They won't."

"But if they do, I just want you to know—"

"Keenan," she insisted. She didn't want to hear what he was going to say, but she imagined it was something like 'I'll have to stop you.' She didn't blame him — there would be little of her left anyway at that point. Still, it wasn't the sort of thing she wanted to hear from her boyfriend's mouth.

"If you do, I will follow you." His hands knitted together on the small of her back.

"Follow me?" Melanie scrunched up her nose.

"I will be whatever you need me to be."

She looked into his eyes. They were dark and hungry. He was offering to be a killer just to be with her. Bryan wouldn't even give up fake plastic

225

teeth. Lucas would never have stopped whittling stakes. But Keenan was willing to surrender everything he had fought for, just to be with her.

"You'll never have to." She stood up on her tiptoes and kissed him on the mouth.

Keenan shut his eyes and hugged her tightly.

"I love you," she said in between kisses.

"World without end."

His kisses became more passionate, and they fell together on the floor of the cave.

* * * * *

In all her wanting, there was a part of the fairytale that Melanie had never even considered — the part where the prince and princess grow old together, grow fragile and weak until their skin is as thin as paper. Their kids move away and have stories of their own. The world abandons them. And the true ending to every fairytale is always the same. Happiness is not forever. Love does not conquer all. That victory goes to Death.

But that would never happen to her. She and her prince would remain young forever; each end to a story would merely be a prelude to the next chapter. She would really and truly live, happily ever after.

PART III

End

Chapter 27

"The end." Trevor paused. Kirsten didn't move, so he figured she was finally asleep. He lifted himself off the chair with more than a few groans of complaint from both the chair and his knees.

"Daddy."

Busted. Trevor froze in place, hoping she was just stirring in her sleep. A long quiet pause gave him hope, but just as he resumed heading towards the door, she called out. "You didn't end the story right." Her voice was drowsy. The kid was doing everything she could to stave off sleep. Always the fighter.

"Oh?"

"The monster is supposed to get killed."

"I told you, sweetie, This story is different."

"But the wrong people die."

"Yes," Trevor said, feeling suddenly tired and very sad. "Sometimes, that's just the way it goes."

Kirsten mumbled something into her pillow. He brushed back her hair. "I'm going to check on your brother, okay?"

But now she was really asleep. She sighed and rolled to her side, hugging the covers to her chest. In the harsh, white light from the streetlamp pouring through the window, she looked just like an angel.

Trevor shut the door as quietly as he could and leaned against the wall outside her room. Maybe he shouldn't have told her that story. Look what it had done to her brother, and his twisted imagination. Of course, Lucas was different. Even when he was her age. Goddamn kid never let anything go. Sat on it like a golden egg.

And where had it all led? *Vampires. Christ.* He blamed himself . He should've listened to the goddamn shrink. 'Stick with reality,' she said. 'It's safer.'

He took a deep breath and headed down the hall to Lucas's bedroom. The door was partially open, which made coming in to check on him easier. And between bringing him his antibiotics and pain meds, Trevor had already worn a deep groove into the carpet.

The room had that claustrophobic, hospital room smell to it — a combination of sleep, medications, and something else. *Despair.*

The bruises on Lucas's arms and face were yellow and anemic now. That was poetic justice as far as he was concerned, remembering every time he'd seen Leah with a new mark on her wrists or neck; every time she'd showed up to the house in a turtleneck when it was ninety degrees out. Lucas had it coming. It was about time he picked on somebody who could fight back.

But the rest of the damage — that was just inhuman. Though his nose was still bandaged, he could still see the flattened pulpy mess that had been left when Lucas was first brought to the hospital. With the broken jaw and damages to his lungs on top of it, the kid was lucky to be alive, lucky to still be breathing on his own. Seeing him in the eye patch was just heartbreaking. It reminded him of Lucas's first Halloween costume — a pirate. He limped around happily and held up his hook for a hand, smiling as he peeked out from behind his patch. Difference was, he'd never get to take this one off.

Still, Trevor didn't buy the car wreck story, and he wondered now if the first accident was staged too. He had no one but himself to blame. A lifetime of covering up for the kid, he was bound to pick up a few tips from his old man.

"Dad," Lucas called weakly.

"Yeah, buddy." Trevor sat next to his son on the bed.

"I did it." Lucas smiled but his eyes never opened.

"Yeah, you did, kid." *You pulled through,* Trevor thought. *You survived.* Lucas was a fighter, too, just like his sister. He'd make it through this. Trevor leaned over and kissed his head. For a moment, he got a whiff of gasoline and smoke. *Nah,* he told himself. *Must be left over from the last incident. The scent was just soaked into his mattress.*

Hopefully this was the end of all that craziness. No more talk about hunting vampires and burning down nests. If he could get back together with Melanie, she would keep him in line. She wouldn't put up with his crap.

Hell, since he started seeing her, he'd already changed. He'd washed out that faggy blonde hair dye and taken out those damn fake piercings. He'd even stopped dressing like a GI Joe doll. *Yesiree, just like in the fairytale, this was an ending to a terrible chapter. But the next one had to be better.*

Seeing Lucas like that, Trevor thought about every bruise he had inflicted on Lucas. Every welt. Was he any better than the monsters that had done this to him?

Over the years, Trevor's punishments began to have less and less effect. No TV. No story at bedtime. No friends. No phone. No car. His punishments rolled off Lucas like water off a duck's ass. But the first time he'd hit him — a clean slap across the face — his eyes finally opened. He didn't cry like Trevor expected him to, but he did listen. And things were okay for a while after that.

But Lucas always slipped up, went astray, and the beatings got worse every time. If he had cried, just once, maybe Trevor could have stopped. After a while, he began to wonder if he was punishing him or just trying to break him.

After the first few times, Trevor would lie in bed all night and drink himself to sleep. This wasn't the way things were supposed to be. If Sondra were still here, if that goddamn car hadn't...

His train of thought was broken by the ringing of the phone.

Chapter 28

Melanie added the kitchen as an afterthought. "You know, in case we ever have guests."

Keenan shook his head in mock disgust, but Melanie knew he secretly appreciated all the changes to the house. She threw herself into the work like it was a new art project, and she was pleased to discover she had an affinity for design and decorating.

For three months, there was a steady stream of junkmen hauling debris, repairmen, painters, electricians, and furniture deliverers. She replaced the ancient floorboards, which had become darkened by age and grunge, with polished slats of pine. *Just because we live in darkness doesn't mean we have to live in gloom. Martha Stuart would say said the same thing if she ever joined the ranks of the undead. God help me,* Melanie thought, *I'm becoming domestic.*

She added modern stainless steel appliances that gurgled and hummed and clicked, filling the house with peaceful, unbroken white noise. And she updated the bathrooms in glass and marble tile — again, more for guests.

The fluorescent lighting was a terrible idea and had to be swapped out with low-level track-lights. The harsh white made Keenan's skin look like chiseled marble. And Melanie herself was slowly losing her summer tan. It wouldn't be long, she figured, until she was just as pale as her vampire beau. She wondered if a tanning bed was out of the question.

To her surprise, she was beginning to miss the sun, more so than she thought she would. But three months without so much as a glimpse of natural light made her antsy. Some part of her leftover self kept telling her this was wrong, that she should be depressed, weakened. But she wasn't — in fact, she felt stronger, with her thoughts more focused and ordered than they had ever been. She almost longed to go back to school because she thought she might finally have the concentration necessary for Calculus 101.

Melanie called in a road crew to pave a driveway from the house to the road, marking for the first time in two hundred years that the house was accessible to anyone without a scythe and a really good sense of direction. And all of these workmen, of course, had to be tipped very generously for showing up while it was dark.

This didn't even put a dent in Keenan's fortune though. It seemed the old lady who originally owned the house had left more than just a withered building and a moldy wine cellar. She had carefully stored away precious artworks and ancient books, as well as priceless jewelry and useless currency. All of which sold very well on eBay.

Keenan did most of the listings himself. He complained to no end when Melanie ordered the yard dug up so fiber optic lines could be laid for internet. Now it was all she could do to get him out of the chat rooms. Two hundred years of pent-up conversation had to go somewhere. *God help me,* she thought, *if he ever discovered online porn.*

As a last touch, Melanie had replaced Keenan's wardrobe — all but his combat boots, which reminded her all too much of Lucas. Unfortunately, she couldn't break his unhealthy attachment to them. "Practical and comfortable," he had told her while clutching the worn out shoes to his chest like a favorite purse. She vowed to toss them the moment his back was turned.

She purchased a double-bed for Tristan and Isolde, and then picked out an elaborate platform for them to play. Everyone deserved to be put on a pedestal every now and again. Fortunately, the malls stayed open late.

All of these comings and goings had attracted some attention in town. Keenan had predictably freaked the first time someone knocked on the door, but was soon ordering the Sunday paper and boxes of Girl Scout cookies like any other homeowner — though what he did with the boxes of cookies, she had no idea.

Melanie stayed safely tucked away in the bedroom when anyone came near the house — but now it was more just out of caution — the temptation was no longer there. Keenan had scared her straight on human blood.

She enjoyed running with wild abandon through the woods with him, hopping the different trains, finding increasingly higher places to leap from, learning all of his cool vampire tricks, and of course making love. She had replaced her previous drug and alcohol addiction with sex. And fortunately her new boyfriend was an excellent supplier.

She no longer thought about New York or Paris, going back to college, or killing off Lucas. None of those paths included Keenan, and she wouldn't even consider such a possibility.

* * * * *

Before she knew it, October had rolled in with dry leaves and cloudless evenings, and the smell of fresh cut hay and cool earth.

"Is that what I think it is?"

"Too much?"

Keenan straightened the cherubic-looking vampire cutout that Melanie had hung on the porch. Just next to its lopsided teeth was a caption that read, 'Who needs blood when you've got candy?'

"No." He smirked and folded his arms, regarding the silly Halloween poster like a fine work of art. "I think it's roffle."

"Roffle?"

"Am I not using that right? I read it in a chatroom."

"Oh, 'ROFL.' You are so freaking adorable." Melanie slid her arms around his neck.

"It's part of the curse." He kissed her and grinned, and his eyes lit up. "So, not even close?"

"I'll bet you operate a mean kiln."

"So, that's a no." He frowned.

"You're good at other things." She took his hand and pulled Keenan back into the house. He smiled, pacified.

In the living room, he said, "I got you a little something," and produced a white box from under the coffee table.

"Keenan," she said with a sigh. This wasn't fair. It felt like all she had done was take.

"Please."

She bit at her lip and opened the box. It looked like the pelt of a dead deer.

"Um, thanks." She gingerly picked up the hide with her thumb and forefinger.

"Take it out."

"Okay." She pulled and pulled, but the damn thing kept unraveling. Whatever it was, it was too big to be a deer. Dead sasquatch maybe. When she finally got to the bottom of the box, her mouth dropped open. "Where did you find this?"

"That is the right one, yes? A wooly?"

"Wookie. Chewbacca."

"Wookie," Keenan chastised himself.

"I don't know what to say." She clutched the furry mask to her chest. She'd slept with him, and he was still romancing her like it was a first date.

"How about 'thank you'?"

"Thank you," she said.

Keenan took the mask from her and kissed her neck. "You could always show me how thankful you are."

Melanie ran her fingers through his hair. "I still need to get candy."

"I'll do it," he added a little too quickly and pulled away.

"I'm going to have to go out on my own sometime."

"I know that. I just—"

"Worry. I know. Thank you." Far from insulted, she enjoyed Keenan's concern, his protectiveness. "But I really think I'm ready. I've been coming out of my room whenever someone's come by the house. I even made it halfway down the stairs once."

"So no..."

"None." Melanie smiled honestly. There was too much to lose.

"Okay," Keenan agreed.

"That's it?" She expected much more of a fight.

"If you say you're ready, you're ready. Tristan, hullo boy."

One of the cats ambled down the hall and let out a troubled growl.

"I just put out their food." Melanie's brow furrowed with concern. The cats represented Keenan's tie to the world. If something should happen to them ... she shuddered. *God help us all.*

"Where's your lady friend?" Keenan knelt next to Tristan and stroked his silky black fur. The cat raised its haunches then let out another low meow.

"She hasn't been very active lately."

"I know," Keenan stood up and looked troubled.

"C'mon." Melanie's face brightened, let's go check on her. "I'm sure it's nothing. Probably knocked her water dish over again."

Tristan scampered down the hall to the kitchen where Isolde lay nestled on the heating vent.

"Hey girl," Keenan said to the furry heap, but she didn't move. He looked over at Melanie. "What's wrong with her?" There was a little desperation in his voice.

Isolde's eyes looked dull and glassy.

"Her heartbeat is strong. I don't understand it. Maybe we should call a vet."

Melanie cocked her head to the side. "Wait, listen." She knelt besides Isolde and touched her belly.

Keenan eyes narrowed in concentration, and then his face slowly lit up into a smile, "Two heartbeats."

"Listen again." Melanie smiled.

"Three. You little minx." Keenan stroked her chin and then grabbed Tristan and flipped him on his back and scratched his belly, "You old tomcat."

Briefly, only briefly, Melanie wondered if she could now get pregnant safely. She didn't want kids, at least not now, but it was funny what meeting the right person did to your frame of mind. She shoved the thought aside for later consideration.

"We should probably take her to a vet, unless you know about breeding animals." She wouldn't have been surprised if he did. He seemed to know a whole lot for a guy who didn't get out much.

"I'll get a room ready for them." Keenan winked at her.

Unreal, she thought. He had a two-hundred-year head start on learning. She would never catch up.

Off her look, Keenan added, "Oh, there isn't much to do anyway. Animals were giving birth on their own long before vets came along."

"I'm going to go get the candy, Dr. Doolittle." She kissed him on the cheek.

"Imagine ... kids ... coming here. Amazing." Keenan shook his head in disbelief and grinned to himself. "Hurry back." His hand reached out and touched hers.

"Always." She smiled and let her hand slide across his until only their fingertips were touching. She held them there a moment, then reluctantly broke away and headed into town for the first time by herself since she'd changed.

* * * * *

Melanie had secretly been planning this trip ever since Keenan had single-handedly carried all of her belongings from her apartment straight to his bedroom. By the time she hung up the lace curtains, she had worked out when and how it would go down.

The more Keenan willingly made space for her, the more Melanie wanted to return the kindness, and the more she realized just how little she had to give. So far, it had been pretty one-sided. She was living in his house, spending his money, gleaning all of his knowledge. What did she bring to the party?

That's when it occurred to her. She could give him the one thing he had never gotten before — a birthday.

The present, that was the easy part. She found a simple gold watch online to replace Keenan's Eighteenth-Century pocket watch, and had it delivered to a local jeweler to be engraved. Never really one for poetry or soppy sentimentality, Melanie chose a line from a children's song her father used to sing to her, 'You are my sunshine.' She hoped Keenan appreciated irony.

Blood and Sunlight　　　　Jamie Wasserman

In keeping with her theme, she picked Halloween for his date of birth and made him three years older than she was. She would always be his young plaything, but she wanted to make it official.

Getting a birth certificate proved the real challenge. Ultimately it had taken about two dozen calls, several emails to a guy in Taiwan, and more money than she'd ever admit to Keenan — and that was just to get the name of someone who could help. The person in question turned out to be an old high school classmate who worked at Social Security Administration, who was now selling official documents online to support his meth habit. No wonder she'd been told all her life to forget about counting on social security for retirement. Look who they were hiring.

Once she got a hold of him, the rest was easy. Just a few reminders about certain past episodes involving a police cruiser and some B-and-Es was enough to convince him to help.

* * * * *

Melanie walked slowly towards Main Street, following the twisted, hilly road down past churches and houses crowded on top of another. She smiled to herself as she heard the barely perceptible patter of footsteps behind her. It was Keenan doing his best to stay out of sight, ever vigilant. Just as she predicted.

She slowed her pace even further, buying time for the decorators to get the house ready for his first birthday party. Nothing elaborate. A simple cake that would never get eaten, some streamers and balloons. The guest list was small and, if Melanie had anything to say about it, most of the time celebrating would be spent in the bedroom.

When she hit Main Street, she went right to the old general store on the corner and picked up full size bars of toffee chocolate and fruity candy and coconut chews. Nothing she would have eaten in her previous life, but the smells were irresistible. Never mind that they probably tasted like cardboard to her now.

"Anything else?" the man behind the counter asked without looking up from his newspaper.

He was heavyset with thinning hair and deep lines in his face. Melanie looked at the man's hands — no wedding ring. No jewelry of any kind. The store was empty. She wondered, would he be missed? She could be over the counter in a flash, have his neck open and his blood spilling down her throat before Keenan could even get in the door...

"Miss?"

"What?" Melanie looked up. "Oh, no. Thank you." She frowned. She would need to be more careful.

"I asked what kind of perfume you were wearing." The man had set his newspaper down and was leaning over the counter.

"I'm not." She frowned. A single blue vein twitched on the man's neck. *It would be so easy.* She shuddered.

"How much?"

"$6.50. Really? Maybe it's your shampoo. Smells like..." The man closed his eyes and inhaled deeply.

Christ, he was practically offering himself to her. This would be much easier for the wolf if the sheep didn't cover itself in barbecue sauce first. She threw a twenty on the counter, grabbed up the candy with shaking hands, and bounded out of the store.

Behind her, she heard the man call, "Come back! You forgot your change," but Melanie was already walking up the street to the jewelry store.

Okay, it wasn't pretty and it had been more difficult than she'd imagined, but she had done it. And if she could do it once, if she could push back every natural instinct, she could do it twice. And it would only be easier next time. It had to be.

The street was largely empty, as only the bars and restaurants and a few odd antique stores still remained open. The tourists were gone, and even the street was largely free of traffic.

She lingered in front of the Hyperion Café, enjoying the earthy aroma of coffee and foreign-spiced teas. Keenan was nowhere in sight, but Melanie knew he was close. She closed her eyes and smiled. She could almost smell the sweet cedar scent of his skin, hear his strong but measured heartbeat.

Blood and Sunlight Jamie Wasserman

Okay, more focus, she told herself and crossed the street to the jewelers.

Milton's specialized in antique and estate sale jewelry, though the owner also did custom pieces and engraving. The store was filled with heavy teak furniture and a thick dark carpet which pulled at her feet. The place had a library-like atmosphere to it, and the few times Melanie had gone in, she always found herself whispering.

A bell over the door jingled to announce her arrival. Melanie noted with a sigh of relief that the place was empty. She wasn't sure how she'd react to being around more than one person in close confines, and she was hoping she wouldn't have to put her resolve to the test.

"Ah, you must be here to pick up the watch."

Melanie turned back to the door. An old man was sitting in an ornamentally carved chair with a book in his lap. She had walked right past him and hadn't even noticed. *I can do this,* she told herself.

"Yes," she said.

The man struggled to his feet. "Nice piece. I'm sure he'll love it." He handed her a small gold colored box with a silver bow.

"Thank you," she said, beaming. The last time she had picked out a present for a man might have been a tie for her father. She remembered how he fussed and oohed and ahhed over it, and then how crushed she'd been when she found it still with the tags on while going through his things after he died.

"Mind if I look around for a bit?" she asked, thinking she'd need at least an hour to kill.

"Not at all. Waiting for the missus to finish up." He jabbed a thumb at the backroom and gingerly sat back down in the chair.

She pictured an equally frail looking woman adjusting a wig on her white head. The two of them ambling down the street as the world raced around them. It was equally sweet and pathetic. At one time she might have even envied that kind of devotion. Not anymore. Their love would only last one lifetime. How could that ever be enough?

She passed by a rack of delicate porcelain statues. Some part of her wanted to smash them into fine powder, so she bit her lip and moved on to the charms.

Something in the air made her nose itch. Probably the dust. The place was crowded with relics — antique engagement rings and lavish necklaces. Remnants of a thousand relationships doomed before they even started. *How insignificant they are.* Melanie glanced back at the old man starting to nod off in his chair. *Outlasted by their own trinkets.*

She felt her hands tingle with energy. She could wring his neck before he uttered the first gasp of protest. His wife's grief would be over long before her heart called it quits.

She made a fist and took a slow breath. *Get it together, Mel.* She was feeling a wave of superiority similar to what Keenan had experienced at the height of his rampage. *Remember where you came from, remember how much you stand to lose,* she reminded herself.

Over by the engagement rings, Melanie knelt close to the glass. The jewels sparkled in elaborate settings. Briefly she wondered if Keenan and she would ever get married, then scolded herself. *Till death do us part* no longer applied. It was greedy to ask for more than what she already had.

The hairs on the back of her neck tingled as she caught of a whiff gasoline and smoke. She looked around and sniffed the air.

"Do you smell that?"

But the man was completely out now, his chin resting on his chest.

She scrunched up her nose and listened for Keenan on the streets, but found nothing. Something was wrong.

"Hey!" Melanie called, but the man didn't move.

The smell was stronger now and filled the room.

In a flash she was standing in front of the man. She grabbed him by the shirt and hefted him in the air.

"Whu-?"

"Do you smell that?"

"Put me down!"

Melanie dropped the man in his chair. He grunted and scooted back, frightened.

"Do you ... smell that?" she asked. Her brain was firing off signals left and right, but she couldn't slow her thoughts down long enough to process them.

The man shook his head quickly.

"It smells like something's burning."

"Could be the soldering. Jenny!" He stood up and ran to the back, throwing a puzzled and fearful glance back at Melanie.

But she knew the smell wasn't coming from there. Near the door, it was even stronger. She shoved the door open and the scent hit her immediately — sulfur, gas, heat.

"Keenan?" she looked around. There were a few people standing on the street pointing above the trees where a plume of thick smoke rose in hot blasts. Right where the castle stood. It was black with whatever the flames had devoured. She let out an involuntary whimper.

"Lucas." She whispered his name so quietly, she could barely hear it. "No."

* * * * *

She didn't remember how she got there, but the next moment she was standing in front of the castle. Sharp flames shot out of the lower windows, and black drags of smoke climbed up the walls. Her feet felt rooted to the ground. The animal part of her brain, the part focused solely on survival, would not allow her to take another step.

All of the changes she had made to the house — gone. The new clothes and leftover antiques. Her personal things that she'd saved from her apartment. Keenan's birth certificate. Everything was obliterated.

Even Tristan and Isolde. Melanie was nauseous.

"Keenan!" she shouted, but she knew he wasn't inside. "Keenan!"

She heard the first sirens. Miles away, but wending their way here.

It reminded her briefly of the day Lucas burned down the trailer in back of Hell House, and she felt suddenly too human, too fragile.

Instinctively, she knew where Keenan was. She could almost see him tearing through the woods as clearly as if he had planted the vision in her head; fangs bared, howling in murderous rage. He would go to Officer Tyler's house first. No one would get out alive. And if Lucas wasn't there, if by some chance he finally skipped town, Keenan would destroy anyone and everything that stood between him and revenge.

Melanie shut her eyes and listened beyond the crackling fire, beyond the city and its all too human noises. The cord had been cut, and there was nothing to hold Keenan here anymore.

This was her fault. She had done everything but stencil 'Vampire' on the mailbox or spray paint gigantic arrows from Lucas's house to the grounds. She only hoped it wasn't too late.

The entire forest seemed to hold a collective breath.

Chapter 29

"Is Lucas there?" Melanie demanded, clenching the pay phone receiver tightly in her hand.

"He's sleeping. You from the hospital?" she heard Lucas's dad say.

"Get him out of the house."

"Melanie? Is that you?"

"You need to take Lucas and whoever else is in the house and get the hell out of there."

"What? How did you even know he was here?"

Melanie banged the phone against the wall three times, then yelled into the receiver, "You don't have time. Get the fuck out of there!"

"Are you in some kind of trouble?"

She let out a frustrated scream. "Not me. Now listen!" She cursed to herself. "Death is coming!"

She slammed the phone down. This wasn't getting her anywhere. She ripped the receiver out of the wall in frustration and rushed out at an inhuman pace through the restaurant and into the street, not giving a damn who saw her.

"Hello? Melanie?" Disturbed, Trevor carefully replaced the phone on the hook and glanced to Lucas's bedroom and then to Stacey's. Briefly he toyed with the notion of who he would choose if he could only save one, then gritted his teeth and walked over to check on Lucas. If that boy is anywhere but sound asleep in his room...

He pushed open the door, expecting the worst, but was pleasantly surprised when he saw Lucas curled up in a ball in bed, window shut, the air warm and undisturbed.

"Death is coming," he repeated quietly to himself. If Melanie was trying to scare him, it worked. Had a goddamn grizzly bear shown up at his door, he would have calmly drawn his magnum and shot the bastard between the eyes. But death had been here before — it couldn't be slowed or stopped with guns or silver bullets or a cross. And death never left empty-handed.

Poor kid is probably high, or trying to freak Lucas out. I guess she took the breakup pretty hard. Leave it to him to screw up a good thing. Trevor sighed and started to shut the door when he caught sight of one of Lucas's combat boots sticking out from under the bed. There was mud on the sole, fresh mud on the rug.

"Luke?" he asked reaching out his hand and taking a tentative step closer, but he froze in his tracks when he heard a terrible crash from the front of the house.

* * * * *

Holy Mary, Mother of God, pray for us sinners now and at the hour of our death. Melanie repeated the holy rosary over and over, or at least as much as she could remember. *Get me through this, Lord, and I'll be a believer forever.* And that meant something. She could provide God with everlasting hosannas. *And if you can't save me, please God, don't let Keenan fall.*

* * * * *

A deep roar came from downstairs. It was loud, angry, and Trevor could swear the windows rattled in response.

He glanced back one last time at Lucas's sleeping form, then ran to his bedroom where he kept his gun. He always kept it loaded, always ready for the next disaster. He threw back the safety and cautiously headed to the top of the stairs.

A figure stood in the doorway among the splintered ruins of the front door. Trevor switched on the hallway light and gasped when he saw the man with streaks of ash and grease on his face. Underneath the grime, his face was as white as a skull, and his clothes smoldered as if he had dragged himself out of a fire. With him came the strong odor of gas and burnt wood. *Brimstone,* like the devil himself had come to call.

243

Shit, he thought. *I did smell smoke in Lucas's bed.* "Mister, I don't know what my son did, but I can fix this."

The man smiled, revealing two razor sharp canines that dripped with saliva.

The hair on the back of Trevor's neck stood up straight, and he felt a shiver run through his entire body. This wasn't just a coked up kid or a gangbanger. This was nothing he had ever seen before, but his brain recognized him, if only subconsciously. This was what Melanie was trying to warn him about. Death *was* here. It had emerged in flesh and blood, straight out of the pages of his own fairytale.

"I'm a police officer," Trevor said, and noticed his hands were shaking. He rested his gun on his forearm, forming a cross with his arms. "Get down now!"

But the thing that was Keenan was beyond words now. It only understood that this man was preventing him from reaching his prey. The man had a gun, and it remembered the pain it had suffered once from such a device. It snarled in anger. *Never again,* the creature thought.

* * * * *

"Keenan!" Melanie called, but the house was quiet. Maybe she had gotten lucky. If Trevor actually listened to her and packed up his family right away, they might be safe. Or Keenan might have killed them all already. He could be on his way to Lucas's apartment right now. Someone innocent might have tried to stop him.

"Keenan," she called again. Her nostrils flared with the scent of fresh blood and a lot of it. She sucked in a tight fist of air and held her breath, then followed the smell where it seemed strongest upstairs.

The stillness in the house was troubling. It wasn't the quiet of an empty house; it was the eerie silence that preceded the roar of a tornado, while you cowered in the basement or a storm cellar.

At the top of the stairs, lying in a heap off to the side, was Officer Tyler's body. His neck was open. He gurgled and clutched at the wound.

Melanie could hear a faint heartbeat, the sound of blood rushing out of the body. He didn't have long. She didn't think about finishing him off, drinking him dry. She didn't think of the honey-rich taste of warm blood on her lips. Her thoughts were focused solely on finding Keenan.

"Keenan, please!"

In front of her was a half-open bedroom door; to her left a short hallway and two more doors. Probably the smaller bedrooms she had seen earlier. She could suss out more blood here, weaker though, and several sets of racing heartbeats. *There's still hope!*

She followed the sounds to one of the smaller bedroom doors. "Keenan?"

Besides the bed, Melanie saw two legs and black boots lying sprawled on the floor.

"Lucas. Shit." Keenan had finished off at least two. She walked over to the body. If Lucas wasn't dead yet, she'd make damn sure he would be now. If she'd only done it sooner. She could come back from a kill, she was sure of it. She'd done lots of things she wasn't proud of, and she'd shrugged them off like an old shawl. But Keenan was on such a narrow moral footing. This at least would have been something she could have done for him.

When she got closer to the body the first thing she noticed was the charred black hair. She rushed over and rolled him over. It was Keenan. Melanie's stomach lurched like she had been punched in the gut.

She touched his chest. Two dark wounds blossomed like irises on his chest.

"Keenan?" She lifted his head.

"Hey, Mel."

Melanie looked up. Lucas stood in front of her, a rifle in his hands.

"You're looking pretty good for a dead chick."

Lucas's bad eye dripped a gummy liquid from underneath his eye patch. His hair was grown out and fell in oily streaks across his foreheads. His face was beet red and flattened. *Pathetic.*

Melanie ignored him and looked back to Keenan and stroked his hair. He still had a pulse, faint though it was. She bit her wrist and held it to his lips.

"C'mon, drink."

But Keenan didn't move. She felt his labored breath on her arm and squeezed her blood into his open mouth.

"Not enough," he whispered. "Too late."

"I said get up!" Lucas shouted.

Melanie glanced back towards Lucas. He was shouting, but she didn't hear a word he was saying. Keenan needed blood. Human blood. And Lucas's heart was strong. The blood was rushing to his face, pinking his cheeks. *So warm.*

She got to her feet. There was more than enough blood for Keenan *and* herself. He would be fine. They would be fine.

"Move against the wall!"

Melanie bared her teeth and hissed.

Lucas cocked the gun and carefully aimed it at her heart.

She shook her head and giggled. A gun wouldn't stop her. God himself wouldn't stop her. She took a step forward.

"I mean it. Don't make me do this again!"

Lucas shut his eye and looked away as he pulled back the trigger. But before he could, an arm reached around his neck and pulled him backwards to the floor. A blast shot through the ceiling, raining down dust over the room.

Melanie watched as Lucas's good eye bulged while he struggled, his arms flailing uselessly at the air. She picked up the discarded gun and looked at it curiously, as though it were a strange artifact from an alien civilization.

Lucas's tongue lolled out of his mouth, and saliva and blood foamed from his lips. Trevor had his son by the neck and squeezed tighter until both of their faces were bright red. "No more, son," he pleaded. "No more."

Lucas kicked wildly at the floor and then, just as quickly, stopped moving. Officer Tyler sobbed and rolled out from behind him. His whole body shook.

"I'm sorry Luke, I can't protect you anymore." He crawled over to him then kissed his forehead. "I'm sorry. I'm sorry. I'm sorry..."

Melanie shook her head as if suddenly wakened from a persistent dream.

There was Lucas dead on the ground. His once steady heartbeat vacant and hollow. Trevor weeping at his son's chest, his own heartbeat fading like footsteps down a hall. And the blood. The wonderful, life-giving blood was everywhere.

Keenan!

She wheeled around and helped him upright. His eyes fluttered open.

"I can still fix this," she whispered, and nodded over to Officer Tyler.

"No," he said through gritted teeth.

"Then Lucas. He's already —"

"No," he repeated more firmly. "Not from him. I would never give him the satisfaction." He wheezed and coughed.

"Keenan," she pleaded. She heard a racing heartbeat secreted in another corner of the house. More blood — warm and fresh. There was every chance in the world to fix this, why was Keenan being so stubborn?

"I can't do this anymore. I'm tired of being a fish." He smiled and closed his eyes. "But you've still got a chance."

Some chance. She would be alone again. The prince had fallen off his horse and he didn't even have the balls to pick himself back up again. Melanie thought back to freshman English, of all things, and to Romeo and Juliet. The book hadn't made much sense to her with its stilted language and stupid customs, but the film the teacher showed afterwards really upset her. Not in the sappy, weepy way it had most of the girls in class. No, Melanie was filled with anger. *Did that freaking idiot Romeo even check for a pulse? No. At the first sign of trouble, he offs himself. And then Juliet follows suit. Two people so strongly dependent on one another that reason went completely out the window. And this is the greatest love story of all time?* Melanie did not want that. She did not want stupid, easy love. She wanted it with all the complications, arguments, betrayals and heartache. She wanted to work for it.

Melanie was ready to cast it all aside — the childhood longings, the unyielding simple belief that love should come and go as easily as the tides. Her life was not a fairytale or a wild, wind-swept romance. Things would not go according to plan. Her story would not be pretty and sealed with a ribbon of pink. Fathers would not read it to their daughters at night. It would be whispered around campfires, told in hushed, shaky voices on basement floors. People would die. Innocent people. The wrong people. But the world would go on the way it always does, patient and indifferent, one terrible sunset at a time. And Melanie would, for the first in her life, be a part of that.

"You're right," she smiled patiently, "I do still have a chance."

She picked up Trevor's hulking body and threw him down next to Keenan. Officer Tyler let out a soft moan of protest.

"What are you doing?" Keenan opened his eyes and rasped. Every syllable must have been torture for him. Dark arterial blood dripped from his lips.

"So I'm the only one who gets to be a monster? I don't think so."

"Melanie." Keenan shook his head side to side. "Don't do this."

She bit down on Officer Tyler's wrist, then brought it to Keenan's lips.

"Drink. Or everything you say will have meant nothing. Everything that has happened will have been a lie. Drink it, or I promise I'll go immediately after you."

He lifted his head and reached out his hand. It seemed to take all his remaining strength. "I can't."

"Why?" she asked, near tears. She was running out of ideas.

"It's not enough."

She touched Officer Tyler's shoulder. He was growing cold. She could already hear the blood, what little was left, draining from his veins. "It has to be."

Keenan closed his eyes and gently shook his head. His hand found hers. "Let me go."

"You promised." Melanie was more than angry. She would not allow Keenan to go back on his word. To be just another ex; soon forgotten, a temporary diversion until the next prince appeared, offering golden apples on silver platters that always turned out to be made of wax and tin.

Melanie remembered the heartbeat she heard in another part of the house.

"I'll be right back," she whispered and kissed his forehead.

She got up and followed the sound to the room next door — an even smaller bedroom done up in pink with butterflies on the wall. It wrenched her heart to see the dolls and the bookshelves crowded with fairytale books. *Childhood was a lie. You grow up believing that your dad will never die. That your home is made of stone, not straw. That the prince will wait for you patiently outside a wall of thorns. He will never leave you. Never grow old. That happily ever after actually means something.*

She opened the closet. Huddling underneath frilly pink dresses and tee shirts printed with kitten pictures was a little girl. Lucas's little sister. She had a thin curious face, hair like spun gold, and big grey eyes.

Melanie smiled.

Childhood was a lie, fine and delicate as an antique mirror. You spent every day of your life wiping away a small part of its clouded exterior, expecting magic until the only thing left was your own horrible reflection staring dumbly back, aged now and creased with worry and disappointment. Better that you die before that happens. Better still that you remain forever young. Forever naive.

She looked into the child's frightened eyes and saw only herself staring back. The face she saw was not the delicate princess; it was the leering monster who fed on damsels in distress. She was seeing things clearly for the first time in her life.

The girl let out a whimper, and Melanie, or rather what was left of Melanie, reached out and took the child's hand.

Epilogue

"Are you sure you don't want a bedtime story?"

The little girl shook her head.

"Okay, sweetie." The woman leaned over and kissed her forehead. "No more talk about monsters and angels coming in the room, right?"

"Right."

Out of habit, the woman double-checked the lock on the window. *Bolted shut.* She smiled weakly at the little girl. "Good night, Kirsten."

"Good night, Aunt Sophie."

Sophie turned on the nightlight and softly shut the door behind her. She immediately let out a deep breath she didn't even realize she had been holding.

"Any better tonight?" Her husband was sitting on the floor outside Kirsten's room, reading the newspaper.

"Little by little." Sophie frowned. "I guess I hoped we'd be closer by now. She won't even let me kiss her goodnight. And lately, I feel like she's in a hurry to get me out of her room as quickly possible."

Martin put the paper down and got up. "Give her time." He put his arm around her and hugged her close.

"It's been almost a year. I don't expect her to forget overnight, but the imaginary friends and the monsters and angels coming into her room... I think we need to take her back to the psychologist."

"I had an imaginary friend until I was nine."

"And how did that work out for you, Martin?" Sophie smiled.

"He still writes sometimes." Martin took her hand. "She's a tough little kid. Can you imagine watching your brother and dad kill each other?"

Sophie tensed up.

"Sorry, it's just..."

"It's fine. I didn't know. Nobody did. I should have stayed in Maryland after Sondra died. Maybe..."

"Don't you dare start putting this off on yourself. Listen," Martin said, searching her face, "there is nothing you could have done to stop this. Okay?"

Sophie nodded.

"Anyway, Kirsten's young enough that she'll forget all of this. She just needs time. C'mon, buy you a cup of coffee in the kitchen?"

"Big spender."

"That's why you love me." Martin grinned sheepishly and tugged her away from Kirsten's room.

* * * * *

Kirsten waited until the voices faded down the hallway to get out of bed. She padded barefoot to the window, unlocked it, and pushed it open. Then she got back into bed and pretended to be asleep.

One moment the room was empty; the next moment they were there. The angel with the green eyes and the pretty woman with the long dark red hair. Kirsten watched them with one eye shut.

"You're not really asleep are you?" the green-eyed angel asked.

Kirsten giggled and rolled over.

"Hello, my pet." The red-haired woman smiled down at her.

"Hi."

"How was school today?" the angel man asked

"Good."

"Make any new friends?"

Kirsten shook her head.

"Never mind that. They don't know what they're missing."

"And what about your reading test?" the woman asked.

Kirsten looked down ashamed.

"Oh, sweetie. We studied all night for that!"

Kirsten smiled and said, "I got an A."

"You sneak!" The woman tickled her toes, and Kirsten squealed.

"Shhh."

251

"Sorry."

"Do you want the rest of your bedtime story?" the man asked.

Kirsten nodded.

The woman with the long dark red hair walked to the side of the bed and pulled up the covers, tucked Kirsten in, and then sat next to her. Kirsten loved the way she smelled — like vanilla, only sweeter. She nuzzled in close as the woman stroked her hair.

"Where did I leave off?" the angel man asked, sitting next to her on the other side of the bed.

"The boat."

"Yes." The man smiled. "I was just checking to make sure you'd been listening. And did I tell you about how we need..."

"Blood to survive." Kirsten interrupted. "That's how I saved you, right?"

"Right, my little heroine." He frowned and studied the little girl. "You do know that if you ever want us to stop coming—"

"Keenan!" the woman said suddenly.

"I don't want you to stop. You're my guardian angels."

Keenan glared at the woman. "Yes, that is what Angel Melanie said, isn't it?"

Kirsten looked up at the man. "Angel Keenan?"

"Yes, princess?"

"Is my daddy still sleeping?"

"Yes, dear heart," the woman she called Angel Melanie interrupted. "Right next to your mommy and brother. But we can talk to them. They miss you so much."

"Would you like to hear the rest of the story?" Keenan asked, abruptly changing the conversation.

Kirstin nodded.

"America seemed like this romantic place where I could carve out my own piece of wilderness. And the railroad... I thought if I ever felt trapped or restless, well here was a thing of my own creation that could take me somewhere else."

"You said that already."

"Did I?"

Kirsten nodded her head impatiently.

"Did I mention getting sick onboard?"

"Yes."

"Baltimore harbor?"

Kirsten shook her head 'no.'

"Now we're getting somewhere. Back then, Baltimore harbor was one of the busiest ports in the world..."

* * * * *

Kirsten was asleep now. Melanie brushed a strand of blond hair away from her mouth and studied her intently. "I noticed we've been stuck in Baltimore harbor for a while," she said and cast a sidelong glance at Keenan.

"I'm sure I don't know what you mean."

"You like being around her as much as I do. Just say it."

"I never said I didn't."

"Then what's been bothering you?"

"I just don't think guilt is enough reason to stick around."

"It's not that."

Keenan looked at her curiously.

"Okay, it was at first. She reminded me of ... well, me. We'd both lost a father."

"And now?" Keenan crossed his arms.

"I can't explain it."

"Try."

Melanie stared out the window for a while. The moon was barely a white sickle. Tomorrow it would be gone completely. "I never thought I'd find love."

"Nor did I."

"And I certainly didn't know what to do with it if I found it."

Keenan took and squeezed her hand.

"But now that I have it, it's made me greedy. I want more." She looked at Kirstin. "I want one of those."

"It's impossible," Keenan whispered.

Melanie looked back out the window. "Then I want *her.*"

"We agreed—"

"Yes. As soon as she doesn't want us around anymore, we're gone. Just like we never existed."

"I can delay the story all I want. You can offer up study sessions and let her try on your clothes. It's just postponing the inevitable."

"Which is?"

"Her finding out the truth," he said firmly.

"You don't have to do that."

"She'll need to know. And she'll need to decide what to do with that information when the time comes. I think enough decisions have been made for her."

"And then she'll hate us."

"At first. But could you blame her? Perhaps, after a while, she'll find some place in her heart for you. Maybe she'll even want to remain with us. You're not without your charms, Angel Melanie. You did somehow manage to convince her we were there to save her that night."

"After six months of candy, stories, and letting her jump off the roof with me."

"It's not the gift, it's the giver." Keenan grinned and pulled her to him.

Melanie smiled and wrapped her arms around his neck. "Are you flirting with me, Nineteenth-Century style?"

"Some things never go out of fashion." He stroked her cheek.

She leaned in to kiss him, then froze as the door knob turned.

* * * * *

"Kirsten?" Sophie gently opened the door a crack.

The little girl was asleep, her blonde hair spilling around her like spun gold. Everything was just as it should be.

"I swear I heard something," she said to herself.

"Milk and sugar?" Martin asked from the kitchen.

"Yes, please," she called out as quietly as she could. She watched Kirsten's perfect little face — serene and untroubled. *She's stronger than I ever was.*

Kirsten exhaled a small sigh in her sleep, her lips turning up at the corners into a sly smile.

How wonderful, Sophie thought. *How wonderful it is to be young. If only we could stay that age forever.*

~ABOUT THE AUTHOR~

Jamie Wasserman is a native of Ellicott City, Maryland. His work has appeared in *The Rhysling Anthology, Exquisite Corpse, Star*Line, Magazine of Speculative Poetry, Strange Horizons, Flesh and Blood, Gothic.net, Weber Studies,* and *Magma* (UK) among many others. He has received numerous honorable-mentions from *The Year's Best Fantasy and Horror,* and was nominated for a Pushcart by *Lite: Baltimore's Literary Arts Newspaper.* **Blood and Sunlight** is his first novel.

For more information about the author, visit ***www.penumbrapublishing.com***.

Made in the USA
Charleston, SC
02 October 2011